ONCE BITTEN, TWICE DEAD

A TWO BROOMSTICKS GAS & GRILL WITCH COZY MYSTERY BOOK ELEVEN

AMANDA M. LEE

WINCHESTERSHAW PUBLICATIONS

1

ONE

"What are you doing?"

Tillie Winchester planted her hands on her hips and glared at the bush I'd set afire. She obviously wasn't happy with my effort.

I, on the other hand, was fairly happy. I was a fire witch. I'd managed to hit what I'd been aiming at. That seemed like a win.

I, Stormy Morgan, was starting to see the light at the end of the witchy tunnel.

"What?" I challenged. "You told me to set the bush on fire."

"Yes, but I also told you the aim wasn't to burn the bush to the ground." Tillie sent the bush an apologetic look. "Sorry, Fred. I thought you'd survive this rookie. I didn't realize she was going to go whole fire."

I narrowed my eyes. "Who is Fred?"

"The bush," Bay Winchester replied as she wandered through a gap between the trees and looked around. It was early spring in Northern Lower Michigan, the trees were starting to bud and the grass was trying to turn green. We wore layers, because one moment we were freezing as the frost glistened on the ground and the next, we were sweating through our shirts as the sun beat down and it was suddenly sixty degrees.

"She named the bush?" I tried to wrap my head around that. "Does she name all her bushes?"

"She doesn't really name them," Bay replied. "She just pretends when she wants to get a reaction out of you."

Tillie glared at her great-niece with a mixture of disgust and wounded pride. "That shows what you know. I've named all the bushes on our property. I always have."

Bay didn't look convinced. "Sure. Let's play that game." She flashed a flat smile. "What's that one's name?" She pointed to the Arrowwood bush about fifteen feet from us.

"Ted," Tillie replied, not missing a beat.

"And that one?" Bay gestured toward a Ninebark bush.

"Bill."

Bay made a face. "And those names have nothing to do with the fact that you've been on a Keanu Reeves kick that I happen to know included all three Bill and Ted movies within the last two days?"

"Do you know what I'm going to name the poison ivy clump I throw you into?" Aunt Tillie didn't wait for Bay to respond. "Karma. How do you like that?"

Bay waved her off and turned back to me. "That was good. You set the bush on fire, which was your aim. Aunt Tillie is right, though. The goal won't always be to burn something to the ground. There are different types of fire."

I was new to being a witch. Only a year earlier I'd returned to Shadow Hills, the town I grew up in, after my dreams of being a writer went up in flames. I was forced to work at the family restaurant or live in my car. Upon my return, I'd had a drunken night with my cousin Alice, played with a Ouija board, and woke floating several feet above my bed. It had been nonstop chaos, demons, gnome shifters, and fire ever since.

"What other sorts of fire are there?" I asked.

The Winchesters had taken me under their impressive magical

wings almost from the start. They had different abilities and claimed my magic was rare. So far, all I'd managed to do was conjure a few locator spells and set fires while in trouble. I was looking to branch out.

Unfortunately, when it came to being a student, I wasn't all that diligent. Our training sessions kept falling by the wayside as my fiancé Hunter Ryan and I prepared to move into our dream home. We also were planning—mostly throwing around ideas—regarding our wedding. The magical stuff only seemed important when we were about to fight.

As bad luck would have it, we fought something terrible almost monthly. It was time to get with the program.

"I'm not being funny," I added quickly. "It's just, when I think of fire, I think of things burning. I guess I'm not familiar with the other types of fire."

"That makes sense." Bay never made me feel bad about my lack of magical knowledge. She was infinitely patient.

Tillie, on the other hand, had the patience of a first-time father with OCD trying to babysit a toddler with jam hands. "How does that make sense?" she demanded. "It's not rocket science." She lifted her hand and started ticking things off. "There are fire traps. There are fire arrows. There are fire storms. There are healing fires—the type that burn so hot they kill any and all infections—but you're not ready for one of those yet."

"There are healing fires?" I cast a dubious look to Bay, who merely nodded.

"Back during plague times, hellcats used to try to burn the disease out of villages and cities. Sometimes it worked. Sometimes they expended so much energy they died. Aunt Tillie is right, you're not ready for that yet."

The idea of healing people appealed to me, but I needed to defer to their superior knowledge. "Which of the others am I trying to do?"

"The fire trap sounds fun." Bay had a smile at the ready. "That will be useful."

"What is a fire trap?"

"Exactly as it indicates. Create a circle of fire—use Aunt Tillie as the person you're trapping."

Tillie balked. "I am not your guinea pig."

"There's a little resemblance around your eyes," Bay shot back. "Just stand there. Let her practice."

"Why don't you let her practice on you?" Tillie countered.

"Because you're mean and she'll want to trap you more than she wants to trap me." Bay's tone was reasonable. "Intent matters. Stormy is afraid of her magic. That's why she holds back. Her heart won't be in it if she tries to trap me. You, on the other hand..." She trailed off, a wicked gleam in her eyes.

"You're on my list," Tillie snarled. Her eyes drifted to me. "Bay is a moron. Of all my family members, she's the one with the least amount of brain power."

Bay glared at her.

Tillie said, "She's right about intent mattering. You have to want to do it. If you constantly fear that you're going to screw up, it will become a self-fulfilling prophecy. You don't want that."

"I'm not sure what to do."

"I found a book," Bay volunteered. "It's about the different sorts of fire hellcats have conjured. I'll send it home with you."

I perked up. "Maybe I should focus on the reading."

Tillie shook her head. "Practical application is more important than reading."

"That's why half our spells backfire," Bay said.

"Listen here, smart mouth," Tillie barked, "do you want to find out what it's like to be in every spot on my list?"

Bay ignored her. "It's okay to screw up, Stormy," she said. "We learn by doing. You can't be afraid to screw up because some of our best lessons are learned from the ashes of failure."

I beamed at her. "That was almost poetic."

"She stole that from me." Tillie made an impatient motion with her hand. "Come on. Put me in a trap." She waggled her eyebrows. "You know you want to."

I took a deep breath. Everything they said was true. I needed to get over the fear.

"Start small," Bay advised.

"Here. Take this." Tillie grabbed a stick from the ground and broke it before handing it to me. "Use that to conjure the trap."

I was floored. "Like a wand?"

"Yes, like a wand," Tillie said. "I miss the days of witches with wands."

"Don't give her grief," Bay snapped at Tillie. "It was a fair question." She cocked her head. "Besides, you have a wand."

Tillie jabbed a finger in Bay's direction. "That's for costumes and scaring the tourists. I don't really use it."

Bay glanced at me. "She totally uses the wand."

I looked down at the stick again. "What am I using this for if it's not a wand?"

"To draw with," Tillie replied. "Draw a circle around me. Dig into the ground. Then flow the magic into the lines of the circle. Just the lines. This will help you visualize it."

I licked my lips and dropped to my knees. The circle I drew was probably larger than it needed to be, but I didn't want to burn Tillie to death.

Once the circle was complete, the ends closed, I rolled back on my haunches. "Okay. Now what?"

"You know what we want you to do," Bay said. "Do it."

I held my breath and touched my finger to the line. Initially, nothing happened. Then, slowly, fire started to fill the line.

"This will stop your enemies from killing you," Tillie said. She reached out and smacked the back of my head. "You must be faster."

"Hey!" Irritation bubbled up, and I lost control of the magic. It filled the line I'd drawn and pulsed upward, creating a circle of fire around Tillie.

"Now that was impressive," Tillie said as she turned to take in the fire. It was an odd orange, not red or pink. It had a salmon tint. "Let's see what happens when I touch it." She pointed her finger and dabbed the fire, making a hissing noise before quickly pulling back. "Well, that smarts." She held up her finger for Bay to see through the flicking flames.

"Is that a burn?" I asked, squinting to get a look at the injury. Hurting Tillie was the last thing on my list, but I couldn't help from being a little proud that I'd done what they wanted.

"Not a burn." Tillie cocked her head. "The skin is dead. I have some ointment at the inn."

We'd selected a section of woods not far from The Overlook, the inn Bay's mother and aunts ran in Hemlock Cove. It was far enough away that no one—even curious guests—could see what we were doing, but not so far that we had a long hike back.

"Would someone die if they were to throw their whole body against the fire trying to escape?" Bay asked.

Tillie nodded. "No doubt." She smiled at me. "This is a great new ability. I know just the person we should try it out on."

Bay shot Tillie a withering look. "We're not using it on Mrs. Little."

"Definitely not," I agreed. Margaret Little was Tillie's lifelong nemesis. She was a busybody, always wreaking havoc on the town, but I wasn't throwing her in a trap so she could burn to death.

"Can you build a cage quicker next time?" Bay asked.

There was no hesitation when I nodded. "It was actually freeing to let the magic go rather than hold it inside."

Bay beamed at me. "That's what we want."

"I want out of the trap," Tillie said. "I oohed and aahed appropriately. Now let me out. I'm feeling peckish and want a snack."

I raised my hand, prepared to do as she wished, but Bay stopped me.

"Hold up." Bay raised her hand. The grin that spread across her face promised trouble. "Maybe we should take advantage of Aunt Tillie's predicament and have a discussion about the clown."

The clown was a doll Tillie had enchanted, part of a spell gone wrong. The other dolls she had unleashed on the town were gone. Crusty had brokered a deal to remain behind. Tillie had adopted him as her third sidekick.

"You'll be sorry if you try to negotiate with me while I'm locked up," Tillie warned. She didn't look afraid as much as smug. "Go ahead. Prove what an idiot you are."

If Bay was frightened, she didn't show it. "Gladly."

TWO HOURS LATER, BAY SMELLED LIKE rancid pickles and Tillie still had her clown sidekick. I could tell Bay regretted trying to take advantage of the situation. I was grateful that Tillie hadn't held Bay's plan against me. Hunter would not be pleased if I came home reeking of spoiled food.

I hung around The Overlook long enough for Bay to get the book for me. Then I left for home. I was looking for two hours of downtime —it was one of my days off from the restaurant—before my fiancé Hunter got home from work and we started talking about dinner plans. Living above the family restaurant, we often sought meals away from the apartment. I could eat only so many burgers.

I was lost in thought—debating if the drive to Gaylord for my favorite Mexican place would be worth it—when movement in the road set my heart fluttering. I registered quickly that the movement didn't belong to animals, but people, and slammed on my brakes.

I sat there, gripping the wheel of my car, for what felt like a really long time. In reality, it was only a few seconds. I killed the engine and pushed out of my car to approach the people standing in the middle of the road.

They were young, not even twenty yet.

The woman had scraggly, unwashed dark hair past her shoulders. Her eyes were vacant as she stared at a fixed spot about two feet in front of her. As far as I could tell, she hadn't even registered my vehicle. Her clothes were raggedy, torn jeans and a filthy shirt hanging off her shoulder. She wasn't wearing a coat, unusual for this time of year.

Next to her, the man—or was he still a boy?—stared at the same spot. He too wore jeans. The laces of his work boots were untied. He had a stained flannel shirt on over his white T-shirt.

"Hey." My voice was just loud enough to carry. I held up my hands as I approached them. "I'm Stormy Morgan. Were you in an accident?"

Neither of them looked at me. They didn't react to my voice at all. They just stared.

I looked around, on either side of the road. There was no vehicle. There was no blood. There were no monsters giving chase.

"I'm going to call for help." I pulled my phone from my pocket. "Just hold tight. I'll get help."

2

TWO

I didn't give any thought to whether I was on the Shadow Hills or Hemlock Cove side of the line when I called Hunter to tell him what was going on. He called Chief Terry Davenport to meet him at the scene. They would work together to decide who had jurisdiction.

I'd tried to get the boy and girl to sit. I'd offered them water I had in my car. They continued to stare forward.

Hunter was the first to arrive. He parked behind the kids and hopped out of his truck. He started toward them, then gave them a wide berth when it became apparent they weren't reacting to his appearance.

"Stormy?" He sent me a questioning look from thirty feet away. He'd stopped moving in any direction.

"I'm fine," I assured him. "I didn't get that close to them." Shame filled me when I thought about that for too long. "It's weird, right?" I looked around. "Where did they come from? Who are they?" Swallowing hard, I shook my head. "What happened to them?"

"I don't know." Hunter licked his lips, gave me another once-over, then moved in the direction of the teenagers. "I'm Hunter Ryan with the Shadow Hills Police Department," he said. "Can you tell me where you came from?"

Neither reacted. They just stood there, staring at nothing.

"Creepy," Hunter muttered.

The sound of tires on the road behind me made me turn. It was Terry's official vehicle, and he had Landon Michaels, an FBI agent married to Bay, with him. They hopped out of Terry's truck and hurried over.

"What's this?" Landon asked as he studied the teenagers.

I held out my hands. "They were in the road, so I stopped. They haven't spoken." A memory bubbled up. "Wait ... they weren't in the road. They walked into the road and stopped. That's the movement I saw."

"They walked directly in front of you and stopped?" Hunter asked.

"I remember thinking they were moving too slowly to be deer. They just walked out of the woods and stood there."

"Interesting," Landon said. He walked up to the kids, getting closer than I was comfortable with, and waved his hands in front of their faces in turn. "They may be in shock."

"Are we sure they weren't in an accident?" Hunter asked. "Anybody see any tire tracks?"

"That was the first thing I looked for," I volunteered. "I didn't see anything. I didn't go very far because ... well, you know why."

"That was smart." Hunter sent me a little smile.

"We need help," Landon, still standing in front of the kids, said. "We need someone who can search these woods fast."

I was confused. "Are you calling for backup?"

"Not just yet." Landon shook his head, then flicked his eyes to me. "Call Evan."

Evan, the day-walking vampire with a soul, lived in Hemlock Cove, worked in Hawthorne Hollow, and owned the coveted number one spot on Tillie's list of sidekicks. He'd been a sullen mess when Scout Randall had healed him, essentially shoving his soul back inside of him with her pixie magic. Over the course of the last year, he'd turned into a hardened ally. He had all the strength and abilities of a normal vampire, but none of the weaknesses.

I bobbed my head in agreement. "Good idea." I found him on my contacts list. I could hear the confusion in his voice when he answered. "Stormy?"

"Hey, Evan." My voice was raspy, and I had to clear my throat. "We have a bit of a situation on the highway between Hemlock Cove and Shadow Hills."

"How far out?"

"About eight miles or so from Hemlock Cove." I looked to Terry for confirmation, and he nodded. "Yeah, eight miles."

"I'll be there in three minutes." He disconnected before I could say anything else.

"He's on his way," I said to Landon as I returned my phone to my pocket. "He said three minutes, but I don't know how that's possible."

Landon shrugged. "He's Evan." He went back to staring at the teenagers. "They're in some sort of a fugue state."

Terry and Hunter were searching the tree line on either side of the road. I left them to it and moved closer to Landon.

"They don't react to anything." To prove it, I snapped my fingers directly next to the boy's ear. He didn't flinch or blink.

"Look at the size of their pupils." Landon leaned in so he could have a clear look at the boy's face. "I think they're on something."

"Could be a stimulant, or even LSD," I mused. "Or an antidepressant."

Landon gave me an odd look. "How do you know that?"

"I wrote books in my former life," I reminded him. "You wouldn't believe my search history. I think most writers would run into trouble if they were ever investigated for a crime because of the weird things we look up. I thought I was going to write a murder mystery once and dilated pupils were one of the clues to catch the killer."

"I guess you have a lot of weird information running around inside of your head."

More than I wanted to acknowledge. "Can we check their arms?" I pointed to the boy's arm that was closest to Landon.

"You mean for track marks?" Landon tugged up the sleeve of the boy's flannel shirt. "Wow."

There was a huge bruise on the inside of the boy's forearm. "What caused that?"

"Your guess is as good as mine." Landon shrugged.

"What are we looking at?" a voice asked from behind us. It was so close, I almost came out of my skin.

I found Evan hanging over my back to get a better look. He hadn't driven, which meant he'd run the entire way. His dark hair was perfectly in place.

"Make a noise next time," I complained.

Evan smirked. "That kind of goes against the whole vampire thing." His eyes were serious as he studied the kids. "Can I touch them?"

Landon nodded.

"I just want to ...." Evan trailed off as he tugged the girl's T-shirt sleeve. "She's bruised."

"Could they have been in an accident?" Landon asked.

Evan looked at the bruise again, then looked to Hunter, who was on the side of the road staring into the trees. "We would know if they ran off the road here. The trees don't show any sign of damage."

"What if it wasn't here?" I asked. "What if they had the accident miles away and were disoriented? Maybe they decided to walk for help and got confused. They could have internal injuries." My voice grew shriller with each word as I worked myself up into a frenzy.

Evan's nostrils flared. "They don't smell like death."

"What does death smell like?"

"You'll know when you smell it." Evan gave me a kind smile. Then he leaned in and sniffed the girl's hair. "Mothballs."

Landon frowned. "Why would they smell like mothballs?" He leaned forward to sniff. "I don't smell mothballs."

"No offense, but my sense of smell is much stronger than yours. I definitely smell mothballs."

"Unless you can tell me why that's important, I can't see a reason to get excited about it."

"I don't know why it's important." Evan looked around again, then took a step back. "You need to get them to the hospital. Have you called for an ambulance?"

"We haven't." Landon said. "I'm not sure why. It's just..." He looked to me for help explaining.

"We thought they might turn into monsters or something," I admitted.

"They smell human enough," Evan offered.

"I'll call for help." Landon pulled out his phone. "Maybe, once their systems are flushed and they've gotten some sleep, they'll be able to tell us what happened."

"While you're doing that, Stormy and I will head into the woods," Evan said.

I immediately balked. "Why?"

"You know where they walked from. And you're a witch." Evan's lips curved. "If you're afraid, I can go alone."

There was a challenge. "Oh, no." I swept out my arm. "Lead the way."

Evan's grin expanded, but he didn't comment on the sarcasm. He was used to working with Scout and Tillie. They were way more sarcastic on their best days than I was on my worst.

"Where are you going?" Hunter yelled from down the road when he realized we were leaving.

"A quick walk," Evan called back. "We won't go far ... and she'll be fine. I promise."

Hunter looked torn, but nodded. "Okay. Be safe." He blew me a kiss.

Terry, walking behind Hunter, cuffed the back of his protégé's head. "Don't be gross, kid. You're on duty."

"Sorry." Hunter was sheepish. "She's my girl."

"Yeah, yeah, yeah."

Evan was light on his feet. Jumping from spot to spot so as not to roil up the tracks wasn't difficult for him. I, on the other hand, was a stumbler.

"Here." Evan scooped his arms around my waist and lifted me off the ground for four bounding leaps. I was breathless when he lowered me to the ground again. "They obviously came in through here." He pointed to the ground, as if that somehow proved something.

I didn't see anything. "I don't think I'll ever be hired as a tracker," I said, dragging a hand through my blond hair. "I don't know what I'm supposed to be looking at."

Evan dropped to one knee and pointed. "See that right there?"

I could just make out a faint indentation.

"That's the boy's work boots," he said. "I've seen a few small tracks that must belong to the girl, but he's the easier one to track because he weighs more."

"And the boots are distinctive," I guessed.

"Yeah." Evan's eyes were sharp as we started walking away from the road. "How did you find them?"

"I was at The Overlook. I learned how to perform a fire trap spell. Bay wouldn't allow me to release Tillie from it until she agreed to give up Crusty ... and it turned into a whole big thing."

"How did that turn out?"

"Bay smells like rancid pickles."

Evan chuckled. "And I bet Crusty is still around."

"He is," I confirmed. I was distracted driving home and when I looked up, they were in the road. I stopped the car and called Hunter. The whole thing felt odd. I didn't trust any of it."

"Your survival instincts are developing well."

"But they haven't done anything."

"Maybe not, but the situation is strange. Something tells me we're not looking at a human explanation for what's happened here."

I jerked my eyes to him. "What makes you say that? You said they weren't monsters."

"That doesn't mean that they weren't brought here by monsters ... or chased by monsters ... or used as bait by monsters."

"Bait for what?"

"You stopped, didn't you?"

A chill ran through me, and I jerked my eyes back to the road. "Do you think they're okay?" Fear for Hunter almost overwhelmed me.

"I can hear them, Stormy," Evan assured me. "Even from this distance. The ambulance is arriving. Things are exactly as we left them."

I relaxed, marginally. "Okay."

"You still want to go back." His eyes twinkled.

"Yeah."

"Let's go." He rolled his neck and studied the ground again. "The tracks originate here."

"But there's nothing here," I said.

IT TOOK ONLY A FEW MINUTES TO get back to the road. The paramedics had the boy and girl on gurneys, wheeling them to the ambulance.

"We'll take them to the hospital," a male paramedic told Landon. "I have no idea what's wrong with them, but they're definitely dehydrated."

"Could that cause their current state of disinterest?" Landon asked.

The paramedic shrugged. "They'll get a battery of tests run."

Landon nodded. "Keep me updated if they react to anything on the ride."

"Will do." The paramedic started to the ambulance, then

stopped. "This was in the boy's pocket. It fell out when we were loading them up."

Landon watched as the paramedic deposited a Velcro wallet into his hand. He smiled in thanks. "This will be helpful."

Evan and I remained near the trees until the ambulance left, then emerged to join the others.

"The tracks don't go very far into the woods," Evan volunteered. "There's no car or four-wheeler back there. I have no idea where they came from."

Landon nodded, taking the information in. He had the boy's license out of the wallet and was typing on his phone.

"Got him?" Terry asked when Landon's brow furrowed.

"Um ... yeah," Landon replied. "Eli Eaton. The photo matches. The girl is his sister, Shauna."

"Are they from this area?"

Landon opened his mouth, then shut it. "They were. They both went missing when they were sixteen and fifteen, respectively."

"From where?"

"Shadow Hills." Landon looked as if he was about to melt down. "They've been missing for ten years, Terry."

I thought my stomach was going to make a run for the border. "How is that possible? They were five and six when they went missing?"

Landon shook his head. "They were fifteen and sixteen when they went missing. Eli has his license."

"But they're not twenty-five and twenty-six." There was no way.

"They went missing a decade ago and just showed up looking the same way they did when they went missing."

"Which means?"

"Something very weird is going on."

3
THREE

I had questions—more questions than I could internally wrangle—but I kept them to myself. Hunter sent me ahead because they needed to photograph the scene. Evan promised to check the woods again, cast a wider net, and be in touch. So, as much as I didn't want to leave, there was nothing else for me to do. I climbed behind the wheel of my car and drove home.

It was the dinner hour, and the restaurant was hopping. Knowing Hunter would be tired when he showed up—there would be no romantic Mexican feast tonight—I headed into the restaurant. I would get dinner and take it upstairs to keep it warm.

The evening shifts were often a free-for-all with my Uncle Brad in charge. My grandfather handled the mornings. The afternoons were covered by a hodgepodge of individuals. Brad didn't have an authoritative presence. Nobody, not even the family and friends who worked at Two Broomsticks, respected him.

There was a reason.

"Nobody listens to me when I tell them the truth," Brad complained to my cousin David. They were working the grill, a sign the restaurant was unusually busy. That was normal during spring as people left their warm homes to shed the northern Michigan winter.

"What truth are you telling tonight?" I asked as I plucked a strawberry from the garnish bowl. They weren't very flavorful, and I made a face.

"They won't be sweet for another eight weeks," David volunteered.

David shrugged. "Most people don't eat the garnishes." He flicked my ear. I was an only child so he was closer to a sibling than a cousin. "You're the only weirdo who eats them."

I abandoned the bowl and focused on my uncle. I would regret asking what conspiracy theory had gotten him going this evening, but I had time to burn. Hunter wouldn't be home for at least an hour. "What don't people listen to you about?" I asked again, resigned to my fate.

"The drones," Brad intoned. "They're everywhere, but people won't take them seriously."

The drone story had first bubbled up a few months ago. Hunter and I had laughed about it when watching the news. It seemed odd my uncle would be so many months behind the gossip.

"I thought the drones were discovered to be planes and ... well, drones," I challenged. "It was people who happened to own drones jumping on the bandwagon and trying to torture their neighbors."

"That was the official story," David agreed. He was shorter than me by an inch, and I wasn't tall. He was compact and had a ski-slope nose distinctive to him and his three siblings.

"That's so sad." Brad sent me a pitying look. "You can't trust the official story. Have I taught you nothing?"

It had definitely been a bad idea to engage with my uncle. When I pictured him in his old age, he was always in one of those hospitals where they lock up the glue after craft hour. I pushed forward anyway.

"What's wrong with the official story?"

David shot me a wounded look. "Don't encourage him." he complained.

I shrugged. "Hunter won't be home for an hour."

"You guys are so codependent." David shook his head. "Where is he?"

Sensing an opening, I opted to walk through it. "Do you remember the Eaton kids?"

David's face screwed up in concentration. "I'm not sure. Wait." He bobbed his head. "They were kidnapped by their dad, right?"

"I don't know. Did you know them?"

"They were about three or four years younger than us. Their mother was weird. We never hung out in the same places."

"Weird how? What's her name?"

"I think her name was Sandra." David looked to Brad for confirmation.

"Sandy." My uncle nodded. "She believed the government," he said mournfully. "When they told her that her children were taken by their father, she believed it ... and never got over the loss of them."

I was confused. "You don't think their father took them?"

"Obviously, the people on the drones took them," David said with a grin. Now he was the one baiting our uncle when I had a topic I really wanted to focus on.

Well played, David. Well played.

"Wasn't it proven that most people simply never looked up into the sky until others told them what was going on and everything they were seeing was planes and their neighbors messing with them?" I challenged. The drone conversation was already dragging.

"How can you believe that?" Brad threw up his hands and lost the spatula. David, who had excellent reflexes, caught the spatula before it could hit the floor.

"That's the story I heard," I replied, casting David a wary look. I'd clearly kicked the hornet's nest that was my uncle's busy brain and was already regretting it.

"The government doesn't want us to know about the aliens," Brad replied, "because you'll be aware that we have no control."

I waited for him to continue, but he was seemingly done. "No control over what?" I asked.

David jabbed the spatula at me from behind Brad's back. His message was clear. *I'll pay you back for this.*

"No control over any of it," Brad replied. "The aliens control everything."

"What everything?"

"Everything everything!" He looked at me as if I was an idiot. "They're in control of the government, Stormy. They're in control of the FBI ... and the presidency ... and Congress ... and the Supreme Court."

"Oh." I nodded as if that was the most normal thing I'd ever heard. "I'm glad you told me. That explains a lot about the current state of our government."

"Right?" Brad bobbed his head in agreement. "I'm so glad to welcome you to team Alien Nation." He held out his hand as if he wanted to shake mine.

Because I didn't know what else to do, I shook it. "Glad to be on the team."

David's smirk told me I was going to regret saying that. For now, I pulled my hand back. "So the Eaton kids," I prodded. "I'm not familiar with the story. I don't remember them."

"They didn't go to school with us," David replied. "Their mother homeschooled them. They were wacky religious."

"Like Scientologists?"

"No, more like the people who prep for the end of the world and think their kids are being indoctrinated by copies of *To Kill a Mockingbird.*"

It wasn't all that surprising that people who believed stuff like that would end up in Northern Lower Michigan. There was a lot of open country space where they could establish compounds to hoard their dried beans. They weren't right on top of each other like in the city, and they could carry out whatever weird rituals they fancied without the neighbors all up in their business. That part of it worked out for witches as well, because the Winchesters liked getting drunk on warm summer nights and dancing naked on the bluff by the inn.

"So what happened to the kids?" I asked.

David shrugged. "I guess when Sandra moved up here, she and her husband weren't getting along. They divorced because she was a religious nut, and he saw his kids once a month. He was supposed to take them for a month that summer, but he never returned them."

"The police didn't try to find him?"

"Well, Greg Ryan was in charge at that point."

I scowled. Hunter's father had been a bad cop. The worst cop imaginable. He abused his son and wife. He was forced out of his position and held a grudge against Hunter for remaining with the department. They'd never been close. As far as I knew, Greg had moved into the woods and almost never came to town. I hadn't seen him in the year since I'd moved back.

"Then he dropped the ball?" I asked.

"Hunter will know better than me," David replied. "I was in my early twenties back then. I probably didn't pay as much attention as I should have. Honestly, they were gone a month before anyone—including their mother, apparently—realized it."

"Is their mother still here?" I thought about how she might take the news that her children were back … and didn't look a day older than they had when they disappeared.

"She moved seven or eight years ago. I have no idea where."

I blew out a sigh. This required further digging. It was probably best to do it away from my family, just in case it turned out to be something witchy. It was time to change the subject. "What's on special tonight? Hunter will be hungry when he gets back."

"You haven't told us why you were asking about the Eaton twins," David pointed out.

"Something happened tonight in regard to them," I evaded. It was time to lie. The news would come out eventually, but I didn't want to be the source. Besides, if Brad heard the story, he would turn it into an alien invasion. "Hunter said he'll tell me when he gets here. I need to get dinner ready."

"Do you think they're dead?" David looked alarmed.

"He didn't make it sound like that. Maybe he found some of their belongings or something." I felt guilty for lying to David, but not to Brad. I would apologize later. "I guess we'll find out soon enough."

David looked momentarily troubled. "As for specials, there's prime rib." He gave me a knowing look. "Mashed potatoes and gravy, and green beans as sides."

I almost went weak at the knees. I loved prime rib. "Can I get two servings on plates covered with foil to keep it warm in the oven?"

"I guess I can do that for you."

"Thank you." I gave him a cheeky smile. "I'm going to put together two salads and grab some bread."

"You're such a good provider," David teased. "I can see why Hunter is marrying you."

"He's not marrying me for my cooking abilities. He's marrying me because I provide other gifts." I realized how filthy that sounded too late. "I meant like massages and good conversation."

David was dubious. "If that's your story."

Brad stopped me before I could move too far away. "I'll send you some literature on the drones. We meet once a week. We don't publicize the location until the night of the meeting. It rotates, for obvious reasons."

"Because you don't want the aliens to find out?" I guessed.

He nodded. "They have eyes and ears everywhere."

HUNTER LOOKED TIRED WHEN HE LET himself into our apartment above the restaurant. I was looking forward to moving into our new house in a few months. It was my dream house from childhood. The woman who had lived in it for decades had agreed to sell to Hunter under the stipulation he let her live there until the end of spring. Once she moved out, Hunter said, we would have the carpet replaced, the floors buffed, and the interior painted before we moved in.

I was champing at the bit to get my hands on the house so I could decorate. For now, though, the apartment was warm and welcoming when we cuddled on the couch every night. Now that Easton, my gnome shifter familiar, was living with my best friend, Sebastian Donovan, it didn't feel as if the walls were closing in on us as often.

"Hey." Hunter came straight to me and planted a kiss on my mouth as soon as he'd removed his shoes. "Are you okay?" His eyes, filled with concern, roamed me. "I didn't get a chance to ask earlier."

"You did ask," I argued.

"Yes, but I usually like to ask with my arms and lips."

That made me laugh, then I sobered. "Any word on the Eatons?"

He flopped down next to me. "No change. They still aren't talking. They stare into the distance and don't interact with anyone. Their vitals are stable. They're being hydrated. Everyone is hopeful, after a good night's sleep, that they'll start talking."

"What happens if they don't?"

"That's tomorrow's problem."

I was quiet a beat, then remembered dinner. "Do you know who you're going to love more than anyone in about thirty seconds?"

Hunter's smile was lazy. "Feels like a trick question."

"Me."

"I already love you more than anyone."

"But what if I told you that right now, in our oven, I have not one but two servings of prime rib?" I was excited beyond belief.

"I would still say I love you more than anyone, but I'd have to say it in the kitchen." He was already on his feet and moving to the kitchen. "You'd better not be playing with me, woman."

"Did you just call me 'woman?'" I was appalled ... and a little amused. "That's so sexist."

Hunter didn't respond until he opened the oven and looked inside. "I'll call you whatever you want me to call you, baby." He leaned over and kissed me senseless, then happily grabbed the baking mitts from the countertop. "Go to the table. I'll bring dinner over."

"I have bread and salads too."

"I knew my faith in you wasn't misplaced."

We settled silently at the table. I poured us each a glass of wine— it had been a long day, and we needed to relax—and the only sound after that was silverware clinking against plates. We were halfway through our meal before I couldn't take the silence.

"David told me a bit about the Eatons," I started. When Hunter sent me a sharp look, I held up my hands. "I did not tell him what happened. That information will get out, but not through me."

He relaxed and nodded. "Sorry. It's just ... how are we going to explain this, Stormy? It has been ten years. The doctor said he would place their ages at roughly sixteen."

"Which means they haven't aged at all. How is that possible?"

"I was hoping you could tell me." He watched me with his steady gaze. "You're the magical one."

"Yes, but Bay had to give me a book on hellcats today because I don't know what I'm doing." I was morose. "Do you know, if I get good enough, I can create healing fire?"

"No."

"Neither did I. Today I created a fire trap. Bay wouldn't let me release Tillie until she agreed to dump the clown doll sidekick."

Hunter perked up. "Crusty's gone?"

"No. Tillie found a loophole. Then she made Bay smell like rancid pickles as punishment. Apparently, I escaped retribution because she blamed it all on Bay."

Hunter chuckled. "Sometimes I think they just like to mess with one another out of boredom."

"Landon is going to have to cuddle up with a wife who smells like a rancid pickle tonight. I can't see that making him happy."

"Maybe not, but it won't matter. Landon will cuddle with her regardless."

I scratched the side of my nose. "David said the mother—I think her name is Sandra—moved away years ago. When I asked if anyone interviewed the father—because everyone assumed he took the kids —he said your father ran the investigation and doesn't know if they ever found him."

"The records from my father's reign of terror aren't great," Hunter acknowledged. "I'm getting into all of that tomorrow."

"Will you have to go to him if you don't find what you need?" I was nervous at the thought. Hunter never talked about his father.

"I'm hopeful that won't be necessary," Hunter replied. "I guess I'll find out tomorrow."

"I'll go with you," I blurted. "To see your father." I forced myself to calm down when he made a weird face. "I just meant that you don't have to go alone."

His eyes were soft when they connected with mine. "Thanks, but I don't want you around him. If I need to see him, I'll take Terry."

4
FOUR

Hunter was a wall of heat when I emerged from dreamland the next morning. Our bed was a double—that was all the room could handle without pushing a bed against the wall—so we were always on top of each other.

"Holy crap!" I pushed him away, earning a look of consternation for my efforts. "Sorry," I said. "I thought I was having a hot flash."

"I thought you liked cuddling."

"I do, but not when you're hot."

"Oh, I know." He gave me a knowing smile. "That memo was sent to everyone in town during your vacation from Shadow Hills."

I rolled my eyes. "Everyone, huh? Is that really something you want to brag about?"

"Now that you mention it, probably not," he conceded. He leaned in for a kiss. "Sorry if I overheated you."

That made me roll my eyes harder. "Somebody is feeling full of himself this morning."

His arm snaked around my waist, and he pulled me to him. "I'm feeling romantic, Stormy."

"Is that so?"

"You don't have to work this morning." He gave me a soft kiss. "How about we start the morning off with a bang?"

My eyebrows almost flew off my forehead. "That was quite the double entendre."

"It was meant to be."

"Okay," I said finally. Now that he'd said it, I was in the mood too. "I'm going to want a big breakfast afterward."

"Your wish is my command."

WE HEADED DOWNSTAIRS FOR BREAKFAST an hour later, an extra spring in my step. Normally, I would've started my shift with Grandpa two hours earlier if I had a shift to cover. He was behind the grill working with my cousin Annie.

Briefly, his eyes moved to me, then they skittered away. He'd been this way for weeks, ever since he'd been overtaken by a spell and joined a neighborhood watch, which turned out to be a cult. I wasn't holding a grudge—despite some of the things the cult had done—but he was embarrassed. His way of dealing with the embarrassment was to pretend it had never happened.

"What's up with you guys?" he asked, keeping his eyes on the eggs frying on the grill. "Are you turning into lay-abouts and sleeping your lives away?"

Hunter shrugged. "Stormy didn't have to work this morning, so we decided to sleep in."

Grandpa flashed a flat smile. "Must be nice."

"You don't have to work," I reminded him. "You choose to work because you like hanging out with the coffee crew every morning."

"Whatever." Grandpa's eyes moved back to my face. "When are you moving out?"

The question threw me.

Sensing my discomfort, Hunter put his arm around my waist. "Wow, it's nice out here in left field. Should I take that to mean you want us out soon?"

"No, that's not what I'm getting at."

"We can rent a place for two months if that's what you want." There was no smile on Hunter's face. He seemed to realize—just like me—that Grandpa was mortified over his actions with the neighborhood watch. Rather than apologize, he was being squirrelly. I hated it.

"I'm not kicking you out." Grandpa made a face as if Hunter had suggested the weirdest thing in the world. "Why would you think that?"

"Because you just asked us when we were moving out," I replied. For a split second, I thought about pushing him to acknowledge the neighborhood watch, but it was a waste of time. He would lose his temper, and we wouldn't get breakfast. "We weren't planning on moving for two months. If you need us out before then, just tell us. We'll figure it out." I thought about having to relocate for two months—moving twice in a short amount of time—and sighed. "We should look at available rentals," I said to Hunter.

He nodded.

"Oh, stop being babies." Grandpa's upper lip curled into a sneer. "I'm not asking you to move out. In fact, I don't want you to move out. It's better for me if you two stay another six months."

"Why would that be better for you?"

"Because your cousin thinks she's going to need a place to live with that gaggle of obnoxious kids she insisted on having."

It took me a moment to translate. "Lisa," I assumed. My cousin Lisa was one of my least favorite cousins, and that was saying something because one of my cousins had moved to a compound in the middle of the woods by the Cedar River and was creating booby traps for when the government arrived to take ... well, something, away from him. I didn't know what that something was, but I was sure it involved the eighty million guns he had hidden on his property, and maybe the weed plants.

Grandpa nodded. "After the thing..." He took a dramatic breath. "The thing" was the cult. Lisa and her husband Linc had been dragged into that as well. Linc couldn't keep it in his pants—he slept with anything that moved—and he'd struck up an affair with the mayor's wife during that time. It had to be his twentieth affair, which was why Lisa kept having kids by the man. She thought she could trap him with a new baby whenever she felt him slipping away. He never stopped, and he'd indicated to me that he was never going to. He knew what Lisa was doing and wanted to force her hand so he wouldn't be the bad guy. She needed to be the one to break up with him.

"You mean the thing where everyone in town was taken in by a cult leader, right?" Hunter pressed.

I shot him a quelling look. Grandpa would go surly and clam up if he wasn't careful.

"That's right," Grandpa gritted out. "It seems that Lisa and Linc are having issues seeing eye to eye."

"Meaning that Lisa can't pretend that everyone in town doesn't know about Linc's wandering eye," I guessed.

Grandpa shrugged. "I told her she shouldn't have married him."

"I don't think he should've married her either. It's not as if she's a catch."

"She has limited options," Grandpa agreed. "Their financial situation is not as solid as everyone assumed."

"They have no money?" That didn't make sense. "Linc has a good job."

"Yes, but they spend as if the apocalypse is coming." Grandpa's disdain was evident. If there was one thing he hated, it was people who were fiscally irresponsible. That's why I'd been embarrassed when I'd gotten myself into a financial hole and had to move back to Shadow Hills. He was letting me live in the apartment above the restaurant rent free. Hunter, of course, insisted on paying rent.

"Are you telling me they're going to lose that house?" I sputtered. Real estate in Shadow Hills went two ways: half the houses went for prices considered inexpensive almost anywhere else in the country;

the rest were overblown affairs that the few people in the area with money called vacation homes.

"I'm not privy to everything going on," Grandpa hedged. "She's playing it close to the vest. It seems that if she and Linc separate, the house will have to be put on the market."

"Then she should get half the equity they've built up in that house," Hunter said. "What am I missing?"

Grandpa was grim. "There is no equity. They overpaid for the house because Lisa really wanted it, and Linc is a wuss who wouldn't tell her no. He bought the house even though it was out of their range. They took out a second mortgage when your cousin wanted a new vehicle."

"Oh, geez." I shook my head. I had no room to judge. I'd gotten myself into financial trouble because I was reluctant to come home and admit my writing career had been a failure. I was buried in credit card debt. Thankfully, I owned my car—however rundown—outright and there were no real estate missteps in my past. I had a plan for handling the credit card debt, and it didn't involve letting Hunter pay it off, even though I knew darned well he had every intention of doing just that.

"You're saying Lisa will be homeless if she and Linc split up," Hunter assumed.

Grandpa nodded. "Linc is pushing for the divorce. It seems he's reached his limit. Lisa, of course, wants to pretend it never happened. If she has to admit that marrying him—and then trapping him with a baby whenever he cheated—was a bad idea, she'll never get over the mortification. I'm not sure they have much of a choice."

"You need us to move," I realized. "Grandma won't tolerate Lisa being homeless, even if she is the worst person in the world."

Grandpa scowled. "Your grandmother is making noise about moving them in with us."

I jolted. "You've got to be kidding."

"I wish I were."

"We can find a place to rent," Hunter said hurriedly. "It's only two months. We're going to need at least a week, though. Even if I find a place today, we won't be able to move now."

"Hold up." Grandpa raised his hand. "I'm not keen on the idea of Lisa moving those rugrats of hers—kids she refuses to make behave —into the apartment. I don't trust her not to let them run all over the restaurant at night."

It was one thing for Hunter and me to live upstairs. We weren't going to get bored and come downstairs to play with knives or break the soda machine. Lisa and her kids were another story entirely. "What are you going to do?"

"Lisa can stay in the house until it sells. The house will sell fast. Even if they manage to delay listing for a few weeks and then closing for a month..." He trailed off.

"She'll be homeless right about the time that Hunter and I are moving," I realized.

Grandpa nodded. "I don't want her moving in upstairs. That's better than her moving those kids into my house, though. I don't know what to do."

"What about a rental?" Hunter asked.

"How can she foot that bill?" Grandpa challenged. "She has no job. She's going to have to get one—I've made that clear. Her whole goal was to be a stay-at-home mom. I think that's a noble pursuit. Your grandmother stayed home with our kids. But the situations are different.

"Linc makes a decent living, and he'll pay child support," Grandpa continued. "The thing is, it's not nearly the amount of child support Lisa thinks. She pictures him paying her the same amount of money he currently brings into the household, but that's not realistic.

"On top of that, they're in credit card debt up to their eyeballs," he continued. "They have leases on two new vehicles. They're almost six figures in debt because your cousin insists on shopping like she makes ten times what Linc actually brings in." He looked exasperated.

"They can declare bankruptcy," Hunter suggested.

Grandpa didn't look keen on that idea. He was from a generation of people who didn't declare bankruptcy to shed their obligations. He'd told me—more than once—that people paid their debts. It was his voice I heard in my head as I was figuring out how to deal with my credit card debt.

"They might have no choice but to go that route, but that creates other problems."

"No one will rent to someone who has already walked out on her bills once," I guessed.

Grandpa nodded. "It's a mess. I'm not trying to force you out. I just need a timetable."

"We can get in the house in about five weeks," Hunter said. "We were holding off to change the carpeting and paint, but we can work around that."

Grandpa pursed his lips. "Let me talk to your grandmother again. I keep hoping for a different outcome. I just don't know what that would look like."

"You could always make Uncle Brad deal with it," I suggested. "He is her father. Shouldn't he take her in?"

"I suggested that to your grandmother. She pointed out—and rightly so—that your uncle is a bit nutty."

I liked how he referred to Brad as my uncle rather than claim him as his son. Uncle Brad rubbed Grandpa the wrong way daily. It was only one of the reasons they worked opposite shifts.

"Just let us know what you need," I said. "We'll make it work either way."

Grandpa nodded. "Thanks for that. If you guys want breakfast, put in your orders here. Annie is busy covering both sections today."

I grabbed an order pad and scrawled our usual breakfast orders. "I'll take coffee around to help her."

Grandpa gave me an appreciative smile. This was the friendliest he'd been since the whole neighborhood watch thing. I took it as a good sign that he was moving beyond what had happened. I needed that. Even if he never truly apologized, as long as things got back to normal, I would take it.

Hunter got comfortable at a table and waited for me to take the coffee around. He looked troubled when I joined him. "I wish there was something we could do to help him out," he said.

"I'm not sure there is. I don't have any extra money. And you're not paying my credit card bills," I added quickly, reading his expression.

"We need to talk about that." Hunter was grave. "You paying extra on interest is a bad idea. Why not let me pay them off so all of your money can go toward the house?"

"Because I made this mess, and I have to deal with it."

"But you're wasting money."

"You don't think I deserve repercussions for what I did?" I challenged.

"I don't have any interest in punishing you, and you've learned your lesson. We're building a life together. Doesn't it make sense to spend the least amount of money to clean this up?"

"And then I pay you back?" I was confused.

"We're getting married. My money is going to become your money."

"I don't want that." I vehemently shook my head. "I need to clean up my own mess."

"Geez." Hunter groaned. "You know what?" He held up his hands. "We're not going to argue about this now. We'll fight later. We need to discuss today."

"What's today?"

"I'm going to the hospital to check on the Eaton kids. I thought you would want to come with me." He looked hopeful. It didn't take a genius to figure out why.

"You think something magical happened to them," I said.

He nodded. "There's no other explanation."

"I'll go with you." I flashed a smile I didn't feel. "I'm as invested in this as you are."

He patted my hand. "Maybe on the way to the hospital we can brainstorm some ideas to help your grandfather."

I already had an idea. I traced my finger over his palm. "Thank you for the offer to help pay off my credit cards," I said in a low voice. "I really do think this is something I should finish on my own."

"I get that." Sincerity shone through Hunter's eyes. "The thing is, at a certain point, it's about being smart and not stubborn. If we need to figure out a way for you to pay me back, maybe that's what we need to do. Accruing unnecessary interest is not the way to go."

I didn't disagree with him, but the idea of letting him swoop in to save me after I'd created this mess made me feel guilty. "I'll think about it."

"When you realize I'm right, we'll figure the rest of it out."

5
FIVE

We bandied about ideas on what to do about the Lisa situation. We agreed that Lisa staying in her marriage was a recipe for disaster. Linc wasn't a stand-up guy. In fact, he seemed the sort who would run out for cigarettes one day and never come back.

"Then he'll move to Florida or something and work cash jobs so he doesn't get nailed for child support," Hunter said as we pulled into the hospital parking lot.

"And then he'll find some other woman willing to sleep with him," I said. "She'll get pregnant, and he'll start the whole cycle over again."

I paused in front of his truck. "Lisa is not a good person."

"Not even a little," Hunter confirmed.

"This is going to be a hard road for her, though. I mean, what is she going to do? She wasn't a good waitress when she worked at the restaurant as a teenager. On top of that, how is she going to afford daycare on a server's salary?"

Hunter shrugged. "My guess is that she'll start her hunt for a sugar daddy."

"That might've worked when she was younger. She was gorgeous. But she's had three kids. She still looks pretty good, but she's not the same teenager who didn't have stretch marks and could've doubled as a model. Most sugar daddies aren't looking to take on three kids."

"That's true. There are single men with money who frequent the area. She could start hanging out at the resort looking for one."

"I can totally see her going that route. Until then..." When I tried to picture my grandfather living with Lisa and her kids, I saw bedlam. "Grandpa won't put up with those kids."

"Maybe your grandfather should move to the apartment," Hunter suggested.

I snapped my eyes to him, more intrigued than I probably should've been. "That's interesting."

He laughed at my sudden interest. "I was joking."

"I can see it. He needs his space."

"Would your grandmother allow that?"

Most people assumed my grandfather ran the roost in his house, and they would be right to a certain extent. My grandmother knew how to get what she wanted, though. She was more than willing to force him to sleep on the couch to get her way.

"She wouldn't stop him," I replied as we started to the glass entryway. "She wouldn't be able to stop him. I can see her thinking that it would be a punishment to live alone. And maybe, after several months, my grandfather might believe that. The trade-off to not have to live with Lisa's kids would be worth it to him."

"Then your grandmother would be stuck with Lisa's kids. How would that work out?"

"Not well. My grandmother would be on Lisa about getting her finances in order. Maybe that's the best outcome. The best thing would be for Lisa to move in with her parents."

"Your uncle is crazy."

"That's one of the reasons Lisa is the way she is. He threw money at every problem he had with her when she was a teenager. That's why she's so entitled. He should have to deal with the mess he created."

"Kind of like you and the credit cards?"

I shot him a dirty look. "I thought you were letting that go."

"I figured you'd eventually come to the right conclusion. It's driving me crazy."

"I don't want to argue." I had been using my outdoor voice before we entered and everyone in the hospital lobby turned to look at us.

Hunter had an easy smile at the ready, but the tenseness around his eyes was obvious. "We'll talk about this later."

"You brought it up," I reminded him.

"I thought I was going to win. It's no longer fun."

I didn't want to laugh—that would only encourage him—but I couldn't help myself. "Fine. We'll table the discussion for now."

Hunter marched up to the desk and flashed his badge. "I need to know what floor the Eatons are on."

"They're on the fifth floor," the receptionist replied. Her gaze was appraising as she looked Hunter up and down, then she sent a curious look in my direction. "Do you have identification?"

"She's here as a consultant," Hunter said. "She found them. We're hoping she'll be a familiar face for them. Have they started talking?"

The receptionist jerked her eyes away from me and had a smile at the ready for Hunter. "I don't know. They've shut down reports outside the medical team working with them because they're afraid somebody in the hospital might call the news or something."

"That's a good plan." Hunter winked in his flirtatious—and yet harmless—way. "What room, please?"

"Room 504."

"Thank you." Hunter didn't take my hand. That would cause questions. We weren't in Shadow Hills, where everyone knew we were together. In this moment, we were colleagues. He inclined his head toward the elevators. "Have a nice day."

"You too," the woman called out wistfully. "Have a really nice day."

I waited until we were on the elevator, doors closed, to speak. "Does that happen wherever you go?"

"What?" Hunter was the picture of innocence.

"Oh, don't even." I clucked my tongue and shook my head. "Don't act modest now. You woke up telling me how hot you are."

"No, you woke up and told me how hot I was. I just agreed."

Even though the banter eased some of my anxiety, I had my poker face on when we got to the fifth floor.

Hunter took the lead. There was a doctor outside the room. "Dr. Stiles." Hunter extended his hand. "Hunter Ryan."

"I remember you." Stiles's smile was welcoming. His eyes briefly darted to me. "Who's your friend?"

"Stormy Morgan, this is Dr. Brett Stiles," Hunter volunteered. "Stormy found them last night."

Stiles nodded. "Is it true they were just standing in the middle of the road?"

Hunter and I hadn't talked about what I should say. "Actually, I think they moved out from the woods right in front of me. I was driving, and when I saw the motion, I braked. They just stood there after that."

"They didn't say anything?" Stiles was looking for answers, which suggested things hadn't progressed with the Eatons.

"No," I confirmed. "Are they still not talking?"

"They've made a few noises," Stiles replied. "They act as if they're frightened. They haven't said any words yet."

"Could that be a medical issue?" Hunter asked.

Stiles lifted one shoulder. "Your guess is as good as mine. We're running tests. They're no longer dehydrated. So far, we haven't found any medical reason for concern."

"But?" Hunter prodded.

"My understanding is that these kids disappeared ten years ago, when they were fifteen and sixteen. The tests we've run so far suggest they're the same ages they were when they disappeared. If I didn't know better, I'd say they'd been cryogenically frozen."

"What are our options?"

"I don't know." Stiles looked baffled. "We need them to give us an idea of what happened."

"Maybe we'll have better luck." Hunter pulled open the door and motioned for me to go ahead of him.

My eyes were on the Eatons the moment I walked into the room. They were in their beds, their hands resting on the blankets as they stared at nothing. They reminded me of mannequins.

Then Shauna lifted her eyes to me.

"She sees you," Hunter whispered.

I smiled at her and moved closer to her bed. She was tracking me. "Hey." I wanted to be a safe harbor in what had to be a sea of confusion for her, so I sat on her bed and took her hand. "How are you?"

The second I touched her, my mind was transported. It was a brief flash—darkness and trees everywhere as a scream ripped the air—and then it was gone. I dropped her hand.

"Is something wrong?" Stiles asked.

"No," I lied, shaking my head. I had to force myself not to look at Hunter. That would be a dead giveaway I wasn't telling the truth. "Her hand was colder than I anticipated."

Stiles didn't respond. I hoped he'd leave us alone, but I couldn't request that. He would be suspicious, and that was the last thing we needed.

"Sorry about that." I tentatively reached out to take Shauna's hand a second time. Thankfully, the flash didn't reoccur. "Your fingers are cold." I held them tightly.

"Hello, Shauna." Stiles stepped to the end of her bed. "Do you remember me? I'm Dr. Stiles."

Slowly—almost so slowly it was impossible to track her movement—Shauna shifted her eyes to Stiles. She opened her mouth, but the only sound that escaped was a raspy hum.

"It's okay," I assured her, squeezing her hand. "Take your time."

She licked her lips, her eyes flicking back to me. "W-w-w..." She frowned as she tried to form a word. "Where am I?" Her voice was barely a whisper.

Relief flooded me—she was in there, and I had no reason to believe the same wasn't true of her brother. I kept my smile in place. "You're in Traverse City. Do you know where that is?"

Shauna nodded, but doubt shrouded her eyes. "Where's my mom?"

"We're getting in touch with her," Hunter replied. He stepped forward slowly. "How are you feeling?"

I had to give him credit for not immediately jumping into grilling her. Hunter was good with people, especially traumatized individuals. It probably didn't hurt that he was every teenage girl's dream.

"I don't know." Shauna looked around, as if seeing the room for the first time. "Am I in the hospital?"

"You are," Stiles confirmed. "We're fixing you right up. You were a little dehydrated, but we've got that under control."

"But why am I here?" Shauna's eyebrows moved toward one another. "I don't understand why I'm here."

Hunter took advantage of her confusion—and the way she phrased it—to get to the heart of matters. "That's what we're trying to figure out." He allowed me to serve as her primary contact. "We found you and your brother on the road between Shadow Hills and Hemlock Cove. Do you know why you were out there?"

Shauna screwed up her face. "I don't know where that is."

"You lived in Shadow Hills when..." Hunter caught himself and pivoted. "Shadow Hills is your home. Hemlock Cove is one town over."

Something occurred to me. If Shauna and Eli really had been gone for ten years, the name Hemlock Cove would mean nothing to them. The town had rebranded in their absence. "Walkerville," I corrected. "He meant you were found on the road between Walkerville and Shadow Hills."

Explaining Walkerville being Hemlock Cove, and the town seemingly being taken over by witches was too much at this point.

Shauna looked as if she was concentrating. "I don't … I can't…" Tears filled her eyes. "I don't remember."

"It's okay," I assured her, shooting a warning look to Hunter. "You don't have to remember right this second. Take your time."

Shauna pulled her hand from mine, her gaze roaming the room before falling on Eli. She didn't look shocked to see her brother. It was more like she was staring at him from a great distance and trying to decide if she knew him. "Where's my mom?" she asked.

Either she didn't remember she'd already asked the question or she was more determined.

"We're looking for her," Hunter replied. He cast me a sidelong look. "Listen, I don't want you to worry." His voice was soft. "You need to rest and get better. Dr. Stiles will help you. We'll get your mom here as soon as possible."

Placated for the moment, Shauna nodded. She leaned back against the pillows. "I'm tired."

"You should sleep," Stiles said. "You need your rest." He smiled, but his eyes were troubled.

I left Shauna to nap and stopped at Eli's bed long enough to brush his hair from his forehead. When I touched his skin, I got another flash. It was dark, trees all around. The same voice that had screamed in the first flash screamed in this one.

I was shaky as I walked to the door with Hunter.

"We'll be in touch," Hunter promised Stiles. "We need to find their mother," he added in a low voice.

Stiles nodded in understanding.

Hunter ushered me toward the elevator.

"We need to find their mom?" I guessed.

He nodded. "We need to figure out where she moved to."

"Can you run her through your system?"

"We did last night. She supposedly moved to Grand Rapids. We sent Grand Rapids officers to notify her, but she wasn't at the address listed."

"Could something have happened to her? What about the father?"

"You know everything I do, Stormy. We're going to start digging."

I chewed my bottom lip for the ride down the elevator. "I saw something," I said. "It was very brief, but very visceral."

"What do you think it means?"

"I have no idea."

6

SIX

Hunter ran into three walls before he caught a break. Sandra Eaton was now going by the name Sandy Grant, employing her grandmother's maiden name. She was in Hawthorne Hollow, only thirty minutes away, where she'd been arrested three times in as many years for public drunkenness.

"What do you think that means?" I asked Hunter as we drove to Hawthorne Hollow.

"It means she likes to drink."

I gave him a dirty look. "Does she drink because of the kids?"

"I try not to judge on things like this." He was focused on the road, but I could tell he was giving it some real thought. "She's obviously been through a trauma. For all we know, she was drinking before they disappeared. I don't know that it matters either way."

"It matters because those kids want their mom," I argued. "If she's incapable of being there for them..."

"It's a weird situation," Hunter agreed.

"Oh, you think?"

He smirked at my sarcastic response. "We don't have much on

the father. He seems to be missing. The Eaton kids fell through the cracks."

"Maybe that was by design," I replied. "Maybe there was some sort of magic at work to prevent their disappearance from becoming a priority."

"What kind of magic would do that?"

I shrugged. "I just have trouble believing a mother wouldn't make a huge stink about the cops doing nothing to find her children."

"That's what makes me wonder if she was already drinking then," Hunter replied. "Maybe she was depressed because of the divorce."

I stared out the window. "I don't understand where they were. How can two teenagers disappear and then come back a decade later but they haven't changed? Were they frozen in time?"

"You're the witch, Stormy."

I grumbled under my breath.

"Have you ever considered that I'm a terrible witch?" I asked. It wasn't the first time I'd wondered if that was my ultimate lot in life.

"Why would I consider that?"

"I can't do anything on my own. I need constant help from Bay, Tillie, and Scout." I took a breath. "Maybe I'm bad at it."

"I don't believe that." Hunter was calm. "You're a good witch. You're just afraid to use too much magic."

"Because I'm afraid I'm a bad witch."

"No." Hunter sounded exasperated. "You don't want to expend too much magic because you're afraid you can't control it. That actually makes you a good witch. You're cognizant of what might happen."

I folded my arms over my chest. "That's a little simplistic," I complained after several seconds.

He snorted. "You're contrary to be contrary sometimes."

"I'm just saying it's possible that I'll fail at being a witch just like

I failed at..." I stopped. If I repeated my current stance that I was a failed writer, we would get into a real argument.

Hunter was the only person who still thought I could follow through on my childhood dream. He refused to let me throw my notebooks and computer away. He asked me questions about how I might write a certain story as we watched television at night to keep me engaged.

He was the best partner in the world and still had faith. I, on the other hand, didn't believe writing was in the cards.

"Do you want me to pick a fight over that comment now or later?" Hunter asked when I'd been silent several seconds.

I blew out a sigh. "Can we wait?" I asked, resigned to my fate. "We should focus on the Eatons."

Hunter was blasé as we crested the final hill that led into Hawthorne Hollow. "I can pencil you in for after dinner but before bed."

"You just want to argue so we can make up," I complained.

He smirked. "You know me so well."

SANDY GRANT LIVED IN A TRAILER ON the outskirts of Hawthorne Hollow. Hunter said the area was populated by a group of people who had elevated their social club—a standard Moose Lodge—in importance.

"I don't even know what a Moose Lodge is," I admitted as he parked in front of the trailer that had seen better days. The awning over the door sagged so low I figured Hunter would have to stoop when we knocked.

"Basically, they conduct fundraisers for needy children and seniors," he explained as he killed the engine. "It's also a reason for grown-ups to hang around and play cards and drink."

"So a nonstop frat party but with charities attached."

Hunter took the lead. "Keep your eyes open," he muttered before rapping on the screen frame.

I did a wide-eyed scan of the area around us.

"Well, that wasn't suspicious or anything," he laughed. He blanked his features when the door opened to reveal a small woman with sallow features.

At one time, she was probably pretty. Heck, maybe even gorgeous. She had the right bone structure. She was wrapped in a flannel robe with holes, her blond hair showed three inches of dark root growth, and there were bruised shadows under her eyes, which were red-rimmed. She smelled like a brewery and the stale scent of cigarette smoke wafted through the door.

I took an involuntary step back.

"Ms. Grant?" Hunter asked.

Sandy looked between us, confused. "I paid my rent," she mumbled.

Hunter held up his badge. "We're not here about the rent."

Sandy licked her lips. "Um..."

"You're not in any trouble," Hunter assured her. "We're here about Eli and Shauna."

Sandy let out a shaky breath. "You found them?" She swallowed hard. "Are they dead?"

"They're alive." Hunter made an attempt at a smile, but it fell flat. "We found them yesterday."

Sandy blinked. "I don't ... were they with Craig?"

"Craig Eaton?" Hunter prodded. "Your ex-husband?"

"He took them."

"He wasn't with them when we found them." Hunter paused a beat. "Ma'am, we have some things to discuss with you. May we come inside?"

Sandy glanced over her shoulder. If the scent coming from the open door was any indication, we probably didn't want to go inside. Sandy must have been thinking the same thing, because she waved at the small table under the awning. "Let's do this out here," she suggested.

"Sure." Hunter bobbed his head. "That's fine. It's a nice day."

It was still early spring, but being chilly was preferable to whatever we would find inside the trailer.

We got settled at the table. The chairs were metal and cold. I did my best to push that thought out of my mind and waited for Hunter to drop the bomb on the woman.

"Shauna and Eli are at Munson Medical Center in Traverse City," Hunter started.

"Where have they been?" Sandy asked. "Where was Craig keeping them? I always thought he took them to Canada. He has friends there. That's why they never made their way back to me. They couldn't."

Hunter hesitated, then shook his head. "We don't know where your ex-husband fits into all of this."

"They won't tell you? Of course they won't." Sandy let out a heavy sigh. "They were always loyal to their father."

"It's not that." Hunter exchanged a heavy look with me. This was not going to be an easy conversation. "Ma'am, I don't know how to tell you this, so I'm just going to lay it all out."

He took a deep breath. "Yesterday afternoon, between Hemlock Cove and Shadow Hills, a motorist stopped because there were two people standing in the middle of the road. When she tried to communicate with them, they didn't respond. She called for the police. We couldn't get them to respond either."

Sandy was confused. "I don't understand what that means. Is that why you're here? Did you have to fingerprint them because they weren't talking or something?"

"It didn't get that far," Hunter replied. "When we were loading them into the ambulance we retrieved Eli's wallet. His identification was inside."

"You mean his license from when he was a teenager?"

Hunter nodded. "Ma'am, this is going to sound strange but ... they look exactly the same as when they disappeared."

Sandy's eyebrows moved toward one another. "How is that possible? They've been gone for ten years."

"We don't know," Hunter admitted. "The doctors said they place the age of your children at fifteen and sixteen."

"But..." Sandy was thrown. "That's not possible," was all she said after several seconds.

Hunter leaned back in his chair. "We had trouble tracking you down. The last record we had for Sandra Eaton listed you living in Grand Rapids. We sent officers to check that address, but you weren't there."

"I left Grand Rapids five years ago," Sandy replied. "I thought moving there would make things easier after they were gone. You know, a new atmosphere or something. I don't know what I was thinking. It didn't help.

"I moved to Flint for a year, made some friends, and when they decided to move to Hawthorne Hollow because they had relatives here, I followed," she continued. "I wasn't sure it was going to work —being so close to where it happened—but I got a job at a restaurant, and I'm still here five years later."

Hunter nodded. "I get it."

"No, you don't." Sandy shot him a sad smile. "I appreciate that you're trying your best not to point out that I'm a mess. If you think I don't know that, you're mistaken. I've been a mess since before they were taken."

This was the part of the story I was most interested in, and I nodded encouragingly for her to continue.

"Craig and I never should've gotten married," she started. "We were incompatible. I just wanted to be a wife and mother. I wasn't all that worked up about a job because that wasn't the important part of my life.

"Craig seemed fine with that when the kids were little because I was homeschooling them," she continued. "Once they were older and could do the work on their own, he was always on me about finding a job. He had no problem with me being a waitress and working three shifts at night when the kids were little. But the fact that I was happy being a waitress when they were older bothered him."

"What did he want you to do?" I asked.

She lifted one shoulder. "He thought I should get an office job or something. He kept bringing up working at an insurance agency. His sister owned one. I said I was fine where I was. It caused more than one fight."

She swallowed hard, her fingers drumming against the top of the table. "We fought a lot. I thought that was normal because my parents fought a lot when I was growing up. I just assumed we would keep living our life, but he had other plans."

She took a deep breath. "He had an affair. Then I had an affair to retaliate. Then he had another." Her eyes were glassy when they locked with mine. "It was not a healthy environment for my kids, but I kept at it three or four years. Finally, he had an affair that lasted a full year, and he asked for a divorce.

"I dragged my feet, convinced he'd tire of her and come back," she continued. "It wasn't that I was happy. I just didn't see the need to change things. Then he filed paperwork, and we divorced."

She got to her feet and began to pace. "The judge granted me more child support than Craig wanted to pay. He was annoyed. He moved south and rarely saw the kids. He would show up when he thought it might irritate me and take them for a weekend. He took them in the summer for a month.

"I didn't think anything of it when he took them the last time," she continued. "I was at work. They were gone when I got home. I expected them to call once a week like they normally did when they were with him. They never called."

A tear slid down her cheek as she leveled her gaze on me. "I didn't know there was anything wrong until he didn't bring them home. I hadn't talked to them for the whole month, but I assumed he was just being a jerk. I told the police." Now her eyes moved to Hunter. "Your father. He had some choice words about what a terrible mother I was."

Hunter growled. "I'm sorry about that. My father is no longer with the department."

"Oh, I know." She let loose a hollow laugh. "I've heard the gossip. People say you're a good police officer."

"I try to be," Hunter confirmed.

"I thought Craig packed up the kids and moved and that they would eventually find him," she said. "Then I thought, once the kids were adults and on their own, they would find me. It's not as if they were small children when they left. They knew where I was.

"When that didn't happen, I moved to Grand Rapids. I wallowed in self-pity and started drinking. The drinking continued ... and led to other things." Briefly, she pressed her eyes shut. "I'm sure you've seen my record."

"I'm not here to judge you, ma'am," Hunter assured her.

"I'm judging myself. That's enough." Sandy looked at the trailer, then back at Hunter. "Why are they the same age?"

Hunter helplessly shrugged. "We're trying to figure that out."

"They weren't with Craig this entire time?"

"We don't know. Eli hasn't said anything yet. He's quiet, but stable in the hospital. Shauna has spoken a bit. She said she doesn't remember what happened and then she asked for you."

Sandy made a guttural sound, her shoulders shaking as she lowered her head. "How can I face them? I didn't do enough to try to find them. I was a terrible mother."

"It seems you have a second chance," I said. "Maybe you should get cleaned up, go to the hospital, and start figuring things out."

"They're not supposed to be children any longer. I don't understand any of this."

"We don't either," Hunter said, "but we're going to try to figure it out."

"Where will you start?"

"I'm not sure." Hunter managed a weak smile. "That's next on our list. We'll be dropping in to see the kids from time to time. I think the hospital will want to keep them another day or two. I'm not certain after that." His eyes moved to the trailer door.

"They can't come here like this," Sandy said. "I have to figure things out, get it together. All their stuff is packed away. Some of it was donated."

"Maybe start by cleaning yourself up and visiting them," I interjected. "After that, things might fall into place. You're their mother, and right now you're all they have."

7
SEVEN

B ecause we were in Hawthorne Hollow, Hunter placed a call. He wanted to have lunch with Graham Stratton. Chief Terry had taken Hunter under his wing during the fallout with Hunter's father. Graham had helped, and it was obvious Hunter was struggling with where to turn next. He wanted to talk to one of his mentors, and there just happened to be one nearby.

When we walked into Mable's Country Table I expected to find Graham sitting alone. He had his son Gunner and Scout sitting with him.

"This is a surprise." I smiled at Scout as I sat next to her. "I didn't realize you were coming."

"We were here for lunch and saw Graham," she replied. "He told us what was going on. You found the mother here in town?"

"She's in a trailer near the area where the Moose Lodge people hang out," Hunter volunteered as he sat on my other side, putting him between Graham and me. "I remember you telling me about that area when I was first getting started. You said it wasn't as innocuous as everyone pretended."

"The Moose Lodge is a front," Graham replied. "They hide

behind the good name the lodge has in other areas to cover the fact they're running drugs."

I frowned. "Sandy is running drugs?" We couldn't send Eli and Shauna to live with her if that was the case.

"I'm not sure who Sandy is," Graham admitted. "I don't go out there much."

"But if you know they're running drugs..." I trailed off.

"You're wondering if I'm letting them do it." Graham looked amused rather than offended. "For the record, I am not. We nab shipments coming out of there all the time. We arrest people from that park at least once a month. But not on their grounds."

"Why?" I was honestly curious.

"They're all armed to the teeth and don't trust cops," Gunner supplied for his father. "It's a rough area. I'm not familiar with anyone named Sandy either. Did she say how long she's been there?"

"A few years," Hunter replied. He pulled up his phone. "It says here she's been arrested three times for public drunkenness."

Graham looked at the record. "I know her. Sandra Eaton."

"Yeah, I found a record." Hunter bobbed his head. "She's going by her grandmother's maiden name now."

"I guess I didn't realize she had missing kids." Graham rubbed his cheek. "Makes me feel bad for her."

"Sounds like she was a drunk before she lost the kids and things snowballed." Hunter lowered his phone to the table. "It sounds like she was in an unhappy marriage. She didn't even report her kids missing for more than a month. They didn't call her from their dad's house, and by the time the cops were called in there was no trace of ... anything."

"Who is their father?" Graham asked.

"Craig Eaton. I guess he moved to Kalamazoo. He's been missing as long as the kids. That's why everyone assumed he moved away with them."

"But that's not what happened," Scout said. "Wouldn't the police have pressed harder on two teenagers going missing?"

Graham scowled. "Hunter's father headed up the case." He shot my fiancé an apologetic look. "No offense, son, but your father was a waste of space."

Hunter didn't argue the point. He simply nodded. "The kids fell through the cracks," he said. "It's a shame because they should've been found sooner."

"They're still teenagers and haven't aged a day in ten years," I pointed out. "That suggests whatever happened to them was not of the parental kidnapping variety." Something occurred to me. "Unless the father was magical."

"Did you get a whiff of magic when you saw the kids?" Scout asked. "Graham said you found them."

"That was a fluke." I gave them a rundown on the previous evening.

"We saw Evan last night," Scout said. "He didn't find anything out there, but he can't smell magic like I can. I'm considering taking a trip to the spot to look around."

I was both intrigued and grateful. "Do you think you can find something?"

She lifted one shoulder. "Maybe there's a plane door there."

Now she had my full attention. "You can open plane doors."

Scout smirked. "I'm well aware."

I was a dolt sometimes. "If they were trapped on another plane, you could figure out where they went."

"*If* they were trapped," she agreed. "The thing is, being on another plane doesn't explain their lack of aging. Time still passes on other planes. Sometimes it passes faster, sometimes slower. There's no way of knowing without studying the plane itself."

"What were they doing between Hemlock Cove and Shadow Hills?" Gunner asked. "Say it was a plane door; it would likely open and shut in the same place. Why were they there in the first place?"

"My understanding is that Sandy was at work the day Craig was supposed to pick up the kids," Hunter replied. "She was a waitress. She said goodbye to Eli and Shauna. They were going to their father's place for a month. She didn't expect to see them for four weeks."

"But she expected to hear from them," I argued. "She said she expected them to call once a week."

"She did say that," Hunter conceded. "It's just ... if she was a drunk even then, can we take her word for it? Maybe the kids called and she didn't pick up. Maybe that's why she feels guilty."

"I'm not saying she's a perfect parent—far from it—but she's had a lot of time to reflect since losing her kids. She was pretty matter of fact about being a bad mother and not giving them the attention she should have before they disappeared."

"She also suggested that she didn't push hard enough when she realized they were missing," Hunter argued. "My father may not have been a great cop, but he would've wanted to find missing children for the accolades alone."

Graham tilted his head. "That's true. He would've tooted his own horn across three counties."

"Are you going to try to talk to your father?" Gunner asked. He was well aware of Hunter's father, and he stepped gingerly in pushing forward. "He might have information he didn't include in the reports."

Hunter shifted on his chair, uncomfortable. "I would be lying if I said I hadn't thought about it."

Mable, the restaurant owner, picked that moment to take our orders. Everybody ordered burgers, fries, and iced tea. Then we listened to Mable kibitz about Hawthorne Hollow residents she hated. She talked for a full five minutes before returning to the kitchen to place our orders.

Graham spoke first after she left our table. "Son, if you don't want to talk to your father—and nobody blames you for wanting to steer clear of the man—I can do it." He bobbed his head. "We were never friends, but he doesn't hate me the way he hates Terry."

"Shouldn't that be my responsibility?" Hunter challenged. "This is my case."

"It's your case, but you're not alone in this." Graham was firm. "Let me reach out to him."

"You realize he'll know why you're the one reaching out?" Hunter pressed. "He's going to think I'm afraid of him."

This was an uncomfortable conversation. Hunter's father was a monster—and a half—and nobody would blame Hunter for fearing him after the way he was treated during his childhood. Hunter would never admit to the fear; doing so, for him, would be a sign of weakness.

"If you face off with your father it's likely to come to blows," Graham argued. "You two have a lot of unfinished business. We don't have time for you to beat the crap out of each other. Let me talk to him."

"You shouldn't go alone." Hunter hung his head. "He'll mess with you."

"I'll go with him," Gunner volunteered. "I remember your father well. I wouldn't mind having a sit down with him. I'm sure it will be a pleasant conversation."

"Maybe you should let me go," Scout countered. "I've only heard stories about the guy. I would love to meet him face to face."

"No, you wouldn't," Hunter argued. On a sigh, he shook his head. "I'm not going to stop you from talking to him, Graham. We need whatever information he can provide, but I really don't want to be the one to face off with him. But I'll hate myself if you go and I stay behind."

Graham's voice was kind. "Your father was terrible to you. Nobody blames you for not wanting to see him."

"I just wish we could find Craig." Hunter dragged a hand through his hair. "That would make our lives so much easier."

"That brings up a good point," Scout said. "Everyone assumed Craig Eaton picked up his kids and then whisked them away to a different life. Are we assuming this was because he didn't want to pay child support?"

"That would be my guess," Hunter replied. "What else could it be?"

"I don't know that it matters," Scout replied. "Because—and this is just me spit-balling—isn't it weird that the kids have returned, but their father is nowhere to be found?"

"It makes me angry." Graham shifted on his chair. "If Greg had done his job, he would've at least tracked Craig's credit cards ... or found his car. The three of them shouldn't be able to just disappear into the ether." He pulled out his phone and started typing.

"What's he doing?" I asked.

"Being a super cop," Gunner teased. He knew exactly how to irritate his father. "He's going to prove he's better than Hunter's dad."

"That's not a hard level to leapfrog." Hunter's lower lip jutted out. "My father was probably one of the worst cops ever."

I rested my head against his shoulder in an awkward attempt to offer comfort. He kissed the top of my head to show he was grateful, then slid his arm around my neck and hugged me.

"Oh, so cute," Scout said in her mocking tone. "Do you guys wear matching pajamas at night?"

"Knock it off," I warned. She wasn't happy unless she was irritating someone. Apparently, today, Hunter and I were her best options. "Talk to me about these plane doors. How does it work?"

She shrugged. "It depends. Craig may have taken them out there knowing they were going to cross. That would mean he had knowledge of paranormal worlds. It's also possible they were out there doing teenager stuff—hanging around with friends or something—and accidentally stumbled across the door."

Hunter prodded. "Why wouldn't they come back right away if they realized they wandered into an entirely different world?"

"Maybe they didn't know they had. Many planes look the same. Some plane doors are one-way only. Maybe they couldn't get across."

"But they got back."

"We don't know if they used a different door." Scout turned

thoughtful. Maybe they didn't disappear from the same spot they were found."

"How do we find out where they were?"

"The kids have to tell us. They're the only ones we know for certain were there."

"They don't remember. Eli isn't talking."

"They don't remember *yet*," Scout said. "That doesn't mean they won't remember eventually. Or maybe they do and think no one will believe them."

"Or they don't want to talk about it," Gunner added.

"Is it possible that they were frozen somewhere for ten years? Maybe, from their perspective, nothing did happen to them."

"Oh, you're so shiny," Scout mocked before pressing her finger into my cheek.

I slapped her hand away. "I'm not naive. They didn't age. So in a way, they were frozen."

"Or they could've walked through a door, spent time there and then found a different door back," Scout replied. "Time could've passed differently. We won't know until we talk to them."

Mable brought our drinks, so chatter picked up with her for a few minutes. Once she was gone, I decided to tell them the one thing I hadn't yet revealed. "There is one other thing."

I described what happened when I touched them, the images I'd seen. "It was very brief," I explained. "It was kind of like being trapped in a nightmare."

"Way to leave out the important part," Scout teased. "That could've been another plane. Maybe it was a memory of when they crossed over."

"This is all conjecture at this point. Until we have more to go on —and it doesn't seem as if the mother is going to be any help—we're just firing theories off like fireworks."

"There is one other person who might be able to help," Graham said, drawing everybody's attention to the end of the table.

"Who?" Gunner asked.

"Craig Eaton."

"He disappeared with the kids. We were just talking about that."

Graham gave his son an exaggerated eye roll. "Except he didn't, smart guy." Graham was grim. "Not entirely." He glanced at Hunter. "Your father really dropped the ball on this one, son."

Hunter grimaced. "What did you find?"

"Craig Eaton was in Kalamazoo." Graham moved his gaze back to his phone. "He left Kalamazoo right around the time the kids disappeared, but he didn't completely fall off the map."

Confusion had me leaning forward. "He's still alive?"

"He's alive, and close." Graham tapped the fingers of the hand not holding the phone on the table. "Craig Fields—that's the same last name as Craig's mother; his parents never married—lives about ten miles north of the pack lands."

"The new pack lands?" Hunter asked.

Graham nodded. "It's across the border. His address isn't in Hawthorne Hollow. He picks up his mail at a P.O. box in Charlevoix."

"So he's here?" I was floored. "He's been here the whole time?"

"The last seven years," Graham confirmed. "I don't know where he was before that. There's a three-year gap. However, Craig Fields has the same social security number and driver's license number as Craig Eaton."

"What's the area like where he's living?" Hunter asked.

"Rough," Gunner replied. "Remote. He's mostly on his own out there. It would take him forty-five minutes to get into town."

"Is it possible someone stole his identity?" Scout asked. "Maybe he's dead and someone took over his social security number three years later."

"We can't rule that out," Graham conceded, "but he's kept his license current. This is his old photo from before the kids disappeared." He held out his phone. The clean-shaven man staring back didn't look all that friendly. "This is the current photo for that ID." Graham held up his phone again. The new image showed a man with a full beard and salt-and-pepper hair. He looked as if he'd aged thirty years, but it was clearly the same man.

"I guess I know where we're going after lunch," Hunter said grimly.

"Not alone," Graham said. "We'll go with you." He inclined his head toward Gunner. "Just to be on the safe side. This guy could be off his rocker, ready to kill anybody who crosses onto his property."

"Don't think you're leaving me out of this," Scout said. "I'm invested now. I want to know what Craig Eaton has been doing for ten years."

"And why he didn't report his children missing," I added.

"Maybe he's the reason they were missing," Hunter said. "Maybe he's hiding because he did something to them."

"If that's true, he won't be happy to hear they're back," Scout said. "I can't wait to talk to this guy."

8

EIGHT

G raham drove. He thought it was best to have an official vehicle. Gunner wanted to sit up front with him, but vetoed that idea.

"You sit in back with the other girls," Graham ordered.

Gunner pouted. He also needled his father for the entire ride.

"Have you ever wondered why sons sometimes kill their fathers?" he asked. He was too big to sit in the middle, so he was behind Graham's seat. He kept shoving his big feet underneath the seat and kicking. "I'm not asking for any specific reason," he added. "I'm just making conversation."

Graham growled. "I'll stop this truck right here and let you walk," he threatened.

Gunner didn't look concerned. "Fathers are supposed to love their sons," he lamented. "Where did we go wrong?"

"It could be worse," Hunter interjected. He'd volunteered to sit in the back with Scout and me, but Graham had put the kibosh on that quickly. "You could have my father."

Gunner jerked his eyes to Hunter, realizing he'd miscalculated.

"Dude, your dad is an ass. I'm sorry about him. You can't be an actual sad sack when I'm messing with my father. That's not allowed."

I had to press my lips together to keep from laughing. It was a serious conversation, but Gunner could make almost anything funny.

"If it's any consolation, Hunter, I'd take you over Gunner every single day of the week and twice on Sundays," Graham interjected to ease the tension.

"I'm going to force bonding time if you're not careful," Gunner warned his father. "I'm going to suggest a fishing day. Let's see how you like that."

Graham snorted. "You don't even like fishing. You complain the whole time we're out there."

"But you like fishing. It's no fun ruining something you don't like."

From my vantage point, I could see Graham's profile. He worked his jaw back and forth.

"Let's talk about how we're going to approach this," Graham suggested. "I should do the talking with Craig. I'm the official presence in this area."

Gunner looked smug. "That's what I thought."

"Keep it up," Graham snapped angrily, his calm facade disappearing in an instant. "If you're not careful, I'll suggest a father-son camping weekend. Just you and me around a campfire all weekend."

Gunner opened his mouth, but Graham cut him off.

"No s'mores either," Graham growled.

Gunner made a face. "You really are mean when you want to be," he complained. "Camping without s'mores is cruel and unusual punishment."

"We should go camping," I said to Hunter. "We haven't been since we were kids."

Amusement glinted in his eyes as he turned to look at me. "I don't particularly remember you enjoying camping."

"I had fun."

"We only went to spend quality time together without your mother or my father."

"Yeah, but we had fun." At least I remembered it that way. "Maybe we could all go camping as a group." I turned to Scout for encouragement.

She was already shaking her head. "I'm an indoor girl. Camping sounds about as fun as a root canal without anesthesia."

"How are you an indoor girl?" I asked. "You spend more time in the woods than anyone I know."

"Sure, when I'm hunting. I like going out, killing things, and then coming home to eat fried chicken in bed."

"That's my favorite part of the day too." Gunner sent Scout a lascivious wink. "We could do a camping weekend. The whole group could go."

"And how fun that would be?" Scout agreed. "We'd have Evan and Sebastian fighting over Easton."

"Sebastian has bowed out of that race," I offered. "He sees that Evan and Easton are drawn to one another in a way that Evan isn't drawn to him. We're going to set up a dating profile for him and help him find someone."

Hunter jerked his head. "Who is this 'we' you're referring to?"

I wasn't even going to play that game with him. "You, me, and Easton are going to help him."

"I didn't agree to that."

"You're doing it." Why was he even arguing? "Sebastian is our friend, and he's lonely."

"He's an adult. He can find his own dates."

"Fine." I linked my fingers on my lap and sat primly. "I'll help him myself."

"Of course you will."

"I'm sure it will involve a lot of late nights," I continued. "I'll stay at his place when that happens so he's not alone."

"Now you're playing dirty," Hunter complained.

"Quite frankly, you're all juvenile," Graham said. "You're acting like teenagers. Grow up."

"We can't all be as dignified as you and Marnie," Gunner said, referring to Graham's burgeoning relationship with Marnie Winchester, Bay's aunt. "Three days ago, I saw you helping her garden at The Overlook. That was a mighty pretty gardening hat she put on you to keep away the sun."

Graham scowled. "The sun has damaging effects."

Gunner didn't look convinced. "And the rubber boots with daisies on them?"

"Look!" Graham exclaimed. "We're here."

I turned my attention to the cabin. It was located down a long and winding road. As far as I could tell, there was nothing in the immediate area. It was just the cabin and what looked to be a ramshackle storage shed. Everything else, as far as the eye could see, was trees.

"This is something straight out of a *Texas Chainsaw Massacre* movie," Scout noted as she leaned forward. She related everything to horror movies. I found it both comforting and annoying. "All we're missing is the big guy in a deli apron with a chainsaw and human hanging bodies to be skinned at a later time."

"Thank you for putting *that* image in my head," Gunner muttered.

I was right there with them.

Hunter kept me close as we walked from the truck toward the front door. We probably made for an interesting—and maybe terrifying—sight from inside the cabin. How was Graham going to explain why we were all together?

It turned out that he didn't have to explain anything. When the door opened, the man who stepped out looked resigned.

"Can I help you?" Craig asked. His gaze bounced between our faces. Ultimately, he settled on Graham as the authority figure.

"I'm Graham Stratton." He flashed his badge. "I'm the chief of police of Hawthorne Hollow." He jerked his thumb at Hunter. "This is Hunter Ryan. He's with the Shadow Hills Police Department."

It was the Shadow Hills part that had Craig's shoulders stiffening. "Okay." He flashed a flat smile. "I'm not sure what that has to do with me. I don't bother anyone, and no one bothers me. I can't think of a single reason you'd be out here."

I spoke without thinking. "What about Eli and Shauna?"

Graham shot a glare in my direction. "What did I say?"

I shrank from his anger. "Sorry. I just..." I just what? I couldn't explain why I'd broken from protocol. Instead, I just shrugged and fell silent.

Graham looked pained when he turned back to Craig. "You'll have to excuse her. She's here to observe."

"Like, she's grading your job performance?"

"Something like that."

Craig flicked his eyes to Scout. "And her?"

"I'm the muscle," Scout replied, growing bored with the conversation. She pushed past Hunter to stand directly in front of Craig. "I'm going to cut to the chase because these idiots are going to come in soft thinking that you'll be more likely to talk. We don't have time for that."

Craig didn't say anything.

"Here's the deal." Scout planted her hands on her hips. She made a formidable opponent. I wanted to take lessons from her, because despite her mouth, she always got the job done and people knocked their knees in terror whenever she was on the playing field. "Eli and Shauna appeared out of nowhere yesterday."

Craig balked. "They disappeared."

"They did," Scout agreed. "Everyone thought you took them."

"I didn't take them." Craig's brow furrowed. "I didn't want them."

My heart constricted. "That's a nice thing for a father to say."

Craig didn't apologize. "Judge me all you want. Those kids were ... odd. They were dangerous. They made me see things."

Gunner cocked his head. "What sort of things?"

"I don't know how they did it." Craig had gone pale. "Sometimes they'd brush against me and I'd see horrible images. Like dead animals. Sometimes they showed me dead people. They'd sit at the table and make me see things—crucified people and the like—and then laugh."

Scout didn't look bothered by the assertion as much as intrigued. "It's kind of like *The Ring*."

I gave her a dirty look. "Not everything is a horror movie."

"It was like *The Ring*," Craig confirmed. "I didn't identify with the kids. I'm not even sure how Shauna could be mine. She's not even nine months younger than Eli. Sandy and I were already on the outs when Eli was born. He was a cranky baby, constantly screaming. We were not feeling romantic. Then we found out she was pregnant within weeks of Eli arriving. She had Shauna eight months after Eli was born. How is that possible?"

I wasn't a doctor, but that was suspicious. "You took them," I pressed. "You had visitation."

"I didn't want it." Guilt flashed across Craig's face. "If I didn't take it, I would have had to pay more in child support. It was based on percentage of custody of the kids. I knew Sandy wouldn't give me a break, and I got out of taking them as much as possible, but I couldn't completely get away from them."

I was torn. On one hand, only a monster would admit to wanting to avoid time with his family. On the other, he looked genuinely afraid. I would've discarded the story if it hadn't been for the images I'd seen when touching Shauna and Eli.

"Maybe you should start from the beginning," Graham suggested. "You picked up Eli and Shauna the day they disappeared."

"I didn't." Craig vehemently shook his head. "I had a plan to escape so I wouldn't have to pay child support or see them."

"What a quality father," Gunner drawled.

Graham shot him a quelling look. "Everyone thinks of it at one time or another." He was grim when he turned back to Craig. "Most don't do it."

"I don't know what he's talking about," Gunner sniffed to Scout. "I was a delightful child."

Scout cuffed the back of his head without looking and focused on Craig. "I need to know about these images. What exactly did they show you?"

"The first time, Eli was a baby." Craig worked his jaw. "I was watching him walk between the furniture. He was really good at it. I remember thinking it was odd that he was so steady on his feet at eleven months."

Graham argued, "Gunner was walking at eleven months."

"I was always gifted," Gunner said to Scout. "I told you."

"I'll make you camp in the yard tonight with nothing but a perverted ghost as company if you don't shut up," Scout warned. "This is serious."

Gunner scoffed. "You think they're like the kid from *The Ring*?"

"It sounds as if the kids are demonic, and now Stormy is involved," Scout fired back. "Shut up and let me handle this."

Gunner balked. "Well, *sorree*."

Scout rolled her eyes until they landed on Craig. "What are you?"

The question threw Craig. "I don't know what you're talking about. I'm a man."

"What about Sandy? Is she something?"

"Like what?" Craig challenged. "I don't understand what you're getting at."

Scout slid her eyes to me. "Okay, we're going to save time." She lifted her hand and ignited her magic, a small ball of pink energy appearing in the palm of her hand.

Craig jerked back. "What are you?"

"I'm a witch," Scout replied. "I'm a good witch."

"Like in the *Wizard of Oz*?"

Scout reared back, as if offended. "Gawd no! I'm way better than that. I'm also mean when I want to be, so don't push me too hard."

"She's not lying," Gunner said. "She's definitely mean."

"I'll still make you sleep outside," Scout threatened. "I only showed you that so you'd understand that we're not going to think anything you tell us is strange ... or accuse you of lying."

Understanding dawned. She really was trying to get to the heart of matters. I wouldn't have had the guts.

And that's the problem, my inner voice said. *You need to be bolder. Take a page from Scout's book.*

"Now, give me the rundown on these kids," Scout demanded.

"Why are you asking about them?" Craig challenged. "I thought I was free of them when they disappeared. I figured they were off terrorizing some other corner of the world."

"Well, they're back now," Scout replied. "Yesterday, they walked out of the woods between Hemlock Cove and Shadow Hills looking exactly as they did when they disappeared."

The color drained from Craig's face. "They're back."

"They are," Scout confirmed.

"What are they saying?"

"Not much," Hunter replied. "We saw them in the hospital this morning. Eli wasn't talking. I haven't touched base with the doctor in a few hours. Shauna seemed confused. She said she wanted her mother."

"You can't believe anything she says," Craig insisted. "She lies. They both do. They'll act sweet and innocent and then show you photos of babies being tortured in your head. They're evil."

"Have you considered that maybe you're crazy and they're not really showing you anything?" I asked. It wasn't that I didn't believe him—mostly—but I'd yet to see anything that convinced me the kids were evil.

"Yes," Craig answered without hesitation. "I've been to several doctors. I would've even preferred being diagnosed with schizophrenia. I never could pass all the tests to be diagnosed with anything.

Then Sandy mentioned that she saw things when the kids touched her."

I frowned. "She didn't mention that when we talked to her this morning."

"Sandy's alive?" Craig looked surprised. "I thought she'd have drunk herself to death years ago."

Something clicked inside my head. "Wait ... that's why she started drinking."

"I won't pretend we were good parents," Craig said. "In fact, we were terrible parents, but the kids kept pushing us. Sandy drank. I looked for affairs outside the house so I wouldn't have to sleep under the same roof with them. We were monsters as parents." He leaned closer. "Those kids were literal monsters. I'm telling you, there's something wrong with them."

"How did the timing work out?" Hunter challenged. "How did you happen to disappear at the same time the kids did if you had nothing to do with it?"

"I can't answer that." Craig held out his hands. "I had a plan. I always knew I was going off the grid. I timed it so I wouldn't have to take them for a month. I first left the country. I thought I would be able to stay in Canada. Turns out they don't want us just traipsing around their country willy-nilly." His smile was rueful. "I had to come back a year later. I didn't know where to go, so I jumped from location to location."

"How did you end up here?" I asked. "Why come back?"

"After they were gone for three years, I thought it was safe. This is still my home." Craig looked sad. "What do you think they're going to do to us now that they're back?"

I had no answer. I wasn't even certain I believed the story about the kids.

"Well, for starters, we're going to figure out where they've been," Hunter said.

"Then we're going to determine what they want," Scout added.

"You're not in this alone this time. If there's something wrong with the kids, we'll handle it."

I gave her an odd look, which she met head-on.

"If there's something wrong with the parents, we'll handle that too," she said, ignoring the way Craig protested behind her. "No matter what, you're not alone in this, even though it's much more complicated than any of us thought."

9
NINE

Could the kids be evil?

I wouldn't have thought it was possible. Now I wasn't so sure.

We drove back to town, separated into two vehicles, and then headed for the spot where I'd found the kids.

Hunter and I made the drive in silence in his vehicle. When we parked on the side of the road, Graham's vehicle was right behind us. Gunner and Graham were arguing when they exited.

"You're just being punitive now," Gunner complained. "Putting me in the backseat and putting Scout up front is insulting. I'm your son. You're supposed to want me to ride shotgun."

"Maybe I like talking to Scout more than you," Graham fired back.

"I'm sure listening to Scout run through the plot of *The Ring* was the highlight of your day," Gunner said.

I shook my head and turned back to the road.

"I feel like I'm babysitting," Hunter muttered.

I rubbed his back, then went to the spot where the kids had been standing when I first saw them.

"Here?" Scout asked, joining me.

I nodded. "I saw movement. I was kind of in my own little world thinking about my afternoon with Bay and Tillie. I learned a new trick."

"What new trick?" Scout hunkered down and pressed her hand to the pavement. I had no idea what she was doing, but my guess was that she was trying to feel for traces of magic.

"I built a trap. Tillie was in it. Bay wouldn't let me release her until she agreed to get rid of Crusty."

"The clown?" Scout laughed. "I kind of like him."

"He's creepy," Gunner countered. "No one needs a sentient clown doll running around."

"On that we can agree," Graham said. "I spent the night over there two nights ago and woke up around three o'clock. He was staring at me from the foot of the bed."

Gunner was breathless. "That is my worst nightmare come to life. What did you do?"

"Nothing. He stared. I stared. Then he burst into maniacal laughter and took off."

Gunner shook his head. "That thing needs to die. He's ruined pot roast night for me two weeks in a row."

"Tillie found a loophole out of the agreement and then cursed Bay to smell like rancid pickles," I said. "Anyway, the trap worked. I managed to do it twice. It might come in handy."

"It will," Scout agreed as she stood. "Especially if we're dealing with demons."

I jolted. "How do you know it's demons?"

"I don't, but that's immediately where my mind went when Craig said they were putting images in his head. Demons take the form of kids all the time."

"That's creepy," Hunter supplied. "Now I don't want to have kids."

"Right?" Scout bobbed her head. "It's definitely creepy. I think that's why they do it."

"But it sounds as if Sandy gave birth to both of them," I argued. "How does that work?"

She pursed her lips. "I'm not sure." She moved to the side of the road and looked toward the foliage. "Are we assuming they came from here?"

I nodded.

"Then let's go this way." Scout took the lead through the trees, her eyes bouncing all around.

Gunner scampered to keep up with her. He lifted his nose once we were away from the road and started scenting the air.

"Anything?" I asked, hopeful.

"Maybe," he replied. "Has anyone else been through here?"

"I smell it too," Graham said as he joined his son.

I couldn't smell anything, so I was genuinely lost. "What do you smell?"

"It's weird," Gunner replied. "There's a faint whiff of brimstone, but there's something else I can't identify. It's almost sweet."

"But to the point of being sour." Graham bobbed his head. "I've never smelled that."

"Brimstone?" Hunter cocked his head. "What does brimstone smell like?"

"Like rotten eggs," Gunner replied. "Or sulfur, to be more precise. It's pretty faint here."

"Maybe it will be stronger that way." Scout pointed into the woods.

"Evan and I walked through here," I argued. "He didn't mention the scent of sulfur."

"He might not have picked up on it. He's got a good nose, but Gunner's is better."

Gunner puffed himself out. "Everything about me is better."

"Why are you competing with Evan?" Graham demanded. "It's not as if he's going to steal your woman."

"You did not just call me his woman," Scout growled.

Graham chuckled. "You're so sensitive about that stuff."

"She is," Gunner agreed. "She calls me pet names like 'jerk' and 'idiot,' but if I call her 'babycakes' she threatens to end the world."

I wasn't in the mood to laugh but couldn't help myself. "You guys are hilarious."

Gunner poked Scout's side, then turned his attention to the trees. "What's this?" His gaze was focused on something I couldn't see.

I moved closer to him and looked. There was nothing abnormal about the tree trunk as far as I could tell. "What is it?"

"These marks." Gunner cocked his head. "They kind of look like they're in a pattern."

I stared, confused. Then I realized he was referring to the little pockmarks in the trunk. "Isn't that normal? Couldn't a squirrel have done that?"

"In this pattern?"

Did he see a pattern? I didn't.

Scout joined us. "That doesn't look like much of a pattern. I'm with Stormy. I think a squirrel did that."

Gunner made a face. "You're a squirrel." He poked her side—something he regularly did to annoy her—and kept moving. "The brimstone scent is stronger this way."

Graham nodded. "Everyone stick close together."

He was worried about something. "What does the brimstone scent signify?" I asked.

"It's associated with demons," Scout replied. "It can also be associated with plane doors and other evil creatures. I've faced off with a succubus here and there, and they smelled like brimstone when they used their magic."

"What's a succubus?" Hunter asked.

"A sex demon," Gunner replied. "If you ask me, that's the only type of demon to be. If you're going to overdose on something, it might as well be sex."

"Oh, please." Graham snorted. "You would be a glutton demon."

"I could be both," Gunner countered. "I'm multifaceted gifted."

I left them to snark at one another and kept going. Scout seemed focused on what was ahead.

"What is it?" I whispered as I followed her. Hunter had joined in to argue with Graham and Gunner, and I'd left them behind. "You sense something?"

"It's just ... a feeling."

"Isn't that what sensing something means?"

She managed a small smirk. "The atmosphere here is weird."

"Do you think there's a plane door close?"

"I don't feel one."

Disappointment rolled through me.

When her eyes locked with mine, they were clear. "I know this sounds odd, but it almost feels as if something—or someone—is watching us."

I went ramrod straight, my eyes darting between the trees.

Laughter trilled out as she patted my shoulder and kept going.

"How can you be so cavalier?" I demanded as I forced myself to follow her. "We're talking about two kids."

"Or two demons."

I hated that she had a point. "I can't see them as anything other than kids," I admitted after several seconds.

"I know." She sent me a sympathetic look. "You're still new at this. You never went through a phase when life kicked you in the teeth and things were bad."

"Um ... have you not heard the story about me having to come home to work in the family restaurant?"

That made her laugh. "I'm sorry you're not writing. You'll get over that when you stop feeling sorry for yourself."

My hackles were up. "I don't feel sorry for myself."

"Yes, you do. It's okay. We all feel sorry for ourselves at times. I did when I was shuffled from foster home to foster home. It's hell not being wanted ... even though I didn't want them to want me. At that time, I had no intention of getting attached to anyone."

She hadn't meant it to be pointed. She didn't want me to feel bad. That's exactly how I felt, though. She was right. Scout had been separated from her family at a young age and hidden in the system so people couldn't find her. Bad people. They were looking for a child of the stars. She was a unique pixie witch. To keep her safe, she'd been hidden with magic. Then she'd been bounced between foster homes.

Here I was feeling sorry for myself—and she was right about that too—because my writing career hadn't panned out and I had massive credit card debt. I was always loved during that time, though. My family was frustrating, but they never stopped loving me. Scout had no one to turn to for most of her life.

Then, when she finally found someone to act as her family, Evan had been stripped away from her and turned into a vampire. It was only recently that she'd found a home, her parents, and the rest of her family. She was still adjusting.

My complaints seemed petty in comparison.

"Oh, don't do that." Scout shook her head, correctly reading my mind. "Don't feel sorry for me."

"I can't help it." I opted for honesty. "Your life has been a crap-fest from the very beginning."

"Thanks." Scout grinned.

"I wasn't trying to be obnoxious," I assured her. "You've had real trials to overcome. My stuff is so sad in comparison. I clearly have issues."

Something horrible occurred to me. "Oh, man, I'm entitled."

"Hunter!" Scout barked, causing my shoulders to jerk. "Stormy is being Stormy. I need you to make it stop."

I glared at her as Hunter hurried over.

"What's wrong?" he asked, his gaze bouncing between us.

"She's feeling sorry for herself," Scout replied. "What's worse, she's feeling sorry for me. Make her stop." Scout lobbed her most irritating smile at me and then walked deeper into the woods.

Hunter sent me a questioning look.

"She said I haven't been writing because I've been feeling sorry for myself," I explained. "I said that wasn't true. Then I realized much worse things have happened to her."

"And now you feel bad," Hunter assumed, his arm going around my shoulders.

"I'm kind of a jerk." I buried my face in his chest.

"You're not a jerk. You're softer than she is, and that's okay, because I don't think I could put up with her if she was my fiancée."

Scout's head poked back through the trees. "I heard that."

Hunter smirked at her. "I figured you were loitering to make sure I didn't screw things up."

"You rarely screw things up." Scout looked to Gunner, who was messing with his father. "There's a reason we end up with the people we end up with. You need someone softer. Gunner needs someone to boss him around."

"I heard that," Gunner barked.

Scout ignored him. "You guys are a good match. You're both softer. I wasn't trying to make Stormy feel bad. I was just pointing out that she hasn't lost her writing dream. She's only misplaced it for a while."

Hunter rubbed his hand over my back. "That's something I've been trying to get her to see."

"Then we make a good team." She winked at him. "I found something. Come this way."

I pulled away from Hunter—now was not the time to feel sorry for myself—and started after her. "Is it something good?"

"It makes me think we owe Gunner an apology."

Gunner perked up. "I'm all for that." He practically skipped ahead of Hunter and me.

When we followed them into a clearing it took me a moment to understand what had caught Scout's attention. Then I saw the trees.

They all contained the same marks as the one Gunner had pointed out earlier.

"Is this the same pattern?" I moved closer.

"Looks that way," Scout replied. She traced her finger between the little knots. "These aren't natural to the trees." She leaned closer and sniffed. "I think they've been burned into the wood." She looked at Gunner for confirmation.

He leaned closer, then nodded. "Brimstone," he said. "They have that scent."

"Magic was used to make these patterns." I turned in a circle. All of the trees surrounding us had the same pattern. "What does it mean?"

Scout traced the pattern again, her finger igniting with magic as she moved it between the knots. "I think there's something specific here. It might take some time to figure it out."

I pulled out my phone and started taking photos. "If we load them into a computer we can experiment and maybe find out what the design really is."

Scout backed away from the trees and turned in a circle in the center of the clearing.

"What?" I asked when she stopped and looked directly above us. "Is it a plane door?"

She shook her head. "I don't sense a door. Not here." She hesitated. "That doesn't mean a plane door didn't open here. Some doors can be opened out of thin air. I can do it if I have to."

"What sorts of creatures can open plane doors?" Graham asked. "Your friend Poet can, but she's a loa."

Scout, still looking up, shook her head. "She doesn't open plane doors. She can transport herself—and others—to different places, but she doesn't use doors."

"It's all very confusing," Graham lamented.

"It is," Scout agreed. "The list of who and what can open the doors is not as small as you probably prefer."

"Can demons open them?" Gunner, still sniffing the tree, asked. "This really does smell like brimstone."

Scout nodded. "Some demons can open plane doors. Lower-level demons mostly cannot, although there are some who have that ability, and only that ability."

"What are we thinking the Eaton kids are?" I asked. "They seemed like they were normal kids."

Scout let out a breath. "Maybe I should meet them. I might be able to get a better feel for them."

"We might have to wait until tomorrow," Hunter replied. "I have to come up with a story to get you into their room."

"It might be better to wait until they've been released," Graham suggested.

Hunter bobbed his head. "I'll talk to the doctor again in a few hours. If we don't have another choice, I'll figure out a way to get you in."

"I have a question," I interjected. "If they're demons, why don't they have any memories?"

"What makes you think they're not playing you?" Scout asked. "Demons are masterful liars. You still feel sorry for those kids despite what their father said."

"You're assuming he told us the truth," I said.

"He came across as truthful."

"Maybe he is. Maybe something else is going on here. Maybe we're not even close to figuring this out."

Scout went back to looking at the tree. "Our best bet is to try to figure out a pattern." She snapped a few photos of her own. "That's going to be the key."

"How do you know that?" Hunter asked.

She shrugged. "Just a feeling."

"Well, I hope your feeling is right. We've got a lot of ground to cover."

10
TEN

Back in town, we loaded the photos into Hunter's computer and tried to discern a pattern. We connected the dots ten different ways but nothing stood out. Eventually, we gave up out of frustration. My plan was to curl up on the couch and order pizza.

"We have family dinner at your grandparents' house," Hunter reminded me.

I froze halfway to the couch. That couldn't be right. "That's not tonight," I said tentatively.

He laughed at my discomfort. "Oh, yes it is."

Crap. "Maybe we can call in sick." I was grasping for an escape.

"I don't think that works for family dinner." He kissed my nose. "Do you want to talk?"

The question threw me. "About the Eatons? I don't know what I think. I didn't get an evil vibe from them, but maybe that's the point. If they are demons, they made themselves look like kids so people wouldn't be suspicious."

"That's not what I'm talking about." He rested his hands on my shoulders. "I was referring to the writing thing that you and Scout got into."

I balked. "I wouldn't say we got into it," I hedged. "We weren't fighting."

"Scout would never fight with you."

"Scout fights with everyone."

"Not with you." He shook his head. "She looks at you as if you're a little puppy. She knows you're powerful, but your confidence level isn't there yet, so she had no intention of pushing you."

I frowned. "Was that you trying to make me feel better?" I asked.

"I'm not trying to make you feel better. Not this time. I happen to agree with Scout."

I pulled away from him and turned my back. "You think I'm feeling sorry for myself." I couldn't look at him.

"You're extremely talented, and you'll prove that to yourself eventually." He didn't reach for me, which was abnormal for him. "I know that you think I'm beating a dead horse—"

"I failed!" I shrugged and turned back to him. "I'm fine with it."

"Oh, knock it off." He rarely looked disappointed in me. "I get that you took a hard kick, but you're strong, Stormy. I've never known you to give up after getting knocked down ... except when it comes to this one thing."

I folded my arms across my chest, adopting a defensive position. "I put everything I had into being a writer."

"And you made it."

"Then I failed."

"On one book. You can write another."

"I don't want to fail again. It's hard to have something that you pour your heart and soul into kicked back at you like a soccer ball."

"If you're going to be a writer you have to put up with some bad reviews."

"It wasn't the reviews." That was the truth. "It's not great to get bad reviews, but that happens to all writers. It was my publisher and agent. They lost faith in me."

"And that caused you to lose faith in yourself." He drifted closer and put his hands on my shoulders again. "I don't want you to quit."

"What does it matter? We have a happy life here."

"You won't be truly happy until you're writing again. Don't pretend otherwise."

"I do kind of want to write." It wasn't easy to admit. If he wanted me to be vulnerable, though, he was going to get it with both barrels. "It's just ... things are different now."

"Because you're a witch?"

"Doesn't writing feel less important when someone needs magical help every other week?"

"No."

I waited for him to throw in a "but."

"No?" I challenged after a long stretch of silence.

He laughed at my annoyance. "You can be anything you want. That includes a witch who writes. I don't want you giving up such a big part of yourself."

"But all the stories in my head are different now."

"So?" He cupped my cheek. "There are a lot of different types of books, mystery, horror, science fiction. If you want to tell a different sort of story, you should."

I tried a different tack. "We're about to move into a new house. I don't have time to write, what with my training and work, and moving. And we might have evil demon kids."

"You can still write. You just have to let go of the fear."

I hated how reasonable he sounded. "How about I think about it and you give me a little space to think about it? There's no way for me to focus on writing when we may have demons to grapple with."

"Okay." He gave me a soft kiss. "We'll table this discussion until we figure out what's going on with the Eatons."

"I hate when you're reasonable. Anyone else would pick a fight and storm off."

"I'm not just anyone."

"I know. It's like Scout said. People who are supposed to find one another do."

"I'm glad I found my someone. I always knew I had. You were the one who needed convincing."

I groaned. "Now you're just trying to irritate me."

He laughed, his arm slinging around my shoulders as he pulled me in his side. "I want you to have everything, Stormy. You can't give up on a big part of yourself and get everything. That's not how it works."

He kissed my temple before I could respond. "We'll let this go for the time being." He pointed at the computer, where the photos were still on the monitor. "And we'll let that pattern go for now. We're just going in circles on that. Some distance might do us some good."

"You know what's not going to do us any good? Eating with my family," I said, determined to remain persnickety. "They're going to drive us crazy before the night is over."

"I'm used to it. Some chaos is good. It might help to focus on them rather than this for a few hours."

MY GRANDPARENTS' HOUSE BUSTLED WITH activity when we entered through the laundry room.

My cousin Alice was next to the washer making a face and muttering to herself as we removed our shoes.

"What's wrong with you?" I asked, unsure I wanted an answer. Alice was a bit of a flake.

"My mother is the worst," Alice replied.

I didn't bother to hide my smile. "What did she do this time?"

"I told her she didn't need to make everything about herself—she's mad that Aunt Kori didn't tell her about a mole she had removed and had to find out on Facebook. She blew up and said, 'Fine. I guess you don't need me to talk to you because I'm such a burden on everybody,' and stormed off."

That sounded about right. My family was full of drama queens. "Just leave her be. She'll get over it."

"She said she doesn't want to talk to me for the rest of my life."

"Hasn't she said that a million times before?"

"Yes, but that doesn't stop me from being irritated every time." Alice grimaced at me, then smiled at Hunter. "Hello. You're looking as handsome as ever. How are you?"

Now it was my turn to glare. Alice made a game of flirting with Hunter to irritate me. She knew it got under my skin, so she always went out of her way to purr at him whenever they were in the same room.

"I'm great," Hunter replied. He put his arm around my back. "I'm engaged to the prettiest woman in the world. Everything is absolutely perfect."

Alice's smile disappeared. "You guys suck," she complained. "I hate when pretty people have no problems."

There was a compliment buried in there. Somewhere. "How is the dating scene?" I asked. There was little Alice loved more than talking about her conquests. "Anyone piquing your interest these days?"

Alice flicked her eyes to Hunter. "My interests are spread all around town."

"And on that note..." Hunter grabbed my hand.

I could've made him stay with Alice longer as punishment—after he pushed me into talking about writing when I wasn't ready, it seemed fair—but I didn't have the heart. I still felt bad that his father had been a topic of conversation for so much of the day.

My grandparents had a formal dining room. Half the family was already at the table, sniping at one another. Grandpa sat in his usual chair at the head of the table arguing with Brad.

"You're not listening to me," Brad snapped. "The government is hiding the drones. They're not flying them. That's the aliens. They're just hiding them because they don't want us to know about the aliens. How can you not see that?"

"I can't even believe you share my genes," Grandpa complained, his forehead in his hand. "Please tell me you stepped out on our marriage and he's some idiot's kid," he demanded of Grandma as she breezed past him.

"Sorry." Grandma was all smiles. "He's all yours." Her eyes brightened when she saw Hunter and me. "I'm so glad you made it. I wasn't certain you would when I heard the news."

It took a moment for that to compute. "You mean about the Eatons?"

"Is there other news?" Grandma made a face. "That's all everyone is talking about."

I led Hunter to the far end of the table. There was a children's table, and card tables set up in the corners for some of my irregular cousins, but Hunter and I were always seated at the big table. I had a feeling it was because everybody in my family revered him rather than me.

"If you don't mind me asking, where did you hear the news?" Hunter asked as he reached for the pitcher of water and poured us each a glass.

"You can't keep a story like that quiet," Grandpa said. "Nancy Pritchett told everyone at breakfast this morning." His gaze was contemplative as it fell on me. "I guess I know what you spent your day doing."

"They weren't doing what I would've done with Hunter all day, that's for sure," Alice offered as she sat at one of the card tables. She didn't even try to sit at the big table because she knew she would be booted.

"Knock that off," Grandma chided her. "You're just mad that your mother is mad." She clucked her tongue at Alice, but her smile was bright. Alice was one of her favorites.

"You love me, and you know it," Alice sang back.

"It was the aliens," Brad volunteered.

"What aliens?" I asked, momentarily forgetting.

Grandpa shot me a withering look. "Do not get him started. I can only take so much."

"Sorry." I had to bite back a laugh at his hangdog expression.

"The aliens took the kids," Brad insisted. "They took them and brought them back exactly the same way. There's no other explanation."

Brad wasn't aware of the magical world, and I had no intention of ever telling him. I couldn't even imagine the conspiracy theories he would cook up. "It was totally aliens," I agreed.

"We're still working on figuring out what happened," Hunter said. We were the center of attention. My parents even looked interested in the conversation. "There are a lot of unanswered questions."

"What about the father?" Mom asked. "The story was that he took the kids. Where is he?"

"We found Craig Eaton," Hunter replied. He looked to be choosing his words carefully. "It appears the story might not be true."

"Where has he been?" Mom's forehead creased. "If he didn't take the kids, why didn't he come forward and say so?"

"Because he disappeared for a different reason." Hunter dragged a hand through his hair. "I can't get into too many specifics, but we found him. Their mother, too."

"What do the kids say happened?" Lisa asked. She was at the same table as Alice, her husband Linc across the table from her. They seemed to be making a big show of looking at anybody but each other.

"The kids aren't saying much right now," Hunter replied. "The boy hasn't spoken yet. I called the doctor again right before we came here. He's silent."

"What about the girl?" Grandpa asked. "Nancy said she was talking."

"Nancy has a big mouth," I grumbled.

"Nancy has gotten in trouble over health information violations more than once," Hunter agreed.

"You didn't hear it from me." Grandpa was the picture of innocence. "If anyone asks me to finger her, I won't."

Alice opened her mouth to comment on the unintended double entendre, but Grandma stopped her with a harsh look. "You don't have to be sassy every time."

Hunter rubbed his forehead. "Nancy can't broadcast people's private medical information," he gritted out. "That's against the law."

"How would you know?" Grandpa fired back.

I raised an eyebrow. "Seriously?"

"He's a police officer," Grandma reminded him.

"That doesn't mean he knows the law." Grandpa waved his hand as if Grandma had told him that lemonade could be made with fresh lemons instead of powder. "Give me a break."

Grandma shot Hunter an apologetic look.

"You can't tell those two that they don't know everything," Lisa said. She gave me a furious look. "They get off on telling others how to live."

Hunter pinned Lisa with a glare. "You're going to want to be careful. I don't have to put up with your attitude." He turned to Grandpa. "As for your attitude..."

"Don't let him get to you," I whispered. "He has a lot of issues right now. He can't let things go. It's not who he is."

Hunter seemed to realize I was telling the truth, because he nodded. "Fine." He held up his hands. "Let's talk about something else."

Everybody—including Grandpa—protested.

"We can't talk about anything else," Mom argued. "Two kids who were missing for a decade just showed up and they're the same age as when they disappeared. How can we not talk about that?"

"We don't have any information to share with you," Hunter argued.

He was right, but that didn't mean they couldn't help us.

"Wait." I raised my hand. "You guys probably know a little something about the Eaton kids."

"If you're about to accuse us of doing something to them, you're in big trouble, Stormy," Mom chastised. "Big, big trouble."

"I'm not accusing you. I don't remember them. I'm looking for any stories you might have about them."

Hunter gave me an encouraging nod.

Mom grinned. "We all have a lot of stories. Those were weird kids."

11

ELEVEN

It turned out that no one liked the Eaton kids. In fact, some of my cousins—who were closer in age—were downright afraid of them.

"I remember we were playing basketball at the park," my cousin Blake volunteered. He was six years younger than me. "Eli showed up and wanted to play. We said yes, but then he started sermonizing."

The word threw me. "Sermonizing?"

He nodded solemnly. "He told us we were all going to Hell for the sin of fornication."

"What were you doing at the time?" Hunter asked.

"What makes you certain I was doing anything?" Blake challenged.

"Because I've met you," Hunter replied easily.

Blake scowled. "We might have been talking about a few of the girls on the swings. It was middle school, dude. Everyone checks out chicks in middle school."

"I don't know about everyone," Grandma said. "Middle school is kind of young."

"Oh, please." Blake wrinkled his nose. "Don't tell me that you didn't check out Stormy when she was in middle school, Hunter. I don't believe that."

Hunter shot me an amused look. "I might have." Then, seeing my father's dark look, he hastily retreated. "Not in a gross way. It was totally respectful."

My father didn't look as if he believed him. "Right. You were respecting my daughter when checking her out at twelve."

"It was closer to fourteen," Hunter insisted. If he thought that was better, at least in my father's eyes, he was mistaken.

"I'm not sure I like you any longer," Dad muttered.

"Don't scare him off," Mom complained. "He might be our only shot at grandchildren."

I gave them both dark looks in turn, then took a practical approach. "It's normal for middle schoolers to check each other out. Chalk it up to raging hormones."

"I don't want to hear about Hunter's hormones when my baby was in middle school," Dad groused.

"I'm sorry." I held up my hands in supplication. "I didn't realize this would upset you."

"It was a long time ago," Hunter added. "We're getting married, so all the ogling was for the greater good."

"Don't say ogling." Dad threw his hands into the air. "I want to go back in time and punch you, son."

Now I had to laugh. "Wow." I shook my head, then turned to Blake. "Did you guys push back on Eli's sermonizing?"

"Of course," Blake replied. "He didn't care. He said that we were all going to Hell. Then his sister arrived, and they left together, but not before he told her that we were going to Hell."

"What did she say?" I asked.

"She said she never had a doubt."

"Huh." I glanced at Hunter. I wanted to ask him if he thought demons talked about sending people to Hell, but there were too many people around.

"Anybody else have any dealings with them?" Hunter asked, patting my thigh under the table to tell me he knew what I was wondering.

Alice raised her hand, making me instantly suspicious. "I ran into him while I was on a date. I would've been about fifteen, which means Eli was a year behind me. I was out with Jordan Holbrook. Do you guys remember him?"

"The kid with the mullet?" Hunter asked.

Alice murdered him with a glare. "He did not have a mullet."

I raised a dubious eyebrow.

"He didn't," she insisted. "His hair was glorious."

"It was a mullet," I argued. "It might not have been a Billy Ray Cyrus mullet, but it was shorter on top and longer in the back."

"That was not a mullet." Alice's eyes flashed. "That was a classy hairstyle."

"I remember you had a huge crush on him," I acknowledged.

"Was that before he went to prison for selling meth?" Hunter challenged.

Alice gave him a withering look. It was rare for her to turn on Hunter, but he'd apparently ticked her off one too many times today. "Obviously." She paused for dramatic effect. "I heard those meth charges were trumped up. He was innocent, but whoever arrested him was jealous or something."

"I arrested him," Hunter replied evenly.

Alice looked genuinely surprised. "Were you jealous of him?"

"Why would I be?"

"Well, your hair is pretty boring in comparison."

"So is his now." Hunter was bland. "He had it buzzed off in prison. I hear he's got about three teeth left thanks to the meth. Maybe you should visit him to see if the old feelings are still there."

"Maybe I will," Alice fired back. "Do you want to hear my story or not? I don't need to listen to the judgment otherwise."

Hunter grumbled, but nodded. "Fine. Tell us the rest of your story."

"We were in the alley behind the bowling alley," she started, taking on a wistful expression. "We were just rounding second base and heading to third—"

"I forgot what the bases mean," Grandma interjected. "What's third base?"

"He was feeling her up," I replied without thinking.

Grandpa shot me an "I will kill you look" as Lisa burst out laughing. A quick look at my parents had me back peddling.

"I don't know from personal experience," I lied. "I heard the other kids talking." I should've stopped there. "You know, the bad kids."

"That might have been a dig against me, but I don't care," Alice huffed. "I was younger but saw way more action than you." She gave Hunter a flirty look. "I'm better than her, in case you're wondering."

Hunter looked pained. "No one is better than Stormy." A growl from my grandfather had him readjusting his response. "Not that I have a lot to compare her to." He realized his mistake. "Let's stop with this line of conversation."

I went back to staring at Alice. "Tell us what happened."

"We were in the backseat of Jordan's car," Alice replied. "The windows were really foggy, so it was like being in a different world. We forgot where we were. Then, out of nowhere, Eli appeared. He banged on the window."

She swallowed hard. "He looked really creepy. I swear his eyes were red. Or maybe my eyes were red. There was a little pot smoking going on that night." She wasn't apologetic when glancing at her mother.

"Anyway," I prodded when the silence had stretched too long.

"Anyway," Alice agreed, giggling. "He told us we were being watched, and fornication was going to be our undoing. I said that if God wanted to watch, I was fine with it. I figured God would like the show." She shimmied on her chair until Grandma glared at her.

"Tough room," Alice lamented. "He became even weirder after I said that. He said there was no God. I asked how there could be Hell if there was no God, and he said I would find out."

"And then what?" I asked when she didn't continue.

"That was it. He took off."

"Did you ever talk to him again?" Hunter asked.

"No, but I thought about him when the news came that he'd gone missing. I always assumed he went to some weird religious compound with his father or something. That sort of belief system has to be taught, doesn't it?"

"One would think," Hunter agreed. His hand moved absently over my back. "Anybody have any run-ins with the girl?"

"Shauna?" Grandma asked. "I talked to her once. I always felt bad for the kids. They were home-schooled, and their mother was a drunk. I figured they weren't learning anything, but at the market one day Shauna was behind me in line. She lost her cool when the cashier took too long to figure out change. I remember being impressed that she could do the math in her head so quickly."

"That seems like the bare minimum of education," Hunter argued.

"Not in this day and age." Grandma vehemently shook her head. "Most kids don't know how to figure out change themselves. They have to do it on calculators or their phones. The current generation is losing a lot of basic skills because of technology."

"Is that it?" I asked. "Does anybody have another story?"

We listened to a few more, but they were all variations of what we'd already heard. The Eatons were weird, and even though people felt sorry for them, nobody liked them. They didn't have friends outside their family and were mostly isolated.

AFTER DINNER, HUNTER LOOKED AS IF he'd been through a war.

"Your father threatened me when you were in the bathroom," he said as we hopped into his truck. "He said if I ever made it to third base when we were in middle school he would retroactively castrate me."

I choked on a laugh.

"He was serious. Your father has always liked me. Leave it to Alice to ruin our relationship."

"My father will get over it." I wasn't worried in the least. "He can't stay angry at his golden boy."

"Are you sure? He was mad."

"He gets angry easily. Then he's over it right away. My mother, on the other hand, holds a grudge for fifty years. She still remembers when her sisters stole her bra in middle school and calls them thieves when they argue."

Hunter chuckled. "That's funny."

"Yes, well..." I trailed off, debating how to broach the next subject. He did the work for me.

"I was thinking we should drive to Traverse City to check on Eli and Shauna."

I let out the breath I'd been holding. "Good idea. I was just trying to figure out how to convince you to go."

"You don't have to convince me. The conversation with your family did. It's best we see them ourselves knowing what we do now."

I snuggled into the passenger seat as Hunter headed toward the highway. "Isn't it weird that demons would sermonize? That was an interesting word choice by Blake."

"It's possible they misunderstood what was being said," he countered. "Shadow Hills is a small town. We have one stoplight, three bars, and eight churches. Just because Hell was mentioned doesn't mean their efforts were on behalf of God."

"I didn't even think about that."

"It makes sense when you think about what we discovered today." He pulled onto the highway for the half-hour drive.

"Shouldn't I know that they're demons?" That really bothered me. "I'm not the smartest woman in the world, but I have innate magic. I should have recognized they were magical."

"You're jumping to conclusions, Stormy." He shook his head. "We don't know they're magical."

"What else could it be?"

"Off the top of my head, what if the kids were taken by something magical? Maybe one of the parents is lying and arranged for the kids to be taken."

It was an interesting hypothesis. "But we met both the parents today. I didn't get a magical vibe from either of them."

"I'm not magical, and I agree with you. Craig said he was afraid of them. Maybe he made contact with the wrong person and they took the kids for some nefarious reason."

"The kids were showing signs of being odd long before they disappeared."

"Odd doesn't mean demonic."

"Maybe not, but they were saying creepy things. And I did get the sense that Craig was legitimately frightened by them." I tapped my fingers on my knee. "You don't think Scout is right and this is like *The Ring*?"

"I'm not sure I saw *The Ring*."

"I did. It was creepy."

"What happens in it?"

"There's a video tape. When people watch it they get a call that says 'seven days' and they all die seven days later. A woman's niece receives the call. She's a reporter and starts investigating. She ends up tracking the people in the video to an island where she learns the little girl in the video was thrown into a well and lived seven days after being trapped by her own mother. The twist is that she really was evil. She was putting horrible pictures in people's heads. She never slept. So, when the woman unleashed the spirit of the kid from the well she managed to save herself and her kid, but she unleashed the girl's evil on the world."

"Was she a demon?" he asked.

I shook my head. "They never come out and say so. They only hint is she's magically evil."

"So the only similarity is Craig saying the kids made him see things."

"I guess. You're always so practical."

He laughed, then sobered. "I don't think this one is going to have a Hollywood ending, Stormy. We'll have to do some digging to figure out what we're dealing with."

"I guess that starts tonight with the kids."

"If they'll talk to us."

"Let's not get ahead of ourselves. Maybe there's nothing wrong with them."

WE ARRIVED AT THE HOSPITAL TO FIND THREE police cars and a panicked hospital staff. I knew without really knowing that the hoopla had been caused by Eli and Shauna.

"I was just about to call you," Dr. Stiles said as he strode toward us. "They're gone.

"They were in their room. They had their dinner and when one of the nurses went to collect their trays about thirty minutes later the room was empty."

"Have you searched the hospital?" Hunter asked.

"We have," Stiles confirmed. "We locked down right away. We assumed they were just wandering around, that maybe they'd become bored. We've checked the cameras."

"And?"

"See for yourself." Stiles led us to a room with a security sticker on the door. Inside, a man in a Traverse City Police Department uniform watched a video on one of the screens.

"The camera failed right before they went missing?" the police officer asked.

"Yes," Stiles replied. "The cameras were working fine, then went down one by one, starting with the one on the Eatons' room."

"That can't be a coincidence," Hunter said grimly. "No one saw them leave?"

"No. I'm sorry," Stiles held out his hands. "I don't know how this happened."

12

TWELVE

There wasn't much we could do. The disappearance of the Eatons wasn't Hunter's case. He was handling their reappearance—and original disappearance—but the newest disappearing act fell firmly on the shoulders of the Traverse City Police Department. Hunter wasn't happy, but he didn't have the pull necessary to take over.

So we went home.

I checked the locks—normally his job—then stood in front of the sliding glass doors that looked out on the wooded area behind the restaurant. It was quiet, but I remained uneasy.

Hunter found me standing in the dark—if I turned on the lights, people could see clearly into the apartment from outside—and wrapped his arms around me from behind. "What are you doing?" He nuzzled my neck.

"Wondering if they're out there," I admitted. There was no point in lying.

"You mean out there?" He inclined his head toward the trees. A trail led to a bigger wooded area beyond the storage shed. We'd found our fair share of trouble along that trail.

I shrugged.

"Why would they come here? They don't know who we are."

"If they're demons, it wouldn't be difficult for them to find out. We shouldn't have left them."

"Were you going to sit with them all day?"

I shrugged. "Maybe you should've put an officer on them."

"I don't have a lot of spare officers," he reminded me. "I can't see the residents being happy about me pulling one of them off duty here and sending them to sit in a hospital in Traverse City. Besides, we had no reason to believe they were anything other than victims this morning."

Part of me still wanted to think of them as victims. "I'm not sure what any of this is. It makes me edgy."

"I'm edgy too. There's nothing we can do. Maybe a good night's sleep will give us a few ideas."

I turned in his arms. "You're probably going to have to wear me out before I can sleep."

That drew a wolfish grin. "Now you're talking."

I FELL ASLEEP EASILY ENOUGH. Given the day I'd had, dreaming was inevitable. I emerged into a wooded dreamscape. There was something familiar about the location.

Behind me, in the thick rows of pine trees, I heard whispers. There was no ascertaining if they belonged to men or women, but they were intense. I bolstered myself with a reminder that this was a dream and then walked beyond the tree line looking for a source. I made it only a few feet before fire erupted in front of me. I took an instinctive step back, but the sizzle behind me suggested I was surrounded by fire.

It was a trap, much like the one I'd conjured in Hemlock Cove.

"Stormy." My name carried through the trees on the other side of the fire, followed by a giggle. The voice was that of a teenage girl.

"Shauna?" I called out, relieved when my voice didn't crack with fear.

"Stormy," called out another voice, this one more masculine and even more deranged. "We're coming to get you, Stormy."

I remained rooted to my spot. "What do you want?" I called into the darkness. I'd yet to see either of them.

"You'll find out," the female voice said. It was much closer this time, and I jerked my gaze to the right.

"Sooner than you realize," the male voice said with a loony laugh.

I jerked my attention in the other direction.

"You can't win," the girl I assumed was Shauna said.

"And when you lose, everyone you love will lose too," the boy said.

I opened my mouth to tell them to show themselves or shut up, but the fire exploded around me. I covered my face as the heat forced me down. I felt my skin burning and started to scream.

Hunter shook me out of my dream as I slapped at him. "Stormy!"

I stopped flailing and took in his face, shocked to find the fire gone—it had felt so real—and me safe in my bed. "Hunter?"

"It's me, baby." He pulled me to him and ran his hands over my back. "I'm right here," he assured me. His heart pounded against my face as I pressed it into his chest. "I'm right here," he said again, this time more gently.

"It was a dream." I felt like an idiot saying it. I'd known at the time that it was a dream. The flames had burned so hot that it felt real, however. "It was just a dream." I let loose a shaky breath.

"Just a dream," he agreed, resting his cheek on top of my head. "You scared the crap out of me," he said after a few seconds. "I thought you were being killed or something."

"I was. In the dream, they burned me with fire."

"Who burned you?"

"Eli and Shauna."

"You saw them? You talked to them?"

I hesitated. "I didn't see either of them, but I heard voices."

"How do you know it was them?"

"I just do." Or maybe it was my imagination.

"Baby, look at me." Hunter nudged my chin up, so I had no choice but to look into his eyes. "Tell me what you saw." He settled us back on the pillows, keeping me wrapped tightly in his arms. It didn't take long to tell him.

"That's unsettling," he said as he held me.

A quick look at the clock on the nightstand told me we still had four hours before I had to get up for my shift at the restaurant. "I'm sorry for waking you."

"Don't," he warned in a low voice.

I continued anyway. "You need your rest if you're going to find the Eatons tomorrow."

"I'm fine." He traced a light circle on my back as I closed my eyes and nestled into him.

"I'm exhausted," I said. "A morning shift with Grandpa given his current mood is going to be unbearable if I don't get a little more sleep."

"Then close your eyes. I'll be here holding you the entire time. Try to let go. It was just a dream."

We both knew that my dreams—at least some of them—were far from innocuous.

"You go to sleep too. I can't sleep if you don't."

"We'll sleep together." He held tight. "We'll be together the whole time. It's okay."

WE WERE IN THE SAME POSITION when we woke the next morning. Hunter was careful not to move so he wouldn't wake me, and the first thing I saw when my eyes popped open was his concerned face staring down at me.

I smiled and splayed my hand across his chest. "Morning."

"Morning," he said before pressing a kiss to my forehead. "How did you sleep?"

The dream came back with a vengeance. "Okay. I didn't wake up again."

"I know."

I frowned. "You weren't up all night, were you?"

"I woke up a few times to check on you and then went right back to sleep. I promise I'm well rested."

I wasn't certain I believed him. "I guess I'll let you live," I teased.

He gave me a soft kiss. "Thank you."

We stayed like that for several minutes, basking in each other's warmth. When my alarm went off, I groaned before reluctantly pulling away. "And back to reality."

We showered quickly. Without an idea of where Shauna and Eli had fled to—and no proof that my dream was real—we didn't have anywhere to focus.

By the time we headed downstairs, Grandpa was working behind the grill.

"You're late," he barked.

I glanced at the clock, knowing darned well I wasn't late. "I'm right on time," I countered. "And I don't want to hear how being fifteen minutes early is actually being on time. If you want me here fifteen minutes early, put that on the schedule."

Grandpa rolled his eyes. "You have your mother's attitude sometimes."

"People say Mom has Grandma's attitude." The muscle that flexed in his jaw told me I'd hit a nerve. "How are things with Grandma? Is she still making noise about letting Lisa and her kids move in with you?"

Grandpa's face was a grouchy mess. "I don't understand why she can't move in with your uncle."

"You mean your son?"

"I don't want to claim Brad as my son. He's annoying."

"Have you considered that he's annoying because he's desperate for your approval?"

"He's annoying because he gets a kick out of it."

"Or he's always been desperate for your approval and the only way he knows how to get attention is to be a weirdo."

Grandpa shook his head.

"I glanced over at Hunter. "Do you want breakfast before you head off to work?"

"I can't start my day without breakfast with my girl." He beamed at me before heading to the coffee area. He was familiar with the drill. He grabbed the razor and started opening bags of coffee. He then poured them into filters and stacked the filters. When the rush hit later, we would be grateful we didn't have to stop to open the bags.

I moved closer to Grandpa. "Can you cook us breakfast?"

"I'm not your slave," Grandpa groused.

"This is a restaurant, and you are the cook," I said. "Plus, you're going to make breakfast for yourself. Don't pout."

Grandpa grabbed the tub of potatoes from the refrigerator. It was the afternoon shift's job to boil the potatoes and the night shift's job to shred them. He put a dollop of oil on the grill and checked the temp with a hand close to the surface before dumping the potatoes, where they started to sizzle.

"You would pout if you were in my position," he said. "That's my house. I raised my children. I shouldn't have to bring grandchildren and great-grandchildren under my roof because of poor choices I didn't make."

I could've told him about how it was his choices that led to Brad being Brad. Lisa was the way she was because Brad had been more interested in conspiracy theories than in being a good father. Her mother had a certain reputation around town. Apparently, she wasn't all that faithful either. Brad either didn't know about her infidelity, or chose to ignore it. I leaned toward the latter. That would lead to a fight, though, and this was the chattiest Grandpa had been since the neighborhood watch incident.

"You have to put your foot down with Grandma," I said. "She has to understand that you have a say in how things go in your own house."

Grandpa made a sputtering noise. "We both know your grandmother rules the roost. I'm a victim under my own roof."

I choked on a laugh, then realized he was serious. "You have got to be kidding me. You get your way more than anyone I know."

"Look in the mirror," he fired back. "Hunter spoils you rotten."

I glanced at Hunter, who looked as if he wished he was anywhere but in the middle of this argument. "Is that true?"

He shrugged. "I enjoy spoiling you, but your grandfather is exaggerating when he says you always get your way."

"When was the last time she didn't get her way?" Grandpa challenged. He seemed to think he had a win sewed up.

"Yesterday," Hunter replied. "She wanted me to stop pushing her on writing again, but I kept pushing."

Grandpa stilled. "You're going to start writing again?" I couldn't decide how he felt about the possibility.

I shrugged. "I'm thinking about it."

Grandpa looked Hunter over with fresh eyes. "I'm impressed. I didn't think you'd push her, but here you are."

Hunter chuckled. "When it's important, I push her."

"It's not something I'm considering until we resolve our current problem," I warned them both. "We've already talked about this."

"What is your current problem?" Grandpa asked.

"Other than the kids who returned after a ten-year disappearance looking exactly the same?"

"I figured that had something to do with all that woo-woo stuff you're involved in." Grandpa was never happy when the witchy stuff came up. He liked to pretend it wasn't real. Sometimes I let him off the hook. Today, I couldn't let it go.

"It does," I confirmed. "We just don't know how yet."

"The kids disappeared from the hospital last night," Hunter volunteered.

Grandpa's brow furrowed. "Did someone take them?"

"We don't know." Hunter's shoulders hopped. "The cameras—we're talking every camera in the hospital—was knocked out right before they disappeared. We don't know if they left of their own accord, or if someone came in and took them."

"Which way are you leaning?"

Hunter's gaze landed on me, as if looking for an answer. "We don't know, but if I were a betting man I'd put all my money on them taking off voluntarily."

"Do I even want to know what's going on?" Grandpa asked. "How bad is this going to get?"

"We have no way of knowing," I replied. "We don't know where they were. All we know is that there are strange stories about the kids before they disappeared, the father everyone thought had them was hiding from them, and Eli and Shauna haven't aged a day in ten years."

"So everything is about to get weird and out of control again," Grandpa sighed.

I wanted to disagree, but I couldn't. "That's a pretty apt assessment."

"Great." Grandpa flipped the hash browns before walking to the refrigerator for the bacon and eggs. "That's just what I need. I still haven't gotten over the last woo-woo mess you dropped on this town. Now there's another one banging down our door."

"I didn't drop that mess on anyone," I argued.

"Things like that never happened here before you ... well, you know." His expression was grave.

I wanted to argue with him. "I guarantee all that stuff was going on before I came back to town. You know about it now because I've been dragged into it."

"I preferred not knowing."

"I'm sure you did. We don't always get what we want, though, do we?"

"There." Grandpa snapped a finger and jabbed it at me. "That right there is something your grandmother would say."

Laughter bubbled up. "You're unreal sometimes."

"I'm just saying you have a lot in common with your grandmother."

I was too tired to argue with him. "I'll take your word for it." I headed toward the swinging doors that led to the cafe section of the restaurant. "I'll get things set up and then be back for breakfast."

"I'll miss you while you're gone," Hunter teased.

"Don't push me too hard," Grandpa growled. "I'm already on the edge. I can't deal with you two being mushy on top of everything else."

13
THIRTEEN

I decided to take advantage of my shift. The older crowd often came in for breakfast midweek. They liked to drink coffee, munch on pancakes, and gossip. That gossip would hopefully work to my advantage.

"Good morning." I smiled at Lydia Shields and Genevieve Pope as I approached their table. I placed mugs in front of them and waited for them to get comfortable before pouring. "Do you want your regular orders this morning?"

"Always," Lydia confirmed. Her gaze was wary as she looked me over.

"Is something wrong?" I asked, briefly wondering if I had spinach stuck in my teeth. Grandpa had put spinach in my omelet just to be spiteful because he was still annoyed with everything witchy popping up and ruining his already wrecked week.

"I was going to ask you that." Lydia exchanged a heavy look with Genevieve. "There's a rumor that the Eaton twins were found on the highway coming from Hemlock Cove."

I nodded. "That's true."

"People say you found them."

"They were standing in the middle of the road," I replied. "It's not as if I found them held in a dungeon and saved them. They were right there. I just happened to be driving down the road at that time."

Lydia's smile was flat. "If there were a dungeon involved, those two were the dungeon masters. Those kids were demons."

There was that word again: demons. It had popped up quite a few times the past fifteen hours. Lydia wasn't referring to literal demons. If she knew about the paranormal world, everyone in town would have heard an earful from her.

"You knew them when they lived here?" I asked, avoiding the obvious question. I didn't want to act too eager, it would be a red flag.

"They lived two houses down."

Lydia had lived in her house for almost fifty years. That meant Craig and Sandy had moved in after she'd already been entrenched in the neighborhood.

"Did you see the kids a lot?" I asked. "I understand they were homeschooled."

Lydia's snort was derisive. "Those kids didn't do any learning at all. Have you met Sandy and Craig? They weren't teaching those kids anything."

"I thought homeschooled kids had to take tests to prove they were learning."

"There are ways around those tests." Lydia waved me off. "I've heard about all the tricks. We all talked about it when those kids were supposedly being homeschooled."

"I've talked to them," I replied. "One of them. She didn't seem slow or anything."

"I'm not saying they were slow. I'm saying their parents didn't teach them anything." She leaned closer. "Have you ever wondered how it is that they came across as intelligent as they did when they weren't taught anything?"

"They were younger than me," I said. "I didn't pay as much attention to them as maybe I should have."

"You were better off not knowing them," Lydia insisted. "I saw them from time to time when they were out and about in the yard. Strange little creatures." She made a face. "Honestly, I was relieved when I heard they disappeared."

"You were relieved that they might have been kidnapped?"

"By their father. He was an odd duck too. He never spent any time with those kids. I got the distinct impression he was afraid of them."

"What makes you say that?"

"When he came home at night, he sat in his car for an hour just staring into nothing. He only went inside the house when Sandy came to see what he was doing. Then they screamed at each other for hours. Such delightful neighbors."

I ignored the sarcasm. "Did it ever occur to you the kids acted odd because they had a rough home life?" I asked.

Lydia shook her head. She almost looked as if she wanted to pat me on the head for being so naive. "I'm not saying Craig and Sandy were perfect. Far from it. The kids weren't abused, though. I would've known."

"There are different types of abuse," I argued. "Neglect is a form of abuse."

"Oh, you kids today with the neglect." She clucked her tongue. "Back in my day, once we were three, we were on our own. I turned out fine."

Genevieve nodded in agreement. "Me too."

That was quite a stretch. Still, I managed to maintain an even expression. "I'm just saying that maybe the kids were self-taught."

"Or maybe there really was something wrong with them and that's why the parents were disinterested," Lydia said. "Nobody kicked up a media storm when they went missing. Their mother didn't report it for a month. Their father disappeared with them, yet the current rumor is he never had them. He went into hiding instead."

"I heard that the kids looked exactly the same," Genevieve interjected. "I mean *exactly the same*. They weren't little kids when they went missing, but there's no way they could be exactly the same if there wasn't something wrong with them."

They had a point, loath as I was to admit it. Something still felt off. "Were the kids ever in school?" I don't know why I asked it, other than my interaction with Sandy the day before. She did not strike me as the sort of woman who would've wanted to homeschool.

"I believe they went to the elementary school for a time," Lydia replied. "I don't think they lasted more than a year or two."

"Were there issues?"

Lydia sent me a knowing look. "There were rumors that they were cruel to the other kids, tripping them and stuff. I remember one of the kids threatened Tony Fleet's son. The kid swore they showed him photos of a dead body. There were no photos of a dead body found on them."

"What do you think was going on with them?" I asked. "Do you believe they were evil?"

"They weren't normal," Lydia replied. "The world was probably a better place without them. Now they're back, I don't think that means good things for the town."

I WAS ONLY AN HOUR FROM FINISHING my shift when the two people I didn't want to see strolled through the diner door.

Phoebe Green and Monica Johnson had their heads together, laughing. When they looked up, Phoebe gave Monica a knowing look, then primly gripped her hands together in front of her.

"It was so much nicer when you weren't here the past two days," she said.

"I agree. I prefer not working." I gave her a flat smile, then turned to Monica. My relationship with her was strained, although not in the same way as my relationship with Phoebe. "How are you?"

Monica's eyebrows hopped. We were carefully neutral inter-acting with one another. I found her taste in friends dreadful. I'd always known Phoebe was a monster. How Monica couldn't see that was beyond me. It was Monica's taste in men that was my current irritation, however.

When I'd first come back to Shadow Hills, Monica and Hunter had been together. She was apparently plotting a wedding, and Hunter was just floating along. He claimed he was getting ready to break up with her before he ever laid eyes on me again. I wasn't certain I believed that. Hunter's love-them-and-leave-them reputa-tion suggested she had a few more months before he dropped the hammer on her.

Hunter and I were drawn together, and he dumped her—from her perspective, out of the blue. We didn't have an affair per se. At least not a physical one. Our emotions were twined together from the moment we spoke after a ten-year hiatus.

Monica had tried to put on a brave face, but it was obvious she was wrecked. I felt guilty, but I was also happy for the first time in a long time. Then Monica's next boyfriend, her rebound, turned out to be a paranormal killer and she almost lost her life. That, of course, had made things worse. She claimed to have learned her lesson. I believed her. There was just one problem. Two weeks ago, after playing coy about her current boyfriend, Monica had brought him into the restaurant for breakfast. I recognized him. He was a gnome shifter, essentially the evil counterpart to my white knight shifter. Easton and Weston were two sides of the same coin as it was explained to me. They were cousins locked in a brotherhood on opposite sides of a war. Easton had my best interests at heart— something he'd proven more than once—and Weston was the enemy.

Monica had no idea she was dating the enemy. There was no way Weston was dating her for anything other than cover, but if I told her, I ran the risk of her not believing me. On top of that, if she started spreading my personal business around town—gnome shifters and fire witches were a lot to digest—I would have a whole other problem on my hands.

"Did you hear that?" Phoebe trilled. "She wants to know how you're doing. As if she cares."

I glared at her. One thing I knew for certain was that Phoebe was not Monica's friend. I was convinced that Phoebe had only latched onto the woman—a relative newcomer in Shadow Hills—because Monica was dating Hunter. Phoebe had always carried a torch for my fiancé. He had never once returned her interest, but Phoebe still held out hope. Even now, after she'd been arrested for and convicted of extortion, she thought she had a chance with my future husband.

"I do care," I countered. "Also, it's kind of a standard question, Phoebe. When someone comes in, I ask how they are. Then I seat them, get them some coffee, take their order, and deliver their food."

Phoebe rolled her eyes until they landed on Monica. "Can you believe how ridiculous she is?"

Monica worked her jaw. She cast me a conflicted look. Finally, she sighed. "She's kind of right, Phoebe. It would be weirder if she didn't ask how I was doing."

"The usual rules don't apply when one person steals another's boyfriend," Phoebe pronounced. "She should be on her hands and knees weeping for your forgiveness."

Monica sent me an apologetic look. "I really don't think that's necessary."

I opted to extricate myself from the conversation. "Let's go this way, huh?" I pointed to their usual booth. "Do you need menus or just coffee?"

"Just coffee," Monica replied. She looked relieved that I wasn't going to push things with Phoebe. "We can still get breakfast, right?"

I nodded. "Yeah. You can even get poached eggs if you want. David has taken over the grill from my grandfather."

Intrigue lit Monica's face—she'd been yelled at more than once for ordering the dreaded poached eggs—and then she sighed. "Now that I can have them, I don't think I want them."

I smiled, but it was forced. "I'll get your coffee and be back in a few for your orders."

My mind was bursting with busy energy as I got their coffee. I'd been looking for an opening to talk to Monica about Weston ever since we'd seen them together. Hunter told me there was nothing I could do, that no matter what I said to Monica, it wouldn't end well for me. I still couldn't stop fantasizing about saving her. I couldn't make up for what I'd done to her, even though none of it had been malicious. Still, knowing Weston as well as I did, I very much doubted he was dating Monica because he was attracted to her. He was only in town because of me, something I couldn't reveal to her.

I was still mulling my options as I took them their coffee. Phoebe being Phoebe, decided to take over the conversation.

"So is it true the Eaton twins are back in town?" she asked as she sipped her coffee.

I frowned. "They're not twins. Eli is older than Shauna."

Phoebe made a face. "Everyone referred to them as twins because he was only like eight months older than her. That should've been physically impossible."

"Maybe the sister was premature," Monica suggested.

"I believe that's the case," I said, although Sandy hadn't mentioned that. I'd never considered looking into the circumstances surrounding the kids' births. I made a mental note to ask Hunter later.

"They look alike in a creepy way," Phoebe continued. "Like they could be twins." Her gaze moved to me. "Do they still look creepy?"

"They looked as if they hadn't eaten in a week when I first saw them," I replied.

"How did you find them?" Monica asked. She was aware that I was different. The word "magic" had even been bandied about in front of her. She was careful not to ask too many questions.

"They were just standing in the middle of the road," I replied. "I was on my way back from Hemlock Cove, and there they were." I shrugged.

"You've been spending a lot of time in Hemlock Cove," Phoebe noted. "Were you with that guy?"

I was confused. Was she talking about Easton? "You mean the guy who was temporarily living in my spare room? Easton is living with Sebastian now." I caught my mistake too late. "As friends," I quickly added.

"Friends!" Phoebe snorted. "Right." She gave me the universal "okay" sign and rolled her eyes. "I wasn't talking about him anyway. I was talking about the guy who has been hanging around with Easton and Sebastian."

Evan. Where was she going with this? "What about him?"

"I'm wondering if Hunter knows how much time you've been spending with him."

"Ask Hunter," I suggested, smirking when I pictured her flouncing up to him with her gossip regarding Evan and me. "I'm sure he'd love to hear your ideas on the subject."

Phoebe frowned but didn't respond.

Monica was another story. "Told you." Monica looked triumphant. "He's too good looking to be straight."

So that's where this was going. "Please tell me you weren't going to try to hook up with Evan," I said.

"Don't worry about who I'm going to hook up with," Phoebe fired back. "Worry about the freaking Eatons. Word is spreading that they're missing from the hospital. People say they're dangerous."

"We don't have proof they're dangerous," I hedged.

"We don't have proof they're not," Phoebe noted. "All we know is they disappeared ten years ago, nobody cried too hard about them being gone, and now they're back looking not a day older. If that doesn't point to them being evil, I don't know what evil looks like."

I should've thought before responding, but my insult was automatic. "Try looking in the mirror." I clicked my pen. "What are you having this morning?"

Phoebe glared at me with narrow-eyed hate. "Two eggs basted, corned beef hash, and whole wheat toast."

I nodded and turned to Monica.

"I'll have the same," she said. She looked as if she wanted to apologize, but I wasn't in the mood.

"Go back to talking to me about Weston," Phoebe prodded. "How are things going? You apparently have the only straight new guy in town. I have to live vicariously through you."

"They're great," Monica replied. "I don't want to jinx us or anything, but things are going really well."

My stomach constricted as I marched to the kitchen. *There's nothing you can do,* I told myself. *You can't get involved.*

14
FOURTEEN

Alice practically skipped to the back door when it was time to start her shift. She played with a chain around her neck and giggled, telling me I was about to get an earful about whoever she was dating this week.

"There you are." Alice sidled up as I sat on a crate in the alley and enjoyed the fresh air, clearly happy to see me. "I was wondering if you were still here."

It was difficult to ascertain if she wanted me to be here. We were close, but sometimes it was better to keep distance between us. Alice went through phases when she was a bit of a monster.

"If this is about you flirting with Hunter," I started.

She waved me off as if I was a gnat buzzing around her head. "We both know I only flirt with Hunter because it irritates you."

One thing about Alice was that she owned her bad behavior. She laughed at my annoyance. "Look at you. You're so easy to annoy." She did a little dance, swaying her hips. "Want to see what Noah got me?"

The name was enough to jog my memory. Noah Moore. He'd gone to school with Hunter and me, which made him a few years older than Alice. She'd harbored a crush on him when we were in high school. When she was in middle school, she was desperate to have a high school boyfriend and thought I could somehow secure one for her. Noah had been on her list. Back then he had no interest. Apparently, that had changed.

"What is Noah doing these days?" I asked. I'd seen him once or twice from afar since my return. I didn't remember him coming into the restaurant during my shifts.

"He's part of Danny Anderson's roofing crew," Alice replied.

Given the sorts of people Alice enjoyed dating, Noah was already sounding like a catch. "Roofing is a good job." The second Alice realized I was all for her relationship with Noah she would dump him.

"It keeps him in tip-top shape—you should see his abs—and he makes a lot of money. He's socking it away because he still lives with his mother."

I balked. "I didn't realize he still lives with his mother." My nose wrinkled. "That's less exciting."

"You live in the apartment above the restaurant," she pointed out. "Do you really think you're in a position to judge?"

I didn't like her tone. Also, I didn't like that she was right. "Fair point." I flashed a flat smile. "How long have you been dating Noah?"

"About three weeks." Alice kept swinging her hips, telling me she was going through the euphoria portion of her romance cycle. Things were still going well for her. Given her track record, they would turn poor within the next two weeks.

"Well, I hope things work out." I glanced around the quiet back area. "Have you seen Monica with her new boyfriend?" I asked.

"You're not going to mess with her, are you?" Alice gave me a dark look. "I mean, if you are, I'll help because I don't like her on principle, but that's like kicking a puppy. You already took her one true love."

I glared at her. "I did not."

"I'm not saying that she was Hunter's true love—unfortunately that's you—but he was her true love."

My frown grew deeper. "Why 'unfortunately?'"

"What?" Alice's expression was bland.

"You said 'unfortunately that's you.' Why is it unfortunate?"

"Oh, you know." Alice made a "whatever" motion with her hand.

"I don't."

Alice emitted a disgruntled sound. "I'm just saying that he's always been my crush. When you were gone, I had no reason to believe you weren't over for good. That made him fair game."

"Only he didn't want to play with you," I reminded her.

"Yeah, yeah, yeah." She sent me a mischievous grin. "It's your fault for being older. I always wanted to be just like you."

"So you want to live in the apartment above the restaurant?" I was amused.

"Hey, I would totally take that apartment. It's big, and more importantly, it's free. Plus, you can go downstairs and cook whatever you want late at night."

"I never do that. That seems like it would be against the rules."

Alice snorted. "I'm not a rule follower like you."

That was true. "What's that necklace?" She was still twirling it around her neck, which meant she wanted me to ask about it.

"This? Oh, Noah got it for me." She leaned closer so I could get a look at it. "Isn't it beautiful?"

I was confused at what I was looking at. "Are those stars? They look like a bunch of little dots drawn together by lines."

"It's the constellation Gemini." She gave me a dark look. "Don't make fun of my necklace."

"I'm not. It's pretty." It wasn't the sort of thing I was interested in, but it was pretty. "I just couldn't figure it out." There was something familiar about the way the dots lined up. "You're a Gemini?"

She rolled her eyes. "Of course I'm a Gemini. Like I could be anything else."

I'd never been into astrology much, but I was intrigued enough to keep talking. "What does being a Gemini mean?"

"Gemini is the best sign," Alice supplied. "It means that I'm a social butterfly, but I have two sides to my personality. You know, like the Gemini twins."

My heart rate picked up a notch at the word "twins." That's how Phoebe had referred to the Eatons, and it had stuck in my head. "Keep going."

"You want to hear about being a Gemini?" Alice looked dubious. "Why?"

"Just curious. I don't pay a lot of attention to astrology." That wasn't entirely true. I did occasionally read my horoscope. In general, though, I didn't put much faith in the belief.

"That's because you're an Aquarius. You guys are kind of aloof and annoying."

"It says we're annoying right in our charts, huh?"

She nodded without hesitation. "Geminis are much better."

"Tell me about Geminis." I looked at the necklace again. "Tell me about the twins."

Even though Alice was supposed to be reporting for duty, she jumped at the opportunity. "Geminis juggle a lot of passions. We have a lot of friend groups, unlike some people." She gave me a pointed look.

I ignored it. I was not in the mood to get into an argument about who had better friends. I might not have as many friends as Alice, but I'd surrounded myself with loyal people. She and her friends stabbed each other in the back for sport. And that was exactly the way she liked it.

"Geminis have two parts to their personalities," she continued, warming to her subject. She seemed excited that I was interested in her for a change. "They can be kind and sweet one minute and cold and calculating the next. That's not being two-faced." She gave me a knowing look, as if she assumed I was going to make that assumption. "Geminis are fearless thinkers and are always down to try something new."

"Give me some bad Gemini traits," I instructed.

"Of course you would go right to the bad." Her eye roll was

dramatic. "Geminis are impulsive, anxious, and inconsistent. They're also indecisive and moody."

I took in the information. "What else?" I asked.

"You're so curious all of a sudden." She cocked her head. "What does this have to do with?"

"Just tell me," I ordered.

"Is this about the witchy stuff?" Her nose was still out of joint about that. She'd been with me when I'd first used the Ouija board. When I developed powers after the fact, she'd been jealous. She even said she was jealous and tried to conjure her own powers. When that didn't work, she'd distanced herself from me. She didn't want me to have something—whether it was Hunter or magic—that she couldn't lay claim to.

"Let's just say I think it's important," I said.

She narrowed her eyes. "Does this have something to do with you finding those kids?" She was intelligent on top of her diabolical nature. I hated that about her. "Everyone is talking about that. Everyone who remembers the kids wishes you hadn't found them. Everyone who thinks they're innocent and something terrible happened to them believes you're a hero."

"What do you think?"

She shrugged. "Those kids were weird, but I don't know that I'd say they were evil. Their parents were weird."

"They were closer to your age," I noted.

"I wasn't friends with them. I was with the popular group." She looked proud when she said it, puffing herself out.

"Yes, you were with the popular group," I agreed. "Everyone wanted to be just like you or hang out with you."

"They did." She smiled a bit longer, then frowned. "Except for Hunter."

If she didn't get off the Hunter train, I was going to get annoyed. Okay, I was already annoyed. That's what she was going for. She didn't really want Hunter. She would be bored in five minutes if she ever actually got him. Hunter was far too vanilla for her. She just wanted him because he wanted me. She simply pretended she had a shot because she knew it irked me.

"Anyway," she said when she got the response she was looking for, grinning at my frown, "back to Geminis and their toxic traits." She looked far too happy to be reciting this information. "We're superficial, restless, materialistic, and childish. We're also nosy."

I nodded. "Gemini is part of mythology, too, right?"

She frowned. "Yes, all the astrological signs are."

"Do you know about that?"

She made a face as if I'd suggested the weirdest thing in the world. "Um ... no. I only care about Gemini as it relates to me."

"Okay. Great." I moved to return to the restaurant.

"That's it?" she called to my back. "I have a laundry list of good stuff to go through for Geminis too."

"I'm good for now." I waved her off. It wasn't the astrological sign I was interested in as much as the mythology. A theory was starting to take root in my head.

I DIDN'T HAVE BOOKS TO GO THROUGH—unlike the Winchesters, I didn't have a library at my disposal—so I had to conduct all of my research on my phone.

"What are you doing?" Easton asked, letting himself into the apartment without knocking about two hours after I'd started reading.

I almost came out of my skin. "You don't live here any longer," I reminded him. "You need to knock."

He was even more handsome when he smiled. "Sorry. I thought you were taking a nap. I just came to grab the last of my stuff."

He didn't own much. Everything he did own, I'd purchased for him. "How much more could you have?"

"One bag," he replied. He cocked his head as he looked at the notebook I'd been working in when he entered. "What are you doing?"

"Researching Gemini."

"The constellation?"

I nodded.

"Why?"

"I have a theory about the Eatons."

"Who are the Eatons?"

It was only then that I realized it had been days since I'd even seen him, let alone talked with him. I caught him up, and when I finished, he looked flummoxed.

"You really think these kids are the Gemini twins from mythology?"

"According to mythology, Castor and Pollux were twins but had different fathers," I started. "Craig said he didn't believe he was Shauna's father."

"They're not twins." Easton sat on the couch next to me.

"Yeah, supposedly Shauna was born eight months after Eli," I explained. "That shouldn't be possible."

"Right, they're not twins."

"Maybe they're as close to twins as the magical world allows," I said. "They're boy and girl." I made an impatient movement with my hands. "Let me finish." I said out loud for his benefit as much as my own.

Easton bowed his head. "I know you need to think out loud."

"Castor was the mortal son. Pollux was the immortal son. They were famous for their physical and mental skills, and were members of the voyage to find the Golden Fleece.

"Castor was killed in battle and Pollux begged Zeus to make him immortal. He agreed but only if the twins spent half their time on earth and half their time in the heavens," I continued.

Realization dawned on Easton's face. "Is that what you think? That these twins who aren't really twins went to spend half their time in the heavens?"

"I don't think we can take the story literally," I replied. "We need to take the basics and extrapolate."

"Okay." Easton leaned back on the couch. "Continue."

"There's not much else to tell regarding the mythology angle. The twins have been represented in various cultures, including Babylonian, Arabian, and Egyptian astrology. They're also believed to protect sailors, but I'm not sure how that fits into what we're dealing with."

Easton pursed his lips but remained silent.

"As for the constellation, it's represented by this." I showed him a drawing I'd found online.

"It kind of looks like the pi symbol."

"It does, but there's a line at the bottom," I said. "Now look at this." I showed him a photo of the constellation with lines connecting the stars so they looked like twins.

"I've seen the constellation before," he said. "It lies between Taurus and Cancer to the east. It's prominent in winter skies of the northern hemisphere."

"We're in spring," I said. "I've been wondering if their power built through the winter months, leading them to arrive during spring."

He nodded but waited.

"Anyway," I continued, shaking my head. I kept getting distracted by various tangents. "We found this on the trees near where we believe the Eatons arrived." I showed him the photos on my phone. Then I showed him another photo in which I'd crudely connected the lines.

He leaned forward. "You found the constellation on the trees?" His eyebrows moved toward one another. "Interesting."

"The symbols looked familiar. I took an astronomy class in college. I remember the Gemini constellation."

"You can't be sure that the symbols represent Gemini," he cautioned.

"I'm kind of certain. Phoebe referred to the Eatons as twins this morning. Apparently, a lot of people in town called them twins because they looked so much alike."

"But the girl was born after the boy," he said.

"Yes, but maybe that wasn't supposed to happen. Maybe she was behind him and the fact that it was a boy and girl this time is significant. Maybe the Gemini twins are reborn every hundred years or something and it's special when it's a boy and a girl instead of two boys."

"That's a lot of maybes, Stormy." Easton cocked his head. "Yet I admit it's interesting. The kids haven't been seen since disappearing from the hospital?"

I shook my head. "And last time I checked, Eli wasn't talking."

"Maybe she was waiting for him," Easton mused. "Maybe the trip from wherever they came from was difficult and she recovered quicker. Once he came back to reality, they left together for whatever mission they're on."

"That's what I was thinking," I confirmed, relieved that he'd come to the same conclusion without too much prodding.

"That doesn't explain why they disappeared as children and came back now," he said.

"But it gives us a jumping off point."

"Where are we jumping to?"

I cocked an eyebrow. "We?"

"I am technically your familiar. Wherever you go, I'm going with you."

I was grateful for the help. "Well, to start, we're going to Hemlock Cove. I want to know what the Winchesters think about this."

"Good idea. After that?"

"Let's see what the Winchesters think and go from there."

He bobbed his head and stood. "If they really are a representation of the Gemini twins, we need to get ahead of this."

15
FIFTEEN

When Easton and I walked into the lobby of The Overlook, we heard raised voices coming from the dining room.

"I've had it!" Winnie Winchester shouted. "That clown cannot say. While we're at it, do something about the way Bay smells. I don't want to have to fight the urge to puke whenever I'm in a room with my own daughter."

I exchanged an amused look with Easton. We both naturally slowed our paces to listen ... and to keep ourselves at a safe distance while waiting for Aunt Tillie's response.

"That clown has done nothing to you," Tillie countered. She sounded reasonable. That's why I knew to be careful. When she sounded reasonable she was most likely to fly off the handle. "Give the poor thing a break. He's just trying to find his place in a scary new world."

"This world isn't so scary," a craggy voice I recognized as belonging to Crusty added. "If you had plants that ate people, then it would be scary."

"Thank you for putting that image in my head," Winnie spat. "I'm serious. The clown has to go. He's scaring the guests."

"The last guests checked out this morning," Tillie countered. "We don't get new ones for two days. He's fine."

"What about Bay's scent?" Winnie demanded.

Bay replied with a wail. "There's nothing fine about the way I smell!"

When Easton and I reached the open doorway, we found Tillie sitting in her usual chair, a mug of coffee in front of her. The clown was on the table doing a handstand for some reason. He kicked his little feet in such a way he almost looked cute. Then I remembered he was a sentient clown doll, and he became all the creepier.

"Hey," I said awkwardly, my gaze immediately going to Bay, also in her usual chair at the dining table. I could smell her from ten feet away. "Wow!" I put my hand over my mouth. "Sorry, but is that scent getting worse?"

"So much worse," Bay agreed, frowning.

I would moan too if I smelled like a rancid pickle.

"And how are you?" I asked Winnie, who stood over Tillie, hands on hips, glaring at her aunt.

"I've been better," Winnie replied. "I thought I was well past my child-rearing years, but here's Aunt Tillie to prove me wrong. What about you? I heard about those kids disappearing from the hospital. Landon and Terry told us over breakfast this morning. Have you seen them?"

I shook my head. "No, but I think I might have found something. If you guys are busy, though…"

"We could use the distraction." Winnie slapped Crusty's feet, causing him to flop over. "What did I tell you about doing gymnastics on the dining room table?" she demanded.

Crusty, his face red and full of annoyance, sneered at her. "Tillie is right," he said. "You are the worst one."

"I can be a whole lot worse," Winnie threatened. "Stop being a pain. Stormy obviously has something serious to tell us."

"How is me doing a handstand being a pain?" Crusty asked.

"Because I said so." Winnie's smile was sweet and sympathetic when she turned it to me. "Would you like a cookie?"

"No thank you," I said.

"I would," Easton pleaded.

Winnie tousled his hair. "I'll get you cookies," she said before disappearing into the kitchen.

I tried to sit next to Bay. I lasted ten seconds before I sent her an apologetic look and moved to the other side of the table. "Sorry," I said. "I've never smelled anything like that."

The look Bay shot Tillie was withering. "I know. It's foul."

"Maybe there's a little lesson in there," Tillie said primly. "Like, you don't leave your aunt in a fire trap and try to blackmail her."

"Yeah, yeah, yeah." Bay shook her head. "Make it go away. I have an interview with the new owners of the Hex and Curl, and I can't go in there smelling like this. They'll think I'm dying or something."

"Maybe you should have thought about that before you tried to blackmail me." Tillie smiled at Bay, then at me, then sipped her coffee.

When Winnie returned with a plate of cookies—much to Easton's delight—Tillie was still grinning.

"Knock it off with the pickle curse," Winnie barked. "Enough is enough."

"Thanks, Mom," Bay said dryly.

"How does Landon handle that smell?" Easton asked. He didn't look nearly as put off as I felt. "Does he make you sleep on the couch?"

"He wore a mask," Bay replied. "He also pointed four fans at us and tried to get me to bathe in tomato juice."

I tried not to laugh. "It's not like being sprayed by a skunk."

"That's what I told him." Bay held out her hands. "He was determined to try. He'll cry soon if Aunt Tillie doesn't ease up."

"That makes me want to keep it up." Tillie sipped her coffee again, then made a lip-smacking sound designed to drive her nieces to distraction.

"What's up with you?" Winnie asked when she'd finally managed to drag her attention away from Tillie. "You don't usually stop by in the middle of the day. Not that we're not happy to see you," she added hastily.

"I found something, but I need you to tell me if I'm crazy," I started.

Tillie opened her mouth—to say something snarky I'm certain—but Winnie stopped her with a pointed glare. "You don't have to comment on every opening," she said icily. When Winnie turned back to me, her smile was patient. "What did you find?"

"These patterns were carved—or maybe burned—into the trees near where I found Eli and Shauna." I showed them the photos I'd taken.

"Those were on all the trees?" Bay asked as she leaned across the table.

I did my best to pretend her scent wasn't going to cause me to gag. "Not all, but at least fifteen to twenty."

"They're the same pattern," Winnie mused as she scrolled through the images. "Weird."

"This afternoon, when I was finishing my shift, I was talking to my cousin Alice," I continued. "She was showing off a necklace from her new boyfriend. When I placed the Gemini necklace over the photos, the image matched."

Surprise had Bay's eyebrows hopping. "The Gemini constellation carved into the trees?"

I nodded. "It only occurred to me after Phoebe referred to the Eatons as twins this morning ... even though they're not. Shauna was born eight months after Eli."

Winnie started shaking her head. "That shouldn't be possible."

"But that's how it happened."

"That would mean their parents had sex right away after the first birth and the second birth was more than a month premature,"

Winnie argued. "Trust me, after giving birth, no one is in the mood for sex right away. I'm no expert, but twins come from the same womb at the same time." Winnie sent me a kind smile.

"But what if something caused the Eatons to be born separately?" I felt I was on the right track. "What if they were supposed to come together but somehow there was a delay—maybe through a door or something?"

Bay's forehead furrowed. "Like a plane door?"

I shrugged. "Some magical door. The Gemini twins are prominent in mythology. I'm wondering if they were ever represented here on earth."

Realization dawned on Bay's face. "Like every hundred years the Gemini twins take human form and wreak havoc on the world. That plan was screwed up this time and they were born separately."

"And what if their disappearance was them trying to fix the error?" I pressed.

Bay considered it. "I would like to say I've heard weirder stories, but I haven't." She nodded. "It's an interesting idea."

"But you haven't heard of it happening," I realized, deflating a bit.

"That doesn't mean you're wrong."

"We need someone with extensive historical knowledge regarding paranormal creatures," Winnie said.

Bay already had her phone out. "I know who to call."

TEN MINUTES LATER, EVAN STROLLED INTO the dining room. He looked a little windswept from running, and his hair was damp from a recent shower, but he was all smiles as he dropped a kiss on the top of Winnie's head.

"Thank you for inviting me," he said. "I love Winnie's cookies." He snagged one of the chocolate chips and slid Bay a sidelong look as he sat next to her. "Still stinking the place up."

"Make her reverse the spell," Bay barked. "I can't take another moment of this."

Evan laughed. "Right. Because she listens to me."

Bay growled, shot Tillie the finger, then turned to me. "Tell him what you told us."

Evan was already familiar with pieces of the story. When I finished, he had already devoured one cookie and looked thoughtful.

"You know, now that you mention it, those markings on the trees do remind me of constellations," he said. "I should've seen it." He pulled out his phone and looked at his own photos. "And there it is: the twins."

"Except we're not dealing with twins," Winnie reminded him. "Those kids were born eight months apart."

"Which shouldn't be possible," Evan pointed out.

Winnie wouldn't let it go. "They can't be twins if they weren't in the womb together."

"You're basing that on human rules," he countered. "If these are the twins I'm thinking of, they don't have to follow those rules."

"They're demons," I mumbled.

Evan nodded. "The twins have various representations throughout history. The Babylonians, for example, regarded them as minor gods. They've always been demons."

"How many times have they appeared here on earth?" I asked.

He shrugged. "Impossible to say. If I had to estimate, at least thirty or forty times. They usually show up in times of strife. They like to cause mischief, although they'll lie and pretend that one of them causes trouble while the other tries to stop it."

"Playing good cop and bad cop demons," Tillie said.

Evan chuckled. "They do play games."

"Have they ever come as a boy and a girl before?" I asked.

"Yes. They most often appear as two boys, but they have appeared as a boy and a girl at least three times that I know of. They're even more troublesome when they're a boy and a girl."

"How does it work?" I was invested in this. "How do they decide who they're going to become on this side?"

"Usually they're born. They hijack pregnancies at the last second."

"Could that explain why Shauna was born eight months after Eli?"

Evan tilted his head, thinking it through. "It might explain more than one thing. If they timed their entrance to this plane wrong they might have been off from the start. I'm sure you've been amassing stories about the kids," he said to me. "What have you found?"

"Everyone thought they were weird and didn't like them," I replied. "They told people they were going to Hell and talked about fornication a lot. They had no outside friends."

"That sounds about right." Evan bobbed his head. "The stories I've heard involved them stirring up religious atrocities."

I was caught off guard. "Like?"

"They were involved in Aztec sacrifices." When nobody immediately acknowledged what he'd said, Evan sighed. "You guys need to read more," he chided. "For those not in the know, it's estimated that anywhere between 20,000 and 250,000 people per year were sacrificed to honor the gods.

"These sacrifices were conducted for about 800 years," he continued. "The twins weren't there for the whole 800 years, but they served as clerics to whisper in the ears of the leaders to get it going. They also had a hand in the Crusades, the French religious wars, and they were also involved in the Holocaust."

I felt sick. "They caused all of that?"

He shook his head. "No. It's important you understand the distinction. They didn't technically start any of it. They found individuals who were capable of starting it and decided to see how far they could push things."

"That's not much better," Winnie argued.

"My theory has always been the same," Evan said. "These were tests. The demons wanted to test the humans. We always fail because that's what it is to be human. Our weaknesses are counterbalanced by our strengths."

"What could the twins be looking to do?" I asked. "What religious atrocity could they be trying to propel this time?"

Evan tapped his fingers on his forearm as he considered. "Maybe they're not supposed to do something now. Maybe they were supposed to do something ten years ago but things were thrown off course when they didn't arrive at the same time. Maybe they decided to give up on the plan ten years ago and cross back over."

Winnie asked, "Why didn't they stay gone?"

"Maybe it was another error. Opening plane doors isn't easy, and if we're talking a Hell plane..." He held out his hands. "Maybe they came over looking to cause trouble but were thrown because the birth didn't go as planned. In ancient myths, the twins appeared as babies but grew to be teenagers in a month. They liked the theater of it all. They enjoyed the locals revering them as gods."

"They can't pull that off now," I argued. "People would freak out."

"So why not show up as teenagers?" Bay asked. "Why go through the rigmarole of being born?"

"Maybe they had no choice," Evan replied. "Maybe there are rules. Maybe they are controlled by a different demon."

"We don't know anything," I said, feeling deflated.

"That's not entirely true." Evan shook his head. "We know we're dealing with the Gemini twins. There are other celestial counterpoints."

"Who?" I asked.

"How many other astrological signs are there?"

"Are you saying there's a demon for every astrological sign?" That seemed daunting.

"There's a counterpoint," Evan clarified. "Not all demons are created equal. Heck, not all demons are evil. It's better to think of them as elementals than demons."

"You're going to have to explain that to me as if I'm two."

He laughed. "Let's get Scout and Gunner here," Evan said. "I only want to explain this once, and they'll eventually become involved."

"We're having pot roast for dinner," Winnie said. "That should get them here."

"We'll need Landon and Terry too," Evan said. "If you're right about Shauna and Eli being the Gemini twins, they're going to start wreaking havoc in area towns. We need to get ahead of it."

"What sort of havoc?" I asked.

"The sort we need to prevent." He turned to Bay. "Call Gunner and Scout. I have some books back at my house I want to get." He cast Easton a quick look, something unsaid passing between them. "I'll be gone an hour at most."

16

SIXTEEN

We had to wait for Evan to return, so I texted Hunter and told him to come to Hemlock Cove for dinner.

"What's going on?" He gave me a kiss, then eyed my place at the table suspiciously. "We usually sit on the other side of the table."

All I could do was point at Bay. Curious, he edged closer to her. He only made it four feet before he gagged and returned to me. "I get it," he said.

"Thanks," Bay drawled. "I can feel the love." She glared at Tillie for what had to be the tenth time since I'd arrived at the inn. "Don't you think you've punished me enough?"

"The Goddess will tell me when I've punished you enough," she replied.

Whatever else she was going to say died on her lips as Landon and Terry arrived.

"Hey, sweetie." Landon leaned in to kiss Bay, then reared back. "Oh, come on," he complained to Tillie. "Enough is enough."

His response only made Tillie smile wider. "Your wife needs to learn a lesson about messing with me. She's become lax when it comes to proper respect for her elders."

Landon shot his wife an apologetic look, then headed for the drink cart. "This family is too much sometimes."

"The spell is going," Winnie countered. She graced Terry with a fond smile when he moved over to greet her. "How was your day?"

"Sad because I didn't get to spend any time with you." Terry gave her a kiss, which had Bay smiling despite her pickle predicament.

"You can't say things like that when you've banned me from being mushy with Bay," Landon complained.

"I can do whatever I want," Terry countered. "Besides, when was the last time you held back on your mush with Bay?"

"I hold back." Landon shot Bay a saucy wink. "If I was as mushy as I truly wanted, you would've killed me two years ago."

"Don't give me ideas." Despite his bold words, Terry was sympathetic when turning his attention to Bay, who sat alone on her side of the table. "How was your day, sweetheart?"

"Don't ask," Bay replied. "The good news is that Stormy has a magical fight for me to participate in, so there's that to look forward to. I might get to smite some demons."

"Who says you get to smite them?" Tillie barked. "I'm the one who has the most history with smiting demons. I get to do it."

"I beg to differ," Scout said. She took one whiff of Bay and practically tripped over her own feet. "Oh, that is foul. What is the matter with you?" she complained to Tillie.

"I'm going to cry," Bay announced. "Just so you know, you're all hurting my feelings." She crossed her arms over her chest and sniffled.

"Shouldn't you be soothing your wife," Terry said pointedly to Landon.

"I would love to," Landon replied, "but I don't think puking on her will be all that soothing." He turned to Tillie. "What is it going to take for you to drop that spell?"

Tillie's eyes gleamed with victory. "Now that you mention it, I have a price." She rubbed her hands together. "I'm going to need a badge, and no questions asked."

Landon's eyebrows jumped. "Excuse me?"

"You heard me." Tillie suddenly found something fascinating about her fingernails. "No questions asked," she repeated.

"We can't give you a badge." Terry looked appalled.

"Then get used to the pickle smell." Tillie sent Bay a winning smile. "Maybe you'll become accustomed to it."

"I can't deal with this." Scout stomped over to Bay and planted her hand on her shoulder. Then, to my surprise, she motioned for me to join her.

"What do you want me to do?" I asked, afraid.

"Word on the street is that hellcats can burn out sickness," she replied. "If this isn't a sickness, I don't know what is."

"I cannot set Bay on fire."

"Yeah, let's not be hasty." Landon took a protective step toward his wife. "I could learn to love the pickle smell."

"Oh, stop being a baby." Scout shot Landon a look before turning back to Bay. "That goes for both of you." She was calm as she regarded me. "Bay needs your help. Think of all the help she's given you."

Guilt swarmed through me. "I..."

"I'm here to help you," she said. "You've done it before. Well, technically we've done it before. Remember when you were infected and we helped burn out the sickness together? That's all we're going to do."

"You leave that spell alone," Tillie snapped. "This has nothing to do with you."

Scout shot her a "not going to happen" look. "Listen, normally I enjoy watching you work, but this is just mean. We're all here to deal with Stormy's problem. We need Bay, and she can't smell like rotting pickles if we need to sneak up on the bad guys."

Tillie looked caught. "I'll just reverse the spell," she said. "For now."

"Oh, no." Scout clucked her tongue. "It's best Stormy and I handle this. She needs the practice."

"Plus it will be good to know we have a solution in our pocket if this ever happens again," Bay added.

"What if I screw up?" I was nervous. Bay was one of my best friends. I relied on her, and for more than just her witchy knowledge. And taking her away from her family was more than I could bear to think.

"You won't." Scout was firm. "Get over here."

"Touch her here." Scout put my hand on Bay's shoulder, then covered it with her hand. "I'm here to make sure you don't go overboard. I don't have the same fire magic you do, but I can make sure yours doesn't burn out of control."

That made me feel a little bit better.

Tillie made a disgruntled sound. "I said I would handle it."

Scout jabbed a finger on her free hand at Tillie. "You don't want us figuring out we have a way to negate your hexes, which will diminish your power."

"Hey!" Tillie shouted. "Nothing diminishes my power."

"Oh, stuff it." Scout shook her head. "As much as I enjoy you, enough is enough. You can't win every battle. That will only make you more insufferable."

"Maybe you're the insufferable one," Tillie fired back. "Have you ever considered that?"

"Every day of my life." Scout was calm as she regarded me. "You know what to do. Follow your instincts."

Uncertainty clawed through my chest like a face hugger from *Alien*, but I was determined to prove that I could keep up with the rest of them. I extended my magic and began to explore.

Finding the hex inside of Bay wasn't all that difficult. Once I had it isolated, however, I faltered before pulling the trigger.

"Do it," Bay instructed, her eyes clear. "I want to be able to hug my husband."

"So very much," Landon moaned. "Give me back my wife."

"You can't do it," Tillie countered. "You're just posturing." She didn't sound all that sure.

When the hex started burning, I thought I'd made a mistake. It started slow, but the magic picked up its pace, doubling in speed every second. When the hex tried to run from the magic, it was already too late. Everything sour inside of Bay burned fast and hot, and then fell away.

The room was silent. Bay slowly lifted her arm to sniff herself. "I think it worked."

Landon swooped in and rubbed his nose over her head and neck. "Yes!" He pumped his fist. "I can touch my wife again. Praise the Goddess!"

Terry's sigh was that of a father, and he briefly closed his eyes. "Why does he always say the exact wrong thing?"

I laughed and took a step back, relief as well as pride coursing through me. Both of those emotions disappeared when I glanced at Tillie, who looked ready to murder me.

"Now you're on my list," she said darkly.

Evan picked that moment to return. He took in the room, Bay's lack of stench, and Tillie's fury. "What did I miss?" he asked.

"Nothing important," Winnie replied. "Everybody, get seated. We'll bring dinner—"

Now Gunner whooped and pumped his fist.

"Then we'll talk about Stormy's predicament," Winnie continued.

THE FOOD WAS AMAZING, AS USUAL. Winnie and her sisters Twila and Marnie never disappointed. I'd yet to have a single meal at The Overlook that couldn't be termed divine.

"So what did you find?" Bay asked.

We'd filled in Hunter, Gunner, and Scout during dinner, so everybody was ready to hear what would come next.

"I pulled some files from when I was studying to join Spells

Angels," Evan said. "I vaguely remembered a story about the Third Great Awakening. Does everybody know what that is?"

I was already shaking my head when Twila interjected herself into the conversation. "I know." She raised her hand as if waiting for Evan to call on her.

Evan obliged, his lips twitching as he nodded to her. "Twila."

"The Third Great Awakening was a Protestant religious push following the Civil War," she said, as if reciting from a Wikipedia page. "The effort revolved around pushing salvation by institutions. The stronger the church, the stronger the individual who belonged to that church was in their faith."

Everybody sat around the table slack-jawed.

"How do you know that?" Marnie finally demanded.

Twila shrugged. "I know things."

Evan applauded, which made Twila beam with pride. "You're exactly right. During this time, the country was overcome with religious fervor. The First Great Awakening was between the 1730s and 1750s. The second was not long before the Civil War. The third is the one we're interested in."

"I've yet to find anything in this conversation to be interested in," Gunner said.

Evan shot him a quelling look. He was seated next to Easton, the two men shoulder to shoulder and casting each other the occasional smile. "This is important, Gunner."

"If you say so." He didn't look convinced.

"Eat your pot roast, Gunner," Scout ordered.

He shrugged and went back to his dinner.

"The Third Great Awakening was built around one specific premise, that the second coming of Jesus would occur only after the Earth had been completely remade," he explained. "Anybody care to guess why they thought it was happening soon around that time?"

It didn't take much of a stretch to figure that part out. "Because the Civil War changed the entire landscape of the country," I guessed.

Evan snapped his fingers and bobbed his head. "Very good, Stormy."

"What about the rest of the world?" Easton challenged.

"No one here cared about the rest of the world," Evan replied. "That's kind of normal. To be fair, there were religious revivals happening in other countries at the same time. Britain, for example, was experiencing one. What's important about this time is that religions were flexing their power.

"Back in frontier times, churches were places for small gatherings and there was very little money involved, at least here," he continued. "In Europe, religious leaders figured out they could amass great wealth long before that happened in the United States."

"And money leads to corruption," I said.

"Yes." Evan smiled. "The efforts to convert took root in that time and the people pushing the conversation were more educated and wealthier than they had been in the past. Anybody know what one of the biggest motivators was during this time?"

"I'm guessing it wasn't helping former slaves," Bay said dryly.

Evan snorted. "It was prohibition."

I stilled. "Outlawing alcohol?"

"It was the Devil's drink after all," Evan said. "Prohibition happened for numerous reasons. One of the biggest was religion, and do you know who was pushing for prohibition?"

"Are you about to tell me it was the Gemini twins?"

"They were waist-deep in it," Evan confirmed. "I'm not sure what their overall plan was, but they were involved in alcohol being outlawed. Guess what they did after prohibition became law."

Hunter stiffened. "They got involved in bootlegging."

"Give our fine Shadow Hills detective a gold star," Evan said with a wide smile.

"But why?" I asked. "Why would they get alcohol outlawed and then turn around and bootleg?"

"Money," Landon replied.

"And chaos," Hunter added. "Everything we know about the

Gemini twins so far suggests that they're dual natured. They say one thing and do another. They believe one thing and then switch when they get what they want."

"That is the key," Evan agreed. He picked a chunk of carrot off his plate and popped it into his mouth. He could eat human food or drink blood depending on his mood. He often went through the motions of eating with us just for the social aspects.

"So, the information I remembered reading when I was first in the academy—"

"You were always such a dork," Scout complained. "You actually did the reading for our classes when the rest of us were out having a good time."

"Who graduated at the top of the class?" Evan fired back.

"That's not quite the flex you think it is," Scout grumbled.

Evan ignored her. "The story goes that the twins—two boys again—got involved in bootlegging. There were a lot of prominent figures in the bootlegging industry, and the twins moved between them. Sometimes they worked with Bugsy Siegel. Other times they worked with Al Capone. They were instrumental in forging a relationship between Siegel, his childhood friend Meyer Lansky, and two mob figures, Charlie Luciano and Frank Costello. That group pinged between other groups and a lot of people died."

"What was the point?" Landon asked. He was pressed against Bay, seemingly relieved to be able to be close to her again. "What did they want?"

"Nobody knows." Evan held out his hands. "They seem to enjoy creating as much chaos as possible. All I know is that they disappeared when Prohibition was repealed."

"The churches lost?" I asked.

He shook his head. "The economy won. The Great Depression caused a lot of hardship on families, and part of that was because of prohibition. Religion helped bring in prohibition, but economics ended it."

"What does that have to do with what's happening here?" Scout asked.

"Prohibition wasn't repealed just because the people wanted their economy back. They had a little help from another elemental."

"I'm afraid to ask," I muttered. "Does that mean we're going to try to find this elemental?"

Evan nodded without hesitation. "I found the ritual for calling her."

"Her?" I was both intrigued and afraid.

"Aquarius," Evan replied. "She, on more than one occasion, has had a hand in taking down the Gemini twins. I figured we could go to the bluff after dinner and call her."

He said it as if it was the most normal thing in the world.

I looked around to see what the others thought.

"I'm fine with it," Scout said. "Astrology is a bunch of crap, but why not."

Bay shrugged. "It can't hurt. Any information we can get can only help. I'm game."

17
SEVENTEEN

Rituals on the bluffs behind The Overlook sometimes dissolved into drunken dancing. Other times, horrible things happened. I was rooting for the former this time. I would prefer getting hammered and swiveling my hips to whatever might happen when we summoned Aquarius.

I was seemingly the only one nervous.

"Okay, the candles are done," Marnie announced after only a few minutes of setting up. She glanced at me. "Do the honors?"

When I realized she expected me to light all the candles with my magic, I was thrown. With all eyes on me, I didn't have a choice. I held my breath and waved my hand, the magic coursing through my fingertips. The candles flickered, and for a split-second I thought I'd failed. Then they all ignited at the same time.

"Nice." Bay grinned at me. Her mood was much better now that she no longer smelled like pickles that had been left out in the Atlanta heat for a three-month zombie apocalypse. "You're becoming surer of yourself."

I wished that were true. I was fearful whenever I used my magic. Well, except when I didn't have time to think about it and had no choice but to react or die. "Thanks," I said even though I wasn't feeling all that good about my level of commitment. "I'm trying to learn."

"You're doing a good job." She patted my shoulder, then practically skipped to her mother to see what she was doing with the potions they planned to use for the summoning.

"Are you okay?" Hunter asked, moving in at my side. His hand was on my back, and he rubbed it up and down. "You seem a little ... nervous."

"I am nervous." I kept my voice low. "We're calling an elemental that is supposedly just as powerful as the twins, and we've heard stories of the horrible things they've done throughout the centuries. The whole thing is weird."

"It's okay." Hunter pulled me to him for a hug. "Everything will be fine."

How could he know that? Before I had a chance to ask, my attention turned to Evan and Easton, a few feet away, their heads bent together.

"Still no sign of him?" Evan asked. "How is that possible? Shadow Hills is the size of a postage stamp. It's even smaller than Hawthorne Hollow and Hemlock Cove."

"I don't know where he's hiding out," Easton replied. "He's been AWOL for weeks. He's up to something."

"He's dating Monica," I volunteered, drawing their attention to me. "Why don't you stake out her house if you're looking for him?"

Easton's forehead creased. "I thought you saw them together just the one time."

"I heard Monica talking about him this morning. She said things are great between them."

Hunter pulled back far enough to look at me. "You didn't mention that."

"I got distracted by other things."

"She's not safe with Weston," Hunter argued. "We need to get her away from him."

His alarm caused my stomach to constrict, then I reminded myself I was worried for her too. He wasn't afraid because he wanted to be with her. He felt as guilty as I did about how their relationship had ended. He hadn't wanted to hurt her, but that's exactly what had happened. Things were made worse by the fact that he insisted he wasn't interested in me—even though he was—and then he immediately changed his mind and gave her the heave-ho. Everyone in town seemingly knew we were destined to get back together.

There was no reason to be jealous. Hunter was devoted to me, and it wasn't against the law to want Monica to be safe. We both wanted that.

"I agree that we have to do something about the Weston situation." I chose my words carefully. "I think this takes precedence right now."

"What if he's going to kill her?" A stubborn muscle worked in Hunter's strong jaw. "What if we don't have time to waste?"

"Then we probably should've done something the morning we saw them together," I replied. "Now we have to deal with monstrous elementals trying to kill people. We have the Gemini twins to deal with and we're calling Aquarius to help us. Priorities, right?"

Evan laughed. Easton frowned but nodded. Hunter, however, took a step back.

"Maybe we should worry about both," Hunter said. "Weston is only interested in her because he wants to get back at us. This is some plan he has to use her as a weapon against us. After what happened with her last boyfriend ... and me ... don't you think we should save her from herself this time?"

I did, but I didn't have the bandwidth to focus on that right now. "Hunter—"

Winnie clapped her hands to get everybody's attention before I could finish. That was a relief, because I had no idea what to say to him to make things better. "We're ready," she said. "Let's get in position. Bay, Scout, and Stormy should be at the front since they're the strongest."

Tillie made a strangled sound. "What in the spell did you just say?"

"Oh, no." Winnie shook her head. "We're not putting up with your attitude right now. Just do what you're told for a change."

Tillie's expression turned murderous. "I was wrong. You're the one on my list."

"Yes, I'm quaking in my Crocs," Winnie said.

I glanced down to find she was indeed wearing Crocs, bright purple with fake gems. Winnie never struck me as a Crocs person.

"I've got this," Tillie said, determination wafting off of her in waves. "Stop trying to infantilize me. I'm still the head witch here." She gave Bay and Scout haughty looks before grabbing two potions from her great-niece. "This is my show."

"Wait!" Bay seemed to realize what Tillie was going to do at the last second, but it was too late. Tillie threw the potions at the center of the clearing with enough force that they exploded, blowing everybody back as blue fire erupted. The inferno raced outward.

I did the only thing I could do and used my magic to keep it from chewing through us, pushing back with different fire that had the blue fire race down the hill before extinguishing. The bluff went suddenly quiet, and then a figure appeared in the waning flames.

She was about six feet tall and willowy. Her shimmering silver hair fell to her waist. She wore a flowing dress that hung off her shoulders, making her look far too thin for the yards of fabric. Her blue eyes searched our faces as we recovered before focusing on Tillie.

"You rang," she said. She looked amused.

Tillie needed Evan's help to get to her feet. He lifted her as if she weighed nothing and dusted off her back. She slapped at his hand and glared. "I'm not a toddler," she growled.

Evan nodded but didn't leave her side. He kept close, proving even when she annoyed everyone and did the wrong thing, he was still her protector.

"I am Tillie Winchester," the elderly witch announced.

"I am Aquarius," the elemental replied in a singsong voice.

"I'm well aware, since we called you," Tillie replied. "Thankfully, we had one of your talismans handy because Bay is an Aquarius." She pointed to her great-niece, who looked as if she wished she was anywhere but on the bluff dealing with an ancient temperamental elemental. "I'm sure you've heard of me." Tillie waited for the being's response.

"I haven't, but you look interesting enough." To my surprise, Aquarius broke into a smile. "You're a witch. You're all witches." Her gaze wandered over faces, then froze when landing on Easton and Evan. "Except you two." Her finger jutted out toward Gunner, but her gaze stayed on Easton and Evan. "And that one. He's a wolf."

"A wolf shifter," Gunner corrected. "That's better than a simple wolf."

Aquarius snorted. "I'll take that under consideration." She kept her attention on Easton and Evan. "I've crossed paths with gnome shifters before. Your people are treacherous."

Easton didn't deny the past. "I'm not here to be treacherous."

"Your loyalty is easily marked. You feel it for everyone here, but especially this one." She pointed at me. "And that one." She pointed at Tillie. "And of course this one." When she focused her attention singularly on Evan, she smiled. "I have never seen anything like you." She stepped out of the ring of fire and approached him.

Evan kept his eyes forward and didn't move even when she stepped directly in front of him. Little ripples of blue flame worked around her surface.

"You have a soul," she said.

"Some vampires have souls," Evan confirmed.

"You're not supposed to. You're not one of those vampires. You weren't born into this."

"No, I was made," Evan agreed.

"By whom?" Aquarius looked intrigued. "This one?" She pointed at Tillie. Then she answered her own question. "No, she's nowhere near powerful enough."

"Okay, *you're* the one on my list," Tillie sputtered. "That was uncalled for ... and completely untrue. I could've given him a soul if I'd had enough time. I could give out souls professionally."

Aquarius laughed again. "You remind me of my grandmother. She said ludicrous things too." She turned her back on Tillie and allowed her gaze to move to Scout. "You did this."

Scout had an expressive face. She was not good at playing a role, even if there was a stronger being in front of her. When I saw the war she was internally waging flash across her face, I was afraid. I had every right to be.

"I'm multi-talented," Scout agreed. "You would be amazed at what I can do ... and without little bits of blue fire shooting off me." She extended her finger. "You're like Vegas's version of a show demon."

Aquarius's smile didn't diminish. "I'm not a demon. I'm an elemental. One of twelve higher elementals, to be exact."

"Don't you mean thirteen?" I challenged, not realizing I was going to speak until the words were already out of my mouth.

"Thirteen what?" she asked.

"Elementals. Gemini is twins."

"Ah, the twins are back. I should've guessed." She shook her head. "What have they done this time?"

"We don't know," I replied. "They seem to be lost."

"Lost?"

"It's kind of convoluted," I hedged.

"No matter." She stepped forward and grabbed both sides of my head before I could evade her.

I made an "eep" sound, but that didn't stop her.

"Hey!" Hunter moved to push her away but Evan, lightning quick, stopped him.

"I don't think that's a good idea." Evan easily held back Hunter, who fought him hard. Hunter was strong, but he was still just a human. Evan had vampire strength on his side.

Nothing hurt when the elemental invaded my mind. I thought

for a brief moment I should try to keep her out. She was in control before I could do anything about it. After a few seconds of looking around, after accessing my memories of the Eaton kids, she released me and took a step back.

"Those aren't twins," she said.

I was flummoxed by her response. "I know."

"They're not twins and yet they're of Gemini," she mused, tapping her bottom lip. She turned away from me and paced in the other direction, not stopping until she was in front of Winnie and Terry. "Your wedding will be lovely," she said with a smile before turning back.

"I'm not sure what my responsibility is," she said. "Normally, we try to stay out of each other's business unless something truly bad happens. I've had to step in three times where Gemini is concerned. Pisces has stepped in three times. Virgo has tried to kick his butt more times than I can count. That always ends in a century-long blood feud."

I was still a little dazed from her invading my mind, but I asked the obvious question. "Why did you say 'he' when Gemini is twins?"

"Gemini is one elemental. He may have split himself into twins and told outrageous stories about his exploits, but he has the power of only one elemental." She lifted her index finger for emphasis. "His dual nature makes him think he's two. He likes unleashing both sides of his personality to fight one another. He's a putz."

I was caught between laughter and confusion. "Why would Shauna Eaton have been behind Eli Eaton?"

"He probably misjudged his entry." Aquarius didn't look all that concerned. "It has happened before. That's how World War II grew so big. Three of us misjudged our entries to stop that."

"Oh, well, too bad, I guess," I said dryly.

"Judge me all you want; I understand." Her chin was level as she looked into my eyes. "We're not here to balance the scales or win wars. Long ago, that was our purpose. Then we realized there was no balancing the scales. Humans always tip the scales back eventually. You don't need us."

"And yet Gemini is here," I argued.

"He gets bored and likes playing with his pets." She smiled, but it was flat. "You say he disappeared ten years ago and has now returned?"

I nodded even though I didn't like her dismissive attitude.

"He must've been trying to correct his approach." Aquarius sounded as if she was talking to herself more than me. "My guess is that he doesn't have his full powers. He lost ten years of his mission plan trying to adjust the trajectory."

"I don't know what any of that means," I said.

"I don't know what his goal is. For all I know, he might have to live out his life here and die before he's reborn into his previous form." She laughed as she thought about it. "That would serve him right."

I gaped at her. "What if he goes on a killing spree to abate his boredom?"

She lifted one shoulder. "Then stop him."

"You just want me to ... what?" I asked. "Am I supposed to kill them? They look like teenagers."

"Looks can be deceiving."

"Yes, but..."

Aquarius shook her head. "You may be my proxy. They shouldn't be difficult to kill. It sounds as if they don't have their full powers. Just lop off their heads or use your fire magic. You seem to have plenty of that."

I didn't like the sound of that one bit. "What if I don't want to be your proxy?"

"Then let Gemini do whatever he'll do and stop whining. You have control over this situation. All of you." She glanced around. "Three of you fall under my sign. The three most powerful ones. Interesting."

"Hey." Tillie blanched. "I'm a Gemini."

"Yes, and your personality reflects that," Aquarius concurred. "You can't do much to help. I'm sorry. It must be one of you." Her finger danced between Bay, Scout, and me. "All three of you can act as my proxy. This is your fight." Her eyes landed on me. "If you need something, call."

With that, she gathered up her dress and moved toward the trees. "While I'm here, I'll take a look around. It's been a long time since I've visited this plane. I'm curious about what's changed." She paused. "And what hasn't. Humans still have the capacity to be monstrous, right?"

"Doesn't everyone?" Scout challenged.

"Yes, but humans turn it into an art form." She smiled. "Don't get inside your head. Gemini is an elemental, but he's not unstoppable. He's been stopped many times. Looks like it's about to happen again." There was one dramatic pause, then she waved. "Toodles."

She disappeared in a flash of blue fire, just as she'd arrived. It was almost as if she'd never been there.

18
EIGHTEEN

Nobody knew how to respond to Aquarius's disinterest in our plight. Bay suggested we all take the night to think things through, then regroup the following day to figure out what should be done. I agreed because it seemed the only option.

Hunter left me to stew until after we'd let ourselves into the restaurant. He double-checked the main doors, then did the same once we were in the apartment. The sliding glass door in the kitchen was large. Anyone willing to climb the treacherous outside steps could easily throw a brick through it and gain entry.

"Do you want to talk?" he asked when I exited the bathroom after washing my face. I'd changed into a pair of sleep shorts and a tank top, and braided my hair so it wouldn't turn into a rat's nest overnight.

"I don't know what there is to talk about," I admitted as I rolled into bed. It was still early. "Do you want to talk?"

"We could talk about the fact that you're an Aquarius and that thing—whatever it was—said that made you her proxy," he said.

I bit back a laugh. Of course that's what would garner his attention. "Okay." I got comfortable on my side of the bed. "Let's talk about that."

He looked at me. I returned his gaze.

"I don't know what to say," he said finally.

"Neither do I," I admitted, rolling my neck. "It's just so weird. Did you ever think we would live in a world where the astrological signs were represented by elementals and they would be out to get us?"

He slipped his arm around my back and tugged me to him. "They're not all out to get us. Aquarius didn't seem so bad ... other than when she said you're her proxy."

"Yeah, that was weird."

It was too early to sleep—neither of us were in the mood—he pulled out his phone. "Let's look up Aquarians."

My brow wrinkled. "Why?"

"I'm curious. We learned a lot about Geminis. I find it interesting that you, Scout, and Bay are all Aquarians."

Now that he mentioned it, I found it interesting too. "What does it say?" Really, it was just a way for me to delay making hard decisions.

"It says Aquarius women are known for being free-spirited, unconventional, and independent," he started.

"Sounds like Scout."

"It sounds like you and Bay, too, to a lesser degree. Scout always takes things to the *n*th degree because she likes being the center of attention."

He was right.

"Aquarians are also intellectual, have a strong sense of social justice, and march to the beat of their own drum." He smiled down at me. "That's you. You're altruistic, open-minded, and have a strong friend network. That's true of all of you. You're also analytical and good at problem-solving."

"I don't feel all that good about problem-solving at present," I admitted.

"You're just in a bad mood because you're the proxy. Whatever that means." He frowned. It was obvious he was hung up on that part of our conversation with the elemental. "Do you want to hear your bad traits?"

"Probably not, but I guess I should."

"Aquarians are stubborn, may be neglectful of loved ones, are rebellious, and can be unpredictable." He hummed, telling me he agreed with what he read.

"You think I'm neglectful of my loved ones?" I tried to refrain from turning defensive. "I don't neglect you."

"You did when you moved away for ten years."

I scowled. "Well, thanks for reminding me of that."

A small smile quirked at the corners of his lips. "Ah, here's something interesting. Aquarians hide their emotions, are sarcastic, don't trust easily, and are often not open to seeking help."

I made a face. "I ask for help. That's how we ended up out at The Overlook tonight."

He kept reading. "Aquarians are impatient and often feel discouraged." His eyes drifted to me. "You always get down on yourself when it's not warranted."

"Geez," I muttered.

"Aquarians are also extreme, meaning there's no middle ground. You can be happy, but if things don't go your way you're immediately depressed."

"I'm growing bored of this game," I complained.

He ignored me. "Aquarians are most compatible with Sagittarius, Aries, and Gemini."

"So ... you," I teased. "You're a Gemini."

"We do fit. Do you know what signs Gunner and Landon are?"

"I believe Landon is a Sagittarius. I'm not sure about Gunner."

"I bet he's an Aries."

"Why do you say that?"

"It says here that Aries men are impulsive, playful, passionate, and bold. They can also be aggressive and attention seekers."

"That's Gunner in a nutshell," I agreed. "What's it say about the Gemini and Aquarius relationship?"

"Because you want to know how this fight might go?"

I shrugged. "And maybe a little bit about how our relationship will work," I teased.

He chuckled. "Good idea." He typed on his phone, then started reading. "We're both naturally curious and cherish personal space. We have positive energy when together."

"I already knew that."

"As for challenges, let's see." He pursed his lips. "Apparently, both of us can appear emotionally detached. We're fickle." His eyes moved to my face. "You don't feel fickle, do you?"

"Not even a little," I assured him.

"This is interesting," he continued. "It says that when we fight, we're both keen to avoid emotional arguments. That could lead to suppression of emotions."

"We don't suppress our emotions."

"I think we do at times, especially when neither of us is in the mood. I also think we both worry about a big emotional blowout."

"Like we're afraid to fight with one another?"

He shrugged. "I was afraid to fight with you when we first got back together."

Something inside of me constricted. "Why?"

"I thought you might move away again." He didn't meet my eyes. "I don't feel that way now," he added hastily. "Those first few months, though..."

"I don't ever want you to be afraid." I propped myself on an elbow and looked down at him. "Hunter, I missed you the whole time I was gone. I just had it in my head that if I wanted one thing, I couldn't have the other. Or maybe I just assumed when I was ready, you would be here."

I felt guilty. "What kind of person thinks like that?" I said it to myself.

"Stormy, don't." He shook his head and brushed his fingers over my cheek. "You weren't the only one thinking that. I was certain—even though I wouldn't have admitted it to anyone back then—that you were going to come back and we were going to get our happily ever after."

"I guess you were right." I made an attempt at a smile.

"We're going to get everything we ever wanted. You're still reticent—or should I say discouraged?—about the writing thing. That will come together. And before you blame yourself for leaving, I could've gone after you. I didn't because I was too stubborn."

I sighed. "I think things happened the way they had to," I said after a few seconds. "If you had chased me, I would've had all the power in the relationship. I had to come home to know that I belonged here. More importantly, I had to explore a bit to realize that I really did want to be here. The only reason I fought it for so long is because I didn't want to be labeled a failure."

"You're not a failure." He kissed my forehead and pulled me tight against him. "You're just getting started. You don't realize it yet, but I've seen our future, and it's going to be amazing."

This time my smile was legitimate. "I don't want to argue about writing again. Can we table that until after Gemini goes bye-bye?"

There was no hesitation when he answered. "Yes. After that, I think it's time for our first real fight."

"Oh, I can't wait."

"There's that Aquarian sarcasm."

I HOPED FOR A DREAMLESS NIGHT. Or, if I did dream, something tiki-themed wouldn't have been abysmal. Instead, the dreamscape I woke in was the same as the one from the previous night.

I was surrounded by trees. This time the giggling didn't unnerve me as it did before. I decided to be forthcoming when calling out to the Eatons.

"Yo, Gemini." I realized I sounded a bit like Rocky and adjusted my tone. "We should talk."

The whispering stopped and an uneasy silence settled over the woods. None of the noises that accompanied a real trip to the forest after dark were present. No crickets sang. No owls hooted. No animals scampered from branch to branch.

Shauna appeared in front of me. She looked a little older than she had, though still not an adult. "What did you call me?"

There was no point in backing down. "I called you Gemini."

She frowned but didn't respond.

"Are you surprised?" I pressed my advantage. "Did you think we wouldn't figure it out?"

"I'm curious about how you figured it out," she replied. Her voice was uneven, but there was an intense edge of annoyance riding right below the surface.

"A person I don't even like referred to you as the Eaton twins," I replied. "I pointed out you weren't twins. The circumstances of your birth were odd. It's pretty much impossible for one baby to come eight months after the birth of another."

"That was an error on entry." She didn't look happy. "It shouldn't have happened that way."

"It screwed up your plan," I guessed.

She shrugged. "There's always time to adjust."

"We need to come to an understanding." I had to be forceful, I told myself. "Whatever your plan is, it won't work. It's done."

"You're done," she fired back, reminding me of a petulant child.

"We're not playing this game according to your rules," I countered. "I now understand better."

"You don't understand anything." She turned her back, as if daring me to attack.

There was no point. "I met Aquarius tonight," I offered.

She jerked her head back. "She's here?"

I purposely avoided the question. Aquarius had given us some interesting information but had essentially told us we were on our own. "She had some intriguing observations regarding your presence here. Apparently to her, ten years is just a blip."

"Only lesser beings think ten years is a long time," she agreed haughtily.

"You might consider me a lesser being, but it's obvious you're not at your full strength. Where is Eli, by the way?"

Laughter bubbled up behind me. It was of the insane variety. I turned, but nothing but shadows awaited me.

"He's around," Shauna said with a grin.

"What's the plan?" I asked. "I know you like to insert yourself in times of religious strife."

"Human religions are so ... entertaining," she said, crossing her arms over her chest. "You're all so fragile with your beliefs. It's not difficult to manipulate people into doing what we want." She leaned forward. "Do you want to know why?"

I didn't answer. It wasn't necessary.

"Deep down, you want to commit atrocities," she continued. "Doing them in the name of God somehow makes you feel righteous. It also makes you that much more determined."

"What religious upheaval do you plan on causing this time?" I asked. "The world is becoming more secular."

"Which makes those who believe that much easier to manipulate," she replied blandly. "They know that non-believers outnumber believers now and they're desperate for something to hold onto. Those who are on the fence—maybe they believe, maybe they don't—can be swayed by those surrounding them."

"And the nonbelievers?" I prodded.

She shrugged. "The nonbelievers are impossible to manipulate ... unless you come at them from the point of view that atheism is a religion. Those who are militant about it can be swayed just as easily as the true believers."

"And that's enough for you?"

She was noncommittal. "You think we're here to push a specific agenda, but we're not. We don't care what happens, what the ultimate outcome is. We just like to play the game."

"But you're one elemental split into two beings," I said. "Doesn't that make you weaker? Especially since it seems Eli isn't all there."

Her smile disappeared. "If you believe us weak, you have a rude awakening coming." She took a menacing step toward me. "Look to the sky."

Even though I didn't want to follow her edict, I found myself looking up. The constellation Gemini burned brightly overhead.

She made a disgruntled noise. "Not this sky. Look to your own sky."

"What am I looking for?"

"If you can't figure it out, you're not the foe we thought." Her enigmatic smile was back. "We'll be seeing you soon."

The woods began swirling before I could stop her from leaving. I had more I wanted to talk to her about. Given the fact that I knew as much as I did, she probably wanted to take some time to readjust her own plan. I'd just thrown everything into turmoil.

When my eyes snapped open, Hunter was asleep in the bed beside me. The steady rise and fall of his chest told me he was down for the count.

Look to the sky.

Shauna's words echoed in my head, so I carefully climbed from beneath the covers and walked to the sliding glass doors in the kitchen. There, Gemini burned brightly in my sky, even though it shouldn't have been visible until May. Then it would fade into the sunset before the summer solstice. A second constellation burned brightly. It looked vaguely familiar, and yet I couldn't identify it.

I returned to the bedroom to grab my phone. I adjusted the night settings and snapped photos of both constellations. When I was certain that I had what I needed, I scanned the trees behind the restaurant.

There were no signs of movement, no shadows flitting to and fro. Despite that, I felt eyes on me. Was it both of them? Was it only Shauna? Now that I'd landed on Eli being defective, I couldn't shake the idea that I was right. That would mean she was doing all the heavy lifting. I checked the photos one more time to make sure they were clear, then returned to the bedroom and plugged my phone in to keep it charged. Hunter was in the same position, so I curled into his side, enjoying the way he murmured as he wrapped his arms around me.

I didn't think I would sleep, but slipped into oblivion within a few minutes.

19
NINETEEN

I showed Hunter my photos as soon as he woke up. He was annoyed I didn't take him with me to the sliding glass doors, but I pretended the irritation was lost on me. We showered, got ready for the day, then headed downstairs. Grandpa was already at the grill.

"Breakfast?" he asked without looking up.

I glanced at the clock on the wall and realized I was fifteen minutes early for my shift. In Grandpa's mind, that meant I was on time. "That would be great," I said as I headed around to the refrigerator to grab hash browns and eggs.

Hunter wasn't expected to work, but he always pitched in. The coffee filters had become his job, so he started opening bags and pouring the contents into filters.

"You two are quiet," Grandpa announced when no one had spoken for several minutes. "What's wrong?"

"With us?" I asked, confused.

He nodded. "You're not fighting, are you? I need you to move out on time so I can move into the upstairs apartment. I don't think the three of us would do well as roommates."

I arched an eyebrow as I tried to conjure that image.

"There would be no funny stuff," Grandpa continued pointedly. "If we're all living together, you would have to be celibate."

"That seems like something we don't want to deal with," Hunter said, choosing his words carefully. He gave me a serious look. "I'm thinking we could move into the house early if we have to, take over a guest room, and then just deal with the dust and upheaval for a few months."

I had to bite the inside of my cheek to keep from laughing. The fact that Hunter was willing to sleep on a mattress on the floor rather than share an apartment with my grandfather was telling.

"I don't know that it'll come to that," Grandpa hedged. "I've explained my misgivings about Lisa moving in with us to your grandmother. She doesn't appear to be on my side, though."

"What did she say?" My grandmother was sometimes difficult to read. She was stronger than my grandfather when it came to certain things. Abandoning her granddaughter—and, more importantly, her great-grandchildren—simply wasn't in her wheelhouse.

"She said that Lisa married a bad man, and we couldn't allow her to stay with him." Grandpa made a face. "I pointed out that Linc married a bad woman, but your grandmother didn't want to hear it."

"She doesn't believe bad stuff about us. Even when we're in the wrong, she pretends that's not the case. She can't help herself. Once, Alice got into a fight with a girl in school and tried to run her over with a car. Grandma swears to this day that Alice was having a seizure."

Grandpa scowled. "I remember. She tried to use your grandmother's car to do it."

I bobbed my head. "Luckily, that girl—I think it was Sherry Dalton—managed to jump into a bush to save herself."

"Your cousin is a menace. I hear she's dating someone new. He actually has a job, so you know she'll dump him before the month is out and show back up with some loser she claims is the love of her life five minutes later."

"She does have a pattern," I agreed.

"What about you two?" Grandpa's eyes bounced between us. "You're settled? You're not going to move out, then break up and ruin my bachelor pad life and try to move back in?"

"Your bachelor pad life?" I was amused. "That's not the plan. We don't really fight."

"No, you're all goo-goo-eyed at one another. The honeymoon period only lasts so long. Eventually, you'll fight."

"We're not fighting now."

"We found out last night that we don't like to fight," Hunter supplied.

"You found out?" Grandpa was confused. "How?"

"We compared our astrology symbols."

Grandpa froze.

Hunter realized he'd made a mistake. "Or we found out in a way that doesn't make you think less of me."

Grandpa's eye roll was pronounced. "You compared astrology symbols? Geez." He sent me a wounded look. "You're supposed to be the smart one."

All I could do was shrug. "I don't base my decisions on my astrological sign," I replied. "But some of it is interesting. Given what we're dealing with now—"

"I don't want to hear any of the weird stuff," Grandpa barked.

I held up my hands in supplication. "Let's just say astrology is part of our current game plan and leave it at that."

Grandpa's eyes narrowed. "I don't like any of this weird stuff that you get yourselves involved in. Why can't you just be normal?"

"I believe you have your mother to thank for that," I reminded him. It was his mother—my great-grandmother—who passed the hellcat gene on to me.

"Don't remind me." Grandpa looked pained. "She's threatening to come up again in a few weeks."

My great-grandmother lived in Florida and visited once a year.

When she came, she took over my grandparents' house and drove my grandmother insane.

"How is that going to work if Lisa and her kids are living there?" I asked.

Grandpa momentarily perked up. "I didn't consider that. Hmm." He swung his hips a little as he dumped hash browns on the grill. "That might make things easier."

"How?" Hunter asked. "Will Lisa not be able to move in because your mother is coming, or will your mother not be able to visit because Lisa will be there?"

"I'm not sure which is more preferable," Grandpa admitted. "I'll have to give it some serious thought."

I should've kept my mouth shut. "I would love to see Great-Grandmother. A lot has happened since she was here last. She would be a good person to talk to."

Grandpa glared at me. "Don't put something like that out into the world. It's better for all of us if she doesn't visit."

"She's not going to live forever. She's your mother. Shouldn't you want to see your mother as often as possible before it's too late?"

"You only visit your mother once a week because she forced your hand," Grandpa reminded me. "You're one to talk since you live in the same town."

I frowned. "My mother is irritating. Yours is interesting."

"Not from my point of view." He shook his head. "Either way, I have some thinking to do. I have to figure out how this is going to work. I'm still trying to talk your grandmother out of letting Lisa move in with us."

"I saw them at your house the other night. Lisa and Linc. They seemed tense."

"As far as I know, he's sleeping on the couch," Grandpa said. "That's probably for the best, because your cousin's way of 'fixing' her marriage involves getting pregnant with another kid she can't take care of each and every time."

"Linc knows what she's doing," I replied. "He admitted as much.

Hopefully this time he won't allow himself to get dragged into an even bigger mess."

"Listen, that guy isn't the type to stick around." Grandpa was no nonsense. "It's only a matter of time until he packs up in the middle of the night and takes off. Your cousin won't see a dime of child support after that. If you ask me, Linc is plotting his escape right now."

"You need to put your foot down," I said. "Lisa has a bunch of kids and still acts like a kid herself. She needs to take responsibility and be the adult."

Grandpa rolled his eyes.

"She has to at some point," I insisted

"Certain people never get it together. Lisa is one of those people. So is Alice. I blame your grandmother's genes."

"Does that mean you're taking responsibility for me being like I am?"

"I'll take responsibility for you getting your life together, learning from your mistakes, and picking a good man." He jerked his thumb at Hunter. "I will not take responsibility for the other stuff." He shuddered at the thought. "That stuff is better ignored."

Oh, if only. "Well, I'm sure everything will work out. Be calm and rational when you talk about your concerns with Grandma regarding Lisa moving in. She's rational. She might listen."

"Yes, because that's how my life works."

HUNTER PROMISED TO KEEP ME UPDATED—finding the Eaton siblings was still at the top of his to-do list—and I did the same. Work kept my mind from wandering too much. It was a busy morning. When Annie arrived to help, I was relieved.

I kept my eyes open for Monica. I still didn't know how I was going to talk to her about Weston without rocking the boat, but she and Phoebe didn't come in at their normal time.

I floated into the last two hours of my shift, already making plans for what I was going to do after, when I heard raised voices behind the dishwasher station.

Confused, I started a new pot of coffee and made my way in that direction. I froze when I saw who my grandfather was arguing with.

"This is an employee door," he barked, pointing to the heavy door that led outside. On the other side, Tillie, Evan, and Easton stared back at him. "Only employees can use it."

Tillie, who didn't have what could be considered a congenial rapport with my grandfather under the best of circumstances, merely stared back at him. "There's no sign," she drawled.

"What do you mean there's no sign?"

"If a door is for employees only, there should be a sign," Tillie insisted. "I've seen them at hardware stores. You should get one."

Grandpa's cheeks flushed. He would never admit that she had a point. "It's a given that the back door of any business establishment —whether it's a store or restaurant or bank—is for employees only."

Tillie remained calm, but probably only because she knew that would irritate my grandfather further. "Who says that's a given?" She glanced at Evan and Easton in turn. "Do you think that's a given?"

"Oh, don't drag us into this," Evan complained. "This is your battle."

Tillie shot him a narrow-eyed "we'll talk about this later" glare before turning back to Grandpa. She was the picture of innocence, which meant she was about to do something dastardly. "I don't think it's a given," she said.

"Of course it is." Grandpa gestured toward the door. "Do you see anyone else using this door?"

"I saw your dishwasher use it."

"He's an employee."

Tillie glanced at the messy dishwashing station. "Not a very good one."

"That's neither here nor there." Grandpa was fired up. "You're not an employee. You can't use this door."

"You need a sign to enforce that." Tillie was insistent. "It's a law or something."

"Like you follow the law." Grandpa threw up his hands, his eyes drifting to me. "I'm guessing they're here for you." His tone was accusatory.

I offered a conciliatory smile. "I'll handle it."

"You'd better." He started to stomp away, then stopped and swiveled back. "You're squirrelly." He pointed at Tillie for emphasis. "If they had awards for being squirrelly, you'd take the gold medal."

Tillie's smile broadened. "I do like to win."

"That wasn't a compliment." Grandpa muttered a series of complaints under his breath as he stalked away.

I watched him go, conflicted, then focused on the incoming trio. "I'm guessing you're here for a specific reason."

"We're hunting for the twins," Tillie replied. "I've never fought an elemental before and I love new adventures. I've decided their heads will look great on my monster head trophy wall."

I frowned. "You have a monster head wall?"

"In here." Tillie tapped her temple for emphasis. "I'm going to take out those twins so you don't have to worry about it."

"Oh, well..." I glanced at Evan, an unsaid question passing from me to him.

"It's better to go with her when she heads out on a mission," he explained. "She'll go by herself regardless, and it's often easier to clean up the mess as we go."

"Right." I rolled my neck, then remembered the photos from the night before. "Actually, I'm glad you're here." I reached into my apron and retrieved my phone. "I had a dream last night."

I filled them in quickly. Grandpa would have a meltdown if I dawdled. When I got to the part about the second constellation appearing in the sky, Easton and Evan were intrigued. Tillie? Not so much.

"Why do we care about constellations?" she complained. "We

know who the enemy is. The enemy needs to be slayed. It's as simple as that."

I pretended I hadn't heard her and showed the photos to Evan and Easton.

The vampire looked intrigued. "I've never seen that," he said.

Easton went ashen.

"What is it?" I kept my eyes on his face.

"It's not a constellation," Easton replied in a raspy voice.

I looked at the photo again. There were four points, some closer than others. "It looks like a constellation."

"Well, it's not. Or, I guess it kind of is, except it uses stars from other constellations to form a new one. It's more symbolic than anything else."

I waited for him to finish.

"That's our sign." Easton was grim.

"Whose sign?" I was confused.

"My people. My immediate people." He looked straight into my eyes. "Each of us has a direction that our magic is associated with. My magic comes from the east."

I looked at the image again, realizing that the star that was dragged farthest from the others was the western star. "Then this is Weston's sign," I realized.

He nodded.

"What does that mean?" Evan asked. His body had gone rigid.

"Weston is feeling powerful," Easton replied. "I was worried about this. I haven't been able to find him for weeks. Now Gemini shows up?" He shook his head. "It's not good."

"Are they working together?" I asked.

"I don't know." Easton looked torn. "Weston doesn't play well with others. My understanding is the Gemini twins don't either. It's possible they're working toward the same goal."

Only one possible goal entered my busy brain.

"We're on it," Evan said, correctly reading my mind. Weston was here for me. Shauna had clearly marked me as an enemy. If they were working together, I was the likely target.

I nodded. "Okay, as soon as I'm done with my shift I'll be in touch. We can meet up."

Evan leaned in. "Don't worry about this. We have a bigger army. We won't let them ruin anything."

That was nice of him to say, but it was a promise he couldn't keep. Weston was a wild card. He was familiar with how we operated. If he joined with the Eatons, all bets were off.

20

TWENTY

I was hoping to escape early, but the mid-morning rush continued far later than it normally did. When Phoebe showed up—alone—I had no choice but to wait on her.

"No Monica today?" I looked out at the parking lot, hopeful to see the other woman. She served as a buffer between Phoebe's vitriol and me some days. My heart sank as Phoebe shook her head.

"Not today," she replied. She didn't look happy about it either. "She's with her boyfriend."

I froze, my arm halfway to a menu. Phoebe didn't need one, but it was a habit. "Have you met him?"

"West? He's really cool ... and hot." Phoebe let loose a sigh. "I wish Monica hadn't seen him first."

"West?" It made sense that Weston had shortened his name for whatever game he was playing.

"Isn't that a cool name?" Phoebe was apparently in the mood to be chatty. On a normal day I would've been irritated. I decided to take advantage of her inability to be alone with her thoughts today.

"Very cool." I led her to her regular table. "What do you know about him? What does he do for a living?"

"He's a writer." Phoebe sent me a cagey look. "I guess you have that in common. Is that why you're asking?"

"I don't know anything about him," I lied. I had to stop myself from gritting my teeth after hearing that he'd chosen that profession, clearly a dig at me. "I met him once. Monica brought him here for breakfast a few weeks ago."

"I think she's doing that to make Hunter jealous." Phoebe had no qualms about gossiping about her supposed best friend. "That's why we come here so often. She's hoping to see Hunter."

She'd given me an opening, but I wasn't certain I wanted to walk through it. In truth, I believed Phoebe was the one hoping to see Hunter. There were days he stopped in to have coffee, or a late breakfast if he didn't get a chance to eat with Grandpa and me first thing in the morning, before heading out.

"Do you think Monica still has feelings for Hunter?" I decided it was best to play the game according to Phoebe's rules. That was the only way I was going to get any tangible information.

"Of course she does. It's obvious." Phoebe rolled her eyes as she sat. "I told her that he was going to run back to you as soon as I heard you were coming back. She didn't believe me."

The smile Phoebe unleashed was Machiavellian. She was about to mess with me on top of badmouthing her best friend. I would put up with it as long as she delivered other information as well.

"You've always been the safe choice for Hunter," Phoebe explained. She kept her voice light, as if she was doing me a favor instead of insulting me. "You're not a dynamic individual. The most interesting thing you ever did was leave town, but that didn't last because you weren't very good at professional writing."

"Right," I said. I wanted to choke her with a pancake.

"It was inevitable that you'd return," she continued. "It was only a matter of time. I think Hunter knew that deep down too. He never really invested in a relationship with anyone else. He only chose people he knew he could break up with after a few months. If he'd ever allowed himself to be with someone who could've upended his world, things might have been different, but he was too guarded."

"Like you?" I guessed.

She shrugged. "Hunter would've had a more adventurous life with me—there's no doubt about that—but I've come to realize that he doesn't want that. That's why he spent years pining for you. You're not adventurous."

If she only knew I was hunting her best friend's boyfriend because he was an undercover gnome shifter with nefarious intentions who was apparently working with a demonic elemental that had split himself into two different people and one was crazier than a Kardashian who had to go a week without lip gloss.

"I'm definitely not adventurous," I agreed evenly. "I'm the exact opposite."

"Right?" Phoebe's eyes flashed with victory. "Hunter might've been open to the idea of adventure at one time, but he convinced himself that waiting for you to return was better. I have no idea why." She turned to me, expectant. "Do you?"

"Um..."

"Are you gifted in bed or something?" She looked legitimately curious. "Some people are just naturally good at it. I am. You don't seem the type, but sometimes people surprise you."

"Sometimes," I agreed. "As for my prowess in bed, you'd have to ask Hunter."

"Oh, I have." She rolled her eyes. "He said I was disrespectful and to stop asking."

"Well..." I needed to direct the conversation back to Weston. "I'll ask Hunter and get back to you."

"Awesome." She took the menu and glanced at it. "Is your grandfather cooking?"

"Yes."

"If I order poached eggs, he'll probably come out and dump them on me, right?"

"Probably."

"I guess I'll have two eggs over-medium, hash browns, and whole wheat toast."

"I'll put your order in and be right back with your coffee." I formulated a plan while I did just that, and when I returned, I was prepared. "If Monica still has feelings for Hunter, how do you think that West plays into things? How did they meet?"

"I'm not sure." Phoebe added creamer to her coffee. "That's a very good question. She didn't really say anything specific. I think they ran into each other downtown, maybe at the coffee shop. She mentioned getting to know him over coffee."

That sounded plausible. Weston was the type to plant himself downtown until he found who he was looking for. "And he's an author? What does he write?"

"He's a travel author. He writes those books for big cities. Like, if you were going to visit New Orleans you'd pick up his book and be able to find the best restaurants and hotels."

"Ah, so nonfiction." That was laughable. It sounded as if Weston was spinning one hell of a yarn for Monica.

Phoebe sent me a derisive look. "I think he writes important books."

"Yes, because everybody knows the names of the people who write the travel books," I said. "How long have he and Monica been dating?"

"About a month. They kept it quiet at first. She slipped him into conversation without mentioning his name about three weeks before I met him, so it's been about six weeks now."

I stilled. Six weeks? I was thinking a month at most. Monica had mentioned dating someone to me about a week before I saw her with Weston. If it had been going on for six weeks, she was even more entrenched than I imagined. "So are things getting serious?"

"I have no idea. She seems pretty serious. I still think she'd take Hunter back if he looked her way."

If she thought that was a dig, or that I was going to seethe with jealousy, she was wrong. "I don't think Hunter will do that."

"Probably not." Phoebe seemed to consider it for several seconds, then sighed. "I just wish she didn't make her whole life about who she's dating. Whenever she gets serious, she forgets all about me."

"You could try finding someone to date," I pointed out.

"In this town?" Phoebe rolled her eyes. "I can count on one finger the people I would lower myself to date here."

And his name was Hunter. "What about Hemlock Cove?"

"There's a really hot FBI agent there. I met him last month in the diner. Turns out he's married." She lowered her voice. "And happily so. He didn't even look at me."

She was talking about Landon. "Bummer. He's not the only guy in town."

"That's why I was asking about the guy you've been hanging around with," she said. "I thought if you weren't dating him maybe I could. Or, if you were, I could help Hunter get over his heartbreak. It's just my luck he turned out to be gay."

"Yes, how sad for you," I agreed.

"That guy who was living with you turned out to be gay, too," she said. "I have the worst luck."

"Yes, it's all about you," I agreed. "Poor Phoebe."

She held out her hands in a "what are you going to do" motion. "Maybe I'll start looking in Hawthorne Hollow."

I pictured Gunner if she started hitting on him. Then I imagined Scout's face when Phoebe tried to square off with her. "Yeah, that might be fun."

AFTER WORK, I RAN UPSTAIRS TO SHOWER and change. Then I went to Sebastian's funeral home. I'd texted Easton to find out where he stood with his hunting party, but he didn't reply.

Sebastian was on the little settee in the middle of the funeral home, flipping through a gossip rag.

"Do you know who I feel sorry for?" he asked when he looked up and saw me. "Amanda Bynes. That girl has been through the wringer."

I stared at him a beat, uncertain. "Um … okay." I did feel bad for Amanda Bynes, but I wasn't in the mood to talk about her. "Are Easton and Evan here?"

Sebastian made a face, then covered quickly. "I haven't seen them."

"Isn't Easton living with you?"

"He left this morning. I didn't ask where he was going." The response was delivered with a bit of attitude, indicating that despite his best efforts—and what he knew to be true in his heart—he was still bitter about Easton wanting to be with Evan.

"If this is a tough subject I can come back later," I offered.

"Why would it be a tough subject?"

"I know you had feelings for Easton." Lying wasn't going to get either of us anywhere.

"'Feelings' could mean anything," he responded. His expression indicated I'd picked the wrong topic on which to fixate. "Was I attracted to Easton? Yes. I don't know that we got to actual feelings."

I debated what to say, then sighed. "I'm sorry. I know you're kind of heartsick, but I really do need to find Easton and Evan."

"Have you tried texting them?"

"Yes. They're off with Tillie on an elemental hunt."

Sebastian frowned. "I have no idea what that even means."

I gave him the rundown, feeling mildly guilty about the fact that he was so out of the loop. He frowned, and when I finished, he shot me an accusatory look.

"I can't believe you cut me out of this," he whined.

"I didn't cut you out. I just, well, it's been a busy few days."

"I heard the gossip. I didn't realize it was so dire." He slowly got to his feet. "What does all of it mean?"

I didn't have a good answer for him. "Nothing good," I replied. "From what I've been able to gather, Eli came through wrong. Shauna is calling the shots. He seems like a loon."

"Sounds creepy."

"Oh, it's creepy," I readily agreed. "I'm not sure if that makes him more dangerous than her, but it's not good either way."

"What are Easton and the others doing?"

"Hunting for elementals. Tillie said she wants to put their heads on her wall."

Sebastian's nose wrinkled. "Please tell me she doesn't have a wall full of heads." He didn't wait for me to answer. "What if they stare at her when she's sleeping?"

"She doesn't have a wall of heads. She wants to be the one to take them down. When we talked to Aquarius last night, she kind of dismissed Tillie as a sideshow."

"That wouldn't sit well with Tillie. She's not fun when she's not shown what she considers the proper respect."

I let loose a sigh. "I wanted to find them so I could lead them on a Weston hunt—the more I hear about his relationship with Monica, the more worried I get—but they're not responding."

"I could try texting Easton," Sebastian offered. "I doubt he'll respond if he's not responding to you."

"They're probably in the thick of things."

"How about a locator spell to find them?" Sebastian looked hopeful. He liked going on adventures with me. There was a time, after he was almost killed, that he pulled back. He'd gotten over it, though, and was happy to be back in the thick of things.

"I'm going to leave them alone," I replied. "If they need me, they'll find me. We should go on our own Weston hunt."

Sebastian perked up. "That might be fun. Where do we start?"

"Right now, I only know one place to check: Monica's house."

"Ah." Sebastian nodded in understanding. "If you go to her house, she'll assume you're up to something."

"How can I say that I'm there to see Weston and not get the stink eye? She already doesn't trust me. Her last boyfriend turned out to be a paranormal monster, and she knows at least a little of the truth."

"Let's play it by ear," Sebastian suggested. "We'll go, and if she answers the door, we'll make up an excuse. We can at least go and spy on her. If we see him, we'll approach him. If we don't, we'll decide if we want to knock."

"Maybe we'll luck out and Monica won't be there."

"Didn't Phoebe say she was hanging with her new boyfriend?"

I scowled. "Phoebe says a lot of things, and most of them turn out to be stupid."

"Ah, I see she needled you. She's good at that."

"She's a monster," I agreed. "I had to pretend I was actually interested in what she was saying."

"Oh, you poor thing." Sebastian pulled me in for a hug. "That had to be horrible. Tell Uncle Sebastian all about it. What horrible things did she say?"

I grinned. He always knew how to lighten my mood. Then I turned serious. "I need to talk to Weston. It's been weeks, and now it appears he's working with a very serious enemy."

"Then let's go to Monica's house. We'll decide what we want to do when we get there."

21

TWENTY-ONE

Monica lived on a nondescript street in one of the nondescript neighborhoods just off Main Street. I'd been by her house before—never for a social visit—but it felt weird to park on a side street and spy.

"Someone is in the house," Sebastian said. He had his phone out and was zooming in on windows from our spot beneath a maple tree, shrouded in shadows. "Monica's car isn't in the driveway."

"Maybe it's in the garage," I suggested. I was feeling antsy and yet paralyzed by fear at the same time.

Sebastian shook his head. "It's a detached garage. Nobody parks in those unless we're going to get a foot of snow, and we're well past that."

He was right. I never understood the appeal of detached garages. "We should just go up there and knock."

"Are we going to use the one author talking to another author angle?"

I shrugged. "Seems as good as anything. Monica is already suspicious of me. If she gets more suspicious..."

"She'll probably think you're trying to steal another man from her."

I gave him a dirty look. "Can you not phrase it that way? I didn't steal Hunter."

Sebastian cocked a dubious eyebrow.

"I didn't," I insisted. "We were destined to be together." It made me feel better to look at it that way.

"Listen, I don't doubt for a second that you and Hunter were destined to be together." Sebastian was matter of fact. "However, you did steal her man. Hunter should've admitted it was over the second he learned you were coming back. He didn't, so now people will always look at you a certain way."

"I should just sew a scarlet A to my shirt and be done with it," I grumbled.

"Ooh." Sebastian bobbed his head. "That would be a bold move. I love it."

I glared at him. "You're on my last nerve."

He motioned toward the house. "Are we doing this or not?"

"We're doing it." I was resigned as I killed the engine and exited my car. The worst that could happen was that Monica would distrust me even more than she already did. That was hardly a loss.

My shoulders slumped as I marched up the sidewalk to the front porch. I hesitated a split second before knocking. There was a rustle of curtains at the front window.

"Just let us in, Weston," I ordered. "You don't want us coming back with the cavalry."

I could hear the gears in his mind working on the other side of the door.

"The faster we do this, the faster we'll be out of your hair." I was considering dragging him out by his ear and physically removing him from Monica's life.

The door opened slowly, and Weston peered at us through the foot-wide gap. "We're not welcoming solicitors today," he said primly.

I glared at him. "Why do you have to be ... you?" I asked. "Can't you ever not be a sneaky sneak?"

That earned a grin, and he opened the door wider. "I don't have time for you. My girlfriend will be back in about an hour. She won't be happy if she finds me entertaining another woman—especially you—in her house. Leave." Despite his words, he didn't move to shut the door in my face. He knew better.

"We need to have a talk," I insisted. "It's important."

"I'm not talking to you about my relationship. I don't want to jinx it."

"Oh, we're going to talk about your relationship." I took us both by surprise when I gave him a mighty shove. "That's not my biggest concern right now, though." I forced my way into the house, Sebastian trailing closely behind, and waited until the door had fallen shut behind us. "You're in big trouble."

"Geez." Weston made an exaggerated face before throwing himself on the couch. He was in jeans and a white shirt, his feet bare, and his hair freshly washed. "Why must you be so dramatic? Is it a girl thing? I've noticed the females of your species tend to overreact."

"Misogyny, party of one, your table is waiting," Sebastian drawled.

"You're dramatic too," Weston added. "You're kind of like a girl."

I reacted without thinking and mimicked a spell I'd seen Scout use. It resulted in a magical slap across Weston's cheek. He reared back, cupping his cheek and looking shocked.

"That was interesting." He narrowed his eyes and lowered his hand. "Has someone been practicing?"

"Yes, and I'm in the mood to show you exactly what I can do." My tone was menacing.

"What do you want?" he asked.

"What are you doing with Monica?"

"I like her. She has ... personality."

I crossed my arms over my chest and glared at him.

"She's nice," he insisted. "And she hates you. We have that in common."

"She has a reason to hate me," I said. "You're following some edict from people who have never met me and want all hellcats wiped out simply because it benefits your place in the magical world."

"Actually, that's no longer the mission." Weston shook his head. "Your line is not the only hellcat line being reawakened."

I filed that away.

"We can't stop what's happening, so we've decided to embrace a different tack." His smile was a little too cat that ate the canary for my liking. "We've decided the smartest move is to join forces with you."

I snorted. "No thanks."

"Oh, come on," he protested. "You know you want to get with the winning team."

He was so smug I couldn't stand it. "What makes you think that you'll win?"

"I have the more powerful allies."

"Not so far." I shook my head. "I'll bet on the Winchesters, Evan, and Scout over you any day of the week."

His facade slipped. "The pixie witch is troublesome," he confirmed. "In all the futures we looked at before coming up with our plan, she wasn't present in any of them. Why is that?"

"I have no idea. Her own prophecy is leading her. Her destiny was always set in stone."

"Or maybe you weren't supposed to meet her and something nobody foresaw took place."

"Like what?"

"If I knew that I'd act on it." He looked bored. "I've thought long and hard, and my best guess is that it's the vampire. He and Easton bonded when I don't think they were supposed to." He cast a derisive look at Sebastian. "It would've been best if you'd kept Easton with you."

"Well, thanks for your input." Annoyance ran over Sebastian's features. "I don't know what I would've done without your opinion on the subject."

"Things aren't going as planned," Weston acknowledged. "That has forced ... adjustments ... on our part."

"Is Monica one of those adjustments?" I demanded.

"Monica is a surprise." Weston's smile grew. "I needed a place to hunker down, somewhere you wouldn't come looking for me. I had to recuperate if you remember."

He'd almost died, but we'd managed to save him. "You decided to pay us back by taking advantage of Monica? Hasn't she been through enough?"

He shrugged. "I was in a pickle. I thought it would be a short stay. She's a gracious hostess." His expression turned lascivious.

"You're a pig," I snapped.

"And I like her." He sobered. "Staying here might have been a means to an end, but I genuinely like her."

I didn't believe him. He'd proven himself an adept liar. "You need to get out of here."

"I'm good."

"You also need to tell me about Gemini," I added. I couldn't drag things out too long. "Why was your sign in the sky last night along with their constellation?"

Weston opened his mouth, then shut it. His eyebrows moved toward one another. "Come again?"

"Oh, don't play games. I'm not in the mood. And, as you so helpfully pointed out, we don't have time. Monica will be home soon. I very much doubt you want her hearing this discussion."

Weston tilted his head, then sighed. "I would prefer not hurting her," he acknowledged. "She's been through enough."

Frustration squeezed my throat. "If you're about to tell me I hurt her and you're here to pick up the pieces I'll kill you."

"My intention was not to pick up the pieces," Weston said. "I came to take advantage of her." He turned sheepish. "I really do like her, whether you believe it or not. As for your part in her pain, I don't know what to tell you. She's a good woman, and she does still feel pain regarding what happened.

"It's embarrassment mostly," he continued. "Everyone told her Hunter would dump her like yesterday's fast food, but she believed him when he said he was over you. Even seeing you together, she knew that it was done, but she clung to him because she really cared. She wishes she had followed her instincts and cut him loose when she first heard the rumors. At least then she could've saved face."

"No one wanted to hurt her," I snapped.

"And yet that's exactly what happened."

Sebastian inserted himself before I could muster a response. "Don't let him derail you. He's playing with your emotions. He doesn't care that Hunter dumped Monica for you."

He was right, of course. Weston was playing with me. "Let's talk about Gemini," I prodded. "We know he's here. We know he's split himself—and his magic—into the Eaton kids. We know something went wrong with their entry and Eli is off his rocker. What I want to know is what that has to do with you."

"Who says it has anything to do with me?" Weston asked. "I've been here playing happy houseguest with Monica. I've been mending her broken heart. I've basically been a saint the last month."

"That's the biggest load of crap." I wanted to kick him. "Just tell us what's going on with Gemini, and we'll leave you to play house with Monica. At least until we deal with him."

"Why would I help you if you plan to ruin the good thing I have going on?"

"I'll ruin it for you now otherwise." It was the only threat I had to drop. We all knew I wasn't going to kill him. Not in Monica's house, and not unless he was actively trying to kill me. Even though he was a turd of the highest order, I didn't have it in me to kill him when he wasn't an immediate threat.

"How will you do that?"

I hated the smug tilt of Weston's head. "I'll tell her you're a gnome shifter bent on killing me."

"She won't believe you."

"I'll show her my magic."

He narrowed his eyes. "You wouldn't expose yourself."

"I would. As you said, guilt is a powerful motivator. I ruined her life. If she tries to tell people I'm magical, they won't believe her. She'll know, and it will get her away from you."

Weston tried to wait me out, get me to admit I was lying. When I didn't budge and stared him down, he growled.

"I'm not working with Gemini," he said. "He approached me to join forces—she is more apt because the boy isn't talking and is just laughing like a third-wheel killer in a *Shudder* horror movie—but I politely declined."

"Oh, come on," I muttered.

"It's true!" Weston's eyes flashed. "Do you have any idea how temperamental the zodiac elementals are? Half of them are crazy. Gemini is the craziest of the group. He's been doing his assassin thing for far too long and has turned it into the only game he cares about."

Confusion knit my eyebrows together. "I don't understand."

"Of course you don't. You're not even a full-fledged witch. You're a baby witch and you let the Winchesters do everything for you."

"I'm learning from the Winchesters," I countered. "There's a difference."

"When will you be done learning?"

"We're talking about you, not me."

"You are so dramatic." He clucked his tongue. "Gemini thinks we have common interests. He didn't realize he was going to be taking on three powerful witches to bring his plan to fruition. The original plan was to knock this area into disarray a decade ago."

"The entry was wrong and Eli was never right," I added. "They disappeared to try reentry to correct the problem. That's why they disappeared for ten years."

"It wasn't ten years for them," he confirmed. "It was only a few hours. They were confused when they returned, discombobulated, and it took them time to realize where—and more importantly—when they were."

"Are Craig and Sandy even their parents?"

He shrugged. "I have no idea what would happen if you tested their DNA. Gemini is Gemini. Those kids have no love for the people who birthed them. They would kill them if they got in the way."

"You don't have to worry about that," I said. "The parents are completely disinterested in the kids. They knew something was wrong with them from the start." That explained why Sandy turned to drink. She was afraid of her own kids, didn't want to admit it, and felt guilty.

"Gemini wants to destroy you. You were never part of his plan. He thinks I want to destroy you too."

"Don't you?" I challenged. "Your previous actions indicate otherwise."

"I told you, the mission has changed." He grew annoyed. "Why can't you ever take what I say at face value?"

Was he joking? "Because you're a liar."

"Yes, there is that." He shrugged.

"You said Gemini was an assassin," I prodded. "What does that mean?"

"Gemini always has a kill list when he decides to wreak havoc on this plane. You weren't originally part of the plan. When you found them, that changed. They fear you."

"Which is why they keep visiting my dreams," I guessed.

"They're aware of the Winchesters, and they're aware of you." He hesitated. "I don't think they're aware of the pixie witch. She's supposed to be separate from all of this, but she's here and she's trouble."

"I'm going to be trouble too." I thought about Aquarius, how she said I was her proxy. That wasn't a story I would share with Weston.

"Leave Monica alone," I ordered. "You don't belong here. She's been through enough."

"I agree, but I'm not leaving. I wasn't lying about caring about her."

I wanted to believe him, but I couldn't. "We're not done talking about this. For now ... don't get involved or you'll get the same treatment as Gemini." I pulled open the door and found Monica standing on the other side, grocery bags clutched in each hand.

"Um ... this is a surprise." She glanced between faces, uncertain.

I was glad to have Sebastian with me. If it had just been Weston and me, she wouldn't have believed anything I said. As it was, I had exactly one lie ready to unleash.

"Phoebe told me that West is an author," I said in a fake chirp. "I thought I would talk to him—I'm considering getting back into publishing—and took a chance that he was here." I smiled even though I wanted to scream. "Turns out, his publisher only does the travel books, so we really don't have a lot in common."

"Oh." Did Monica believe me? I couldn't tell, but she looked relieved. "Well, that's too bad."

I shrugged. "It is what it is." I edged around her. "We'll get out of your hair. Have a nice day."

I felt Monica's eyes on me as we left.

"You too," she called out finally.

22

TWENTY-TWO

Sebastian and I went looking for Tillie, Evan, and Easton after we left Monica's house. Easton said he kept looking for Weston and hadn't been able to track him, but we had such an easy time finding him. I planned to ask him about it the second I saw him.

I tried a locator spell, but despite my best efforts, Tillie, Evan, and Easton were nowhere to be found.

"Can Tillie stop a locator spell from finding her?" Sebastian asked as I parked in front of the funeral home.

"I don't see why not. She's probably trying to stop the Eatons from finding her and we're blocked in the process."

"What's our next step?"

I didn't have an answer ... until my gaze landed on Hunter, who stood outside the downtown deli staring at my car from across the street. I hadn't seen him when I pulled up. "How about lunch?" I asked.

Sebastian brightened considerably. "I can do lunch ... if you guys are buying. It only seems fair since you so ruthlessly cut me out of the gossip."

"Not that you're being dramatic or anything," I drawled.

He shrugged. "I'm also honest."

"Yeah, yeah, yeah." I led the way, greeting Hunter with a hug and kiss. "How is your day going?" He looked as beaten down as I felt.

"Not great." Hunter's fingers were light as he brushed the hair away from my face. "How has your day been?"

"We have some things to discuss."

His expression instantly went dark. "What do we need to discuss?"

"Let's get something to eat." I wanted to delay the inevitable rant. "Sebastian says we owe him a meal for keeping him out of the gossip loop."

"Is that a fact?" Hunter slid his gaze to Sebastian.

Sebastian was solemn. "You've hurt my feelings."

"Well, we can't have that." Hunter slid his arm around my waist and prodded me toward the deli. "Let's get something to eat. Then you can fill me in. I'm sure I'll be thrilled with whatever you tell me."

I ORDERED A ROAST BEEF SANDWICH AND fries. Hunter got the same. Sebastian asked for artisanal chicken and pita chips. Then we settled in the corner away from prying ears.

"You start," I said. "Any sightings of the Eatons?"

"Several." Hunter's eyebrows moved toward one another. "Are you forcing me to go first to make me forget you're going to tell me something to irritate me?"

"I'm appalled you would even think something like that."

He wagged his finger. "I'll go first, but only because I think your stuff is going to be more important than mine."

I sent him a faux sunny smile. "Whatever works for you."

He bit into his sandwich, methodically chewed and swallowed, and then got to the heart of matters. "The Eatons were seen in the town square last night," he started. "After midnight. They were together and doing 'general mischief.'" He used air quotes.

"What does that mean?" Sebastian asked. "Is that code for toilet papering town hall or something?"

Hunter laughed. "As far as I can tell they were hanging around and not doing anything. They were talking to one another when several people, including Linda and James Stevens, approached them."

I frowned. Linda and James Stevens were the sort of residents who gave Hunter indigestion. There was nothing they wouldn't complain about. There were no residents—guilty or innocent—they wouldn't tattle on. "I'm guessing that Linda and James made a stink about the kids being here."

"They asked the kids why they looked the same. Linda said they were rude."

"I've seen her call half the teenagers in town rude. Most of the time they were just being teenagers."

"I agree, and that's why I asked for a rundown of exactly what was said. This comes from Linda, so take it with a grain of salt."

He didn't need to warn me. Linda had even reported me for rudeness when I was a teenager, and I was never rude. I was always on my best behavior around adults and was often called a suck-up.

"Linda said she greeted them and explained that everyone was looking for them. Apparently, Shauna did all the talking, which reinforces what you've been thinking. Shauna told her that she wasn't worried about everyone in the town looking for her because she was on a mission that couldn't be stopped."

I straightened. "A mission?"

Hunter bobbed his head. "Yup."

"What's the mission?" Sebastian asked. "If Gemini likes to instigate religious battles, what could he possibly be interested in here?"

That was a very good question. "Sometimes the churches here feud," I said.

"Over things like who gets the town square for the annual pageant on a certain day," Hunter said. "They don't exactly go to war."

"If you were going to start a religious war, would you come to Shadow Hills?"

"It would make more sense to go the Middle East," Hunter said.

"For all we know, the situation in the Middle East is his doing," I supplied. "That might meet his immediate attention."

"But why come here?" Sebastian persisted. "Say he wanted to spark something like Prohibition again. It's not like Shadow Hills is a good place to launch such an effort. It's not a political powder keg. The biggest thing we fight about here is whether or not we should add another streetlight to the downtown area."

"You forget that their entry was screwed up," I reminded him. "We don't know what time they were aiming at. Supposedly, Gemini likes being born and then aging rapidly."

"He liked to do that in ancient times," Hunter countered. "That was before the internet or good records, and invasive medical tests."

"It's so weird. Aquarius wasn't very helpful either. We're flying blind." I took a bite of my sandwich. "Did anyone else interact with them?"

"A group of kids tried to engage with them, but Shauna was dismissive. Everyone said Eli just kept humming to himself and jumping around like a little kid having a grand old time. They all said he seemed off."

"That's a polite way of saying what he is," I agreed. "He's crazy. Like, serial killer crazy."

"That probably makes them more dangerous," Hunter mused. "If they had a plan, they're way off course. They're plotting on the fly. What could they possibly be plotting in Shadow Hills?"

Once the last fry had been eaten, Hunter turned to me expectantly.

"Your turn," he prodded.

It was too much to hope that he would've forgotten I still had something to tell him. I sipped my iced tea and then turned to face him.

"Tillie, Evan, and Easton came into the restaurant this morning," I started. "I heard Grandpa arguing with someone behind the dishwasher station. I found Tillie and her sidekicks. She said she was going on an elemental hunt."

Hunter frowned. "The last thing we need is Tillie being Tillie."

I nodded. "Evan is a good babysitter. I trust him to keep things under control to the best of his ability."

"Is that saying much?" Hunter arched an eyebrow.

"He's pretty good," I hedged. "The thing is, I went looking for them after my shift. I thought they would be looking for Weston after Easton recognized the second constellation the other night."

Confusion replaced intensity on Hunter's face. "I don't know what that means."

I hadn't told him. "During my conversation with Tillie, Easton, and Evan, I told them about what I saw when I woke up from my dream last night. I took a photo, so I had that to show them."

Hunter waited.

"Easton recognized the constellation, although he said that it shouldn't be that prominent."

Hunter's expression didn't change.

"You're making things difficult."

"You're doing that yourself," he retorted. "I'm waiting for you to finish."

"Easton said that because his immediate brethren all have a direction associated with them, a constellation is associated with all four as well. The constellation I saw belonged to Weston."

Briefly, Hunter closed his eyes. When he spoke again, his voice was low. "Does that mean Weston is working with Gemini?"

"That was my immediate thought," I confirmed. "Easton made it sound as if he would be looking for Weston as well as Gemini while out with Tillie. I had to finish my shift, so they left without me. Then Phoebe came in, alone."

"I hate any story that involves Phoebe," Hunter muttered.

"She was without Monica, so I got her talking. I figured if I played the game her way, she might give me something good regarding Monica's relationship with Weston."

"Am I going to hate this?"

I honestly wasn't sure, so I held out my hands. "Phoebe believes that Monica is only dating Weston because she's not over you."

"I don't think Phoebe is a good source on this particular topic because she's always carried a torch for me and believes the only reason we've never gotten together is because I refuse to look at her with clear eyes. She thinks you clouded my view of her."

I stilled. "Did she tell you that?"

He nodded.

"She's an absolute idiot. That's ridiculous."

The way Hunter tilted his head suggested he believed otherwise.

My stomach dropped. "You believe I clouded your thinking? Like, magically?"

"No," he said hurriedly, shaking his head. He reached over to collect my hand. "That's not what I meant."

I didn't respond.

"You're going to make this difficult," he realized.

"I need to know what you mean."

"I love you so much that I can't see beyond you," he replied. "I've always loved you that way. You're all I ever see. So, yeah, when it comes to other people, I always think about you. Are you the only reason I would never get with Phoebe? Of course not. But you are the reason I could never love anyone else. I was always meant to love you, and I believe that to the very tips of my toes."

"Aw," Sebastian said, his expression turning wistful as I went warm all over.

"That's sweet," I said. "I feel the same way about you."

"But?" he prodded.

"There's no but. I've always loved you the same way. Even when I wasn't here, I thought about you every night before I went to bed. It's just ... the magical stuff gives me pause now. I don't want to be the sort of person who would use that to my advantage."

"You're not," he assured me. "You've always been it for me. If Phoebe picked up on a vibe, that's okay. Even if there was no you—and what a sad world that would be—there never would have been room for her in my life. She's not my type."

I gripped his fingers tightly. "She might be right about Monica still having feelings for you. She didn't want to be the town sad sack, so she let you go. Phoebe has told me on more than one occasion that everyone told her to let you go before I even came back to town, but she didn't listen, and now she regrets it."

"You're giving me more power than I have," he replied. "Monica and I were never going to live happily ever after. I am not happy that she's with Weston now, but there's nothing I can do about it. She's her own person, and she makes her own decisions. It's not as if I can go over there and warn Weston away."

I exchanged a heavy look with Sebastian that wasn't lost on Hunter.

"What did you do?" Hunter whined.

"We went to Monica's after my shift to warn Weston away," I replied. "I felt I had to find Weston. Obviously, the Gemini twins wanted to send me a message by using his sign as a warning last night."

"Did you find him?" Hunter was incredulous.

"Yeah. He's staying with her. She was, thankfully, at the store."

"What did you discuss?" There was an edge to Hunter's tone.

"I told him to stay away from Monica." I was resigned to getting it all out. "He claimed that he has real feelings for her. I'm not sure I believe him. That's not important right now. I asked him about Gemini. He's spoken to them."

"And?" Hunter's eyebrows migrated toward his hairline. "Are they plotting the end of the world together?"

"Wow," Sebastian intoned. "And people say I'm dramatic."

"You are," Hunter fired back. "I'm serious, Stormy. What's their plan?"

"He claims he's not working with them. He said they approached him because they knew that he was brought here to work against me."

"He also said his mission has changed," Sebastian added. "He said he no longer wants to stop the hellcats from coming back into power because it's too late. He wants Stormy to change allegiances."

"That doesn't make me feel any better than when he was working against us openly." Hunter was morose. "I hate this." He rubbed his forehead. "Tell me the rest."

"There isn't much to tell." I was matter of fact. "Weston claims Gemini is something of an elemental assassin, that all of his previous missions coincided with big killings and the religious wars are a means to an end to hit his target."

"Who is Gemini's target this time?"

"He doesn't know, but thinks it might be me." I sent him an apologetic look. This was not what he signed on for. The witch thing. He just wanted a quiet life for us.

"Whatever you're thinking right now, don't," he warned, jabbing a finger at me. "I can tell you're going into your martyr headspace."

My lower lip came out to play.

"Just tell me all of it."

"There's nothing else to tell," I replied. "No one knows why they originally came here. As things stand now, they are focused on me as an enemy. Whether that's because there's no one else to focus on, I can't say."

"And he claims he's not working with them?"

"So he says. Monica came home when we were finishing up. I told her I stopped by to see him because Phoebe said he was working as a travel author and I thought we could touch base. She seemed to believe it."

He waited a beat. "And that's it?"

"That's it," I confirmed.

"I don't know what to make of it."

He wasn't the only one. "There's one other thing," I added. "We couldn't find Tillie, Evan, and Easton. Tillie may have them shrouded. Or they could be in trouble."

"Well, great." Hunter's affect was flat. "What a great, great turn of events."

I had to hold back a sigh. Sarcasm wasn't flattering on him.

23
TWENTY-THREE

I called Bay. She met us at the funeral home, an inventive string of curse words escaping before she even greeted us.

"I think I'm going to die before Aunt Tillie," she announced.

"She's going to kill you with her antics," Sebastian guessed.

Bay nodded. "She makes me feel old."

"At least you don't smell anymore."

"I do have that going for me." A wicked gleam blazed in her eyes. "And we know how to combat the scent spells going forward. She'll hate that."

"I guess that means whenever you're in trouble with her we're going to get a free dinner," Hunter mused.

"Please." Bay made a face. "If you guys came over for dinner every single day my mother would be thrilled. There's little she loves more than doting on you, Landon, and Gunner."

"She especially loves Gunner," I agreed.

"Gunner is easy for someone like my mother to love. He'll eat anything and proclaim it the best meal he's ever had."

"I've yet to have a bad meal at The Overlook," Hunter added. "We need to focus. Last time Stormy saw Tillie, Evan, and Easton, they were looking for the Eatons and Weston. Stormy found Weston but can't find Tillie and the others."

"She probably threw up a protection spell," Bay replied. "She would want to be the aggressor when it comes to the hunt. She might not have considered the possibility that Stormy would want to find them."

"I texted Easton." I chewed my bottom lip. "He almost always responds ... unless he's with Evan." I cast a worried look toward Sebastian. "Not that he covets Evan above anyone else."

"Stop." Sebastian looked frustrated. "I know you feel sorry for me—"

"I don't pity you."

His eyebrows flew up. "Who used the word pity?"

"Sorry." My shoulders hunched. I kept stepping in it where Easton and Sebastian were concerned. I told myself to stay out of their business, and yet I couldn't follow through. I was intrigued by the relationship building between Evan and Easton. Sebastian was so very important to me, and I didn't want him unhappy. "We really should pursue that idea about getting you an online dating profile."

Sebastian rolled his eyes. "I can handle my own dating life."

"But you're not," Hunter said, catching me off guard. "You're wallowing. Stormy is right, we're going to get you online and find someone for you. First, we have to find Tillie and the others. The last thing we need is her blowing up half the town because she gets too excited."

"I doubt she'd blow up the town," Sebastian said.

The look on Bay's face said otherwise.

"If she's blocked anyone from locating her, we're going to have to use different means to find them." Bay, all business now, said. "I only know of one foolproof way." She raised her hands. "*Come*," she boomed, causing Hunter, Sebastian, and I to jolt. Almost immediately, we were surrounded by five ghosts. I recognized a few of the faces.

"Mrs. Parker," I said when I saw the old librarian. She'd been in charge when I was a kid, and she was one of my favorite people.

"Who are you talking to?" Hunter asked, reminding me that he couldn't see the ghosts.

"The old librarian, Gillian Parker," I replied, my stomach constricting. "Why are you a ghost? I thought you died in your sleep."

Hunter's gaze was on me, not the ghost. "You can see her?"

"Jeff Blankenship is here too. Remember him?"

Hunter nodded. "He was in that accident when we were in high school. Why would he be a ghost? He wasn't murdered."

"Ghosts aren't necessarily all murder victims," Bay replied. "If the death is traumatic enough, or sudden enough, they can stay behind because they don't know enough to cross over. I'm not sure why a librarian who died in her sleep would still be here." She cocked her head. "Why are you hanging around?"

Mrs. Parker looked surprised by the question. "Does it matter?"

"It does to Stormy," she replied.

"Let's just say I didn't die of natural causes."

I snapped straighter. "You were murdered?"

"Poisoned," Mrs. Parker replied. "Gordon Jefferson." Her upper lip curved into a sneer. "He broke into my house looking for money three weeks before my death. I turned him in. I never got to testify against him. He made sure of that."

I relayed the information to Hunter. He looked shocked.

"I was new on the job when she died," he replied. "No one ever considered that it wasn't natural causes. I'm not sure I can secure a warrant for an autopsy now."

"Would the toxicology report even be accurate years after the fact?" Bay asked.

Hunter held out his hands. "I'll try to figure something out." He was making the promise to me, not Mrs. Parker. He knew how much I'd loved her when I was younger. She was one of the few people always willing to talk about books with me, a lifeline.

"I'm really sorry," I said to the ghost. "I didn't know."

"Why would you?" As always, her tone was kind. "You were off living your dream." Her eyes flicked to Hunter. "I always knew you would come back."

"My writing career didn't work out," I said.

"You're not done yet." She smiled at me. "You didn't have all the pieces of the puzzle in place." She tilted her head toward Hunter. "You always needed him to get what you really wanted. You're well on your way now."

"How can you be so sure?"

"I always knew exactly how things were going to work out for you. I never doubted you were destined for big things, Stormy. You're the only one who doubted that."

My throat felt thick. "Thank you."

"It's really sweet," Bay agreed, "but we can't dwell on it. We have something else we have to do." She glanced between the ghosts. "You have a mission. Find Aunt Tillie, Easton, and Evan. Report back to me."

Before I could muster a word, the ghosts dissipated. "How long will it take?" I asked.

Bay shrugged. "Normally it doesn't take long. They're not constrained by the same laws of motion and gravity that we are."

"At least we have that going for us."

THE GHOSTS HAD BEEN GONE TEN minutes. We used the time to drum up ideas for Sebastian's dating profile—an endeavor he vigorously fought. Bay and I were not to be deterred, though. We had an idea for a photography session, and even Hunter joined in with suggestions. Sebastian was flustered by the time Mrs. Parker returned.

"I found them." She smiled at me, seemingly genuinely happy to see me again.

"Where?" Bay asked. She abandoned plotting for Sebastian.

"The Manistee River, not far off Clairmont Drive. On the other side of Lakes of the North."

I frowned. "What were they doing out there?" I directed the question to Bay, but she looked as baffled as me.

She held out her hands. "Were they alone?" she asked the ghost.

"I recognized Tillie Winchester." A small smile curved Mrs. Parker's lips. "She's always had a certain reputation. I didn't recognize either man with her. They're both good looking, and ready to stand as her protectors."

"Does she need protectors?" Bay asked.

"The Eatons were there too." Now Mrs. Parker looked puzzled. "They haven't aged a day since I last saw them. How is that possible? The rumor was their father took them."

"The rumor was wrong," I replied. "They disappeared. Their father did the same. He was hiding from them."

Mrs. Parker's eyes went wide. "That is interesting."

"How much trouble was Aunt Tillie in?" Bay demanded.

"Well, there seemed to be some sort of argument going on. Tillie told the Eatons that she was going to stomp them into mush. Then they threw fire at her."

I thought I was going to be sick. "You should've led with that."

"Protect her," Bay ordered Mrs. Parker, using her scary "you're a ghost and you have to do what I say" voice. "Tell her we're coming." Bay stopped the ghost before she could take off. "And tell her she's in big, big trouble when I get to her."

"I'll tell her." Mrs. Parker broke into a wide smile, apparently enjoying herself. "I'll see you soon."

Hunter was already moving to his truck. "Let's go," Bay said. "No one is killing Aunt Tillie but me."

TWENTY MINUTES HAD NEVER FELT SO LONG. Bay knew where to go thanks to Mrs. Parker, who was apparently emitting some sort of ghostly beacon. Once we parked, we had to head in on foot. Sebastian didn't like that in the least.

"Ugh," he complained, giving the dirty soles of his shoes a dubious look. "Why is it so muddy?"

"It's spring and we just had four feet of snow melt," Hunter replied without looking over his shoulder. "The ground is thawing. What could survive those circumstances besides mud?"

"It was a rhetorical question," Sebastian muttered. "I didn't need an actual answer."

Hunter grunted. He was in great shape, but it was work to hike through the woods. The closer we got to the river—and our ultimate destination—the more the air crackled. I looked around, confused, and then focused on Bay. "Do you...?"

"Smell brimstone?" Bay asked. "Yes."

I thought of what Evan had said in the clearing. Now I understood.

"It goes with fire magic," Bay replied.

"But Gemini is an air elemental," I argued.

"They can still wield fire. All elementals are essentially demons. Every demon I've ever crossed paths with has been able to wield fire."

"Thank you for putting *that* in my head," Hunter complained.

Bay didn't apologize. "We have someone else who can wield fire too," she reminded him. "I like our odds in this."

Surprise registered in Hunter's eyes, then resigned acceptance. He glanced at me. "We have a fire witch."

"And we're going to need her," Bay said. She was determined as she pushed toward the sound of raised voices. "Here we go," she said, catching my gaze. "Be ready and follow your instincts. Whatever you think we need to do, don't doubt yourself. Something inside of you knows what to do even if you don't have faith in yourself yet."

I didn't have time to respond. As soon as the words were out of Bay's mouth, she disappeared through the trees.

I took a deep breath and followed her, my magic begging to be let loose. *It's time to play,* a voice inside my head said.

The bank of the river was smoky, and I practically choked on the air. Sebastian lingered back—there wasn't much he could do in a situation like this anyway—but Hunter stuck close at my side.

I had to squint thanks to the smoke and fire raging around us. I used my magic to grab the fire and choke it back. As the fire receded, the smoke thinned.

Shauna stood on the opposite riverbank, her hands glowing as she expended endless fire magic. Eli was behind her, dancing with his hands thrown over his head and laughing that maniacal laugh of his.

Mrs. Parker had guided Bay to the right spot. On our side of the river, Tillie had Easton and Evan under a magical protective dome. Evan looked a little singed, but his glare was fierce as he stared across the river.

Easton started panicking when he realized we were swooping in. "Be careful," he yelled. "They're burning everything to get to us."

"This is why you're the second sidekick," Tillie complained. "If you haven't noticed—and you obviously haven't—the fire is no longer burning."

Easton seemed thrown by the realization. "But how?"

Tillie inclined her head to me. "She's more powerful than she realizes. She can do so much more, but she's afraid to try."

I glared at her. "I'm right here. I can hear you."

"Then use that anger to end them," Tillie suggested. "Start with the girl. The boy is practically useless."

When I swiveled to face Shauna, she was poised to strike again. Fury darkened her eyes and soot stained her cheeks. "Why can't you leave us alone?" she demanded. "This has nothing to do with you."

"It does now," I said. "What's the plan, Shauna? You can't get past the dome. Are you going to burn down the entire forest even though you'll never get to them?"

A muscle worked in her jaw, but she dropped her hands. "Apparently, we're at a stalemate," she said.

"Not really," Bay countered. "We have far more firepower." As if to prove it, she slashed her hands through the air, ordering the ghosts to attack.

Eli screeched and ducked his head. Shauna tried to blow back one of the ghosts with fire. She was knocked from her perch on top of a boulder and driven to her knees.

"Stop!" she screamed.

Bay pulled the ghosts back. She left them ringing the elementals.

"I'm not here for you," Shauna snapped. "At least not yet. We'll agree to leave you be. All we ask in return is that you do the same."

"I don't think we can do that," I replied. It was difficult not to see her as a teen, but deep down I recognized she wasn't. She was something more, something so dangerous she could destroy us all. Worse, she could propel us to destroy each other. "We know what you've done in the past."

"We've done nothing now," Shauna said. "Perhaps you should allow yourself to believe that people can change."

It was interesting that she focused her plea on me. That was likely because she figured I was the weakest. Bay and Tillie looked as if they were ready for war. Easton and Evan would do whatever necessary to protect us. Hunter, as strong as he was, wasn't a threat to them. I was their only hope.

"You should leave," I said. "Not just this river, this place. Go back to where you go when you're not on this plane. You don't belong here."

Shauna narrowed her eyes. "You don't know what you're talking about."

"I know that this world is better without you. I know that part of your plan is acting as assassins. I also know that things didn't work out the way you expected, so you're making it up as you go along."

"You seem to know a lot," Shauna said grimly. "You're wrong, but I'm guessing you don't care to hear the truth."

"I'll listen to whatever you want to tell me," I countered. "I know that whatever you have planned will result in innocent people dying. That's your thing, right? We're not going to stand by as you slaughter people on your way to laughs."

"I said we weren't here for you *yet*. We can change that."

"You're going to do what you do and so will we."

She nodded. "Fine. Have it your way."

I was expecting the wall of fire when she threw it at us and managed to catch it. The intensity was so great it took me a moment to adjust before I could throttle the fire back. By the time I did, Tillie's protection dome was down and the Eatons were gone.

"Well, that was invigorating," Tillie said as I caught my breath.

"I'd pick a different word," Hunter growled, his hand landing on my back. "Are you okay?"

I nodded automatically. "I'm fine." I wasn't certain I was okay, though. Not even a little.

24
TWENTY-FOUR

"That was interesting," Tillie said once it was obvious the Eatons were gone. "Good experiment, huh?" She shot me a thumbs-up.

I had no idea how to respond, so I said nothing. Bay felt differently.

"Good experiment?" Bay exploded. "You could've been killed."

"I had everything under control." Tillie wasn't about to admit she'd made an error. "Why must you always be such a killjoy?"

When Bay turned to me, there was a "can you believe what I have to put up with" look on her face. Under different circumstances, I would've laughed. I didn't much feel like laughing right now.

"Hey." Hunter brushed my hair out of my face as he stepped in front of me. "Are you okay?"

"I'm great."

"You're not great."

"I'm not terrible," I argued. "I'm taking it all in."

Hunter didn't look convinced. He hugged me against him and swayed back and forth.

"What's wrong?" Tillie demanded when I caught her eye. "You kicked their asses."

"Why would you assume something is wrong?"

"He's rocking you like you're a little baby. You're acting like high schoolers in heat."

Hunter wouldn't let me pull away from him. "I'm fine with that," he said.

I was still coming down from the magical high, and I was fine with it too.

"Ignore her," Bay instructed as she stood at the bank of the river and looked across. "She's just trying to get a rise out of you because she knows that she shouldn't have been out here, and if we hadn't come along her power would've eventually waned and she would've died." Bay's tone was laced with judgmental vitriol.

"I had them exactly where I wanted them," Tillie huffed. "I was just about to make my move when you happened to show up."

The look Bay shot her was withering.

"It's true," Tillie insisted. "You weren't in the dome with us. You didn't hear our planning." She looked at Evan for confirmation. "Tell them."

"It was eventually going to get ugly," Evan replied. He ignored Tillie when she sputtered. "We were trying to figure out what to do when you guys showed up. I guess we got lucky."

"Stormy tried to contact you guys several times after her shift," Bay said. "When she started worrying, she called me."

"And you sent ghosts to find us," Evan assumed.

"You're in big trouble," Bay said to Tillie. "Mom is going to take your four-wheeler away when she finds out what you did."

"How is she going to find that out?" Tillie demanded. She didn't wait for an answer. "You're such a tattletale. If you tell your mother, I'll tell her what you and Landon did in my field last weekend."

Bay's expression didn't change, but I thought I saw a faint quirk of her lips. "I have no idea what you're talking about," she said. She wasn't quite the liar Tillie was, so she didn't carry it off as well as her aunt.

"We both know that I know." Tillie flipped her fingers from her eyes toward Bay in the universal "I'm watching you" pantomime.

Bay didn't look all that worried. She focused on Hunter and me. "We should head back to the inn. We need to talk about what happened, and I wouldn't mind bringing Scout and Gunner in on this. We might need them."

"We don't need them," Tillie countered. "I've got this."

All eyes turned to her.

"I hate it when you have no faith in me," she complained. "You'll see. I know what I'm doing now. We don't need help."

"We're calling Gunner and Scout," Bay insisted. "We'll talk about it at dinner."

Tillie muttered something unintelligible under her breath.

"Let's get out of here," Hunter said, his hand rubbing my back. "We've all seen enough of this place today."

SEBASTIAN BEGGED OFF joining us for dinner at The Overlook. He'd had enough excitement for one day and was more than happy to wave us off as we headed out of town. Scout and Gunner were already there—Gunner had inexplicably offered to help in the kitchen, and Marnie, Twila, and Winnie had him dressed in a pink apron and chef's hat.

"Why do you all smell like a campfire?" Scout asked from Tillie's kitchen recliner, flipping through a catalog. Unlike her boyfriend, she didn't appear keen to help.

"Look at this," Gunner crowed before any of us could respond. He held a plate containing a decorated fruit pie. "I made apple pie!"

"He made the crust and everything," Winnie said proudly. "He's quite the little chef."

"I'm looking forward to making him do it all over again—naked —when we get home," Scout said.

Gunner shot her a wicked look. "You think that's a deterrent, but it's not."

Scout laughed. "I'll buy you a special apron."

Gunner sent her an air kiss.

Tillie stomped to her chair and glared at Scout. "You're in my spot."

Anybody else would have scrambled to surrender the chair. That's not how Scout operated.

"Huh," Scout said.

"'Huh?'" Tillie challenged.

"That's what I said." Scout obviously had no intention of backing down.

"Get out." Tillie tapped her foot impatiently.

"You can't sit in this chair," Scout countered. "You smell like campfire. You don't want to stink up your chair."

"That chair can smell however I like," Tillie argued. "Now, get out."

"I'm good," Scout said dryly. Her attention moved to the rest of us. "Why do you smell like campfire?" She focused on Evan. "You and Easton look like you've been fighting. Is this some weird sex thing? If so, feel free not to answer the question."

Evan pinned her with a death glare. "Don't be weird. We were fighting. Not with each other," he added when Winnie sent him a sharp look. "We were fighting the elemental. Or elementals." He cocked his head. "I get that it's Gemini, but because two of them have physically manifested it's weird to refer to them as a singular being."

"Either way, Eli is off," Easton said as he slid closer to Gunner to look at his perfect pie. "That's going to be amazing."

"I think I missed my calling in life," Gunner said. "I should've been a chef."

"I would love you just the same," Scout offered. She was still in a silent standoff with Tillie. "What's your deal?" she demanded when

Tillie extended her hand and made a claw-like gesture. "What are you planning to do with that thing?"

"I'm going to curse you," Tillie replied. "It's going to be grand ... and it's going to hurt."

Scout didn't look bothered. "Have at it." Her eyes flipped to me. "You look drained."

"I'm a little tired," I admitted. "I'm not sure if it's because I'm emotionally wiped or because I expended too much magic."

"We should hear the story from the beginning," Winnie prodded.

Bay related everything. She left nothing out, including every bad move Tillie had made over the course of the afternoon. With each passing word, Tillie's countenance grew darker. By the time Winnie started harrumphing and shooting glares at her aunt, Tillie was practically spitting fire.

"Oh, you're definitely on my list," she said as Bay finished. "In fact, I'm going to start a new list and make you the sole person on it. How do you like that idea?"

Bay shrugged. "You made a mistake today, a mistake that could have cost us all dearly."

Tillie muttered something in a language I didn't recognize. "You'll wish you'd never been born."

"Stop it," Winnie barked, pinning her aunt with a dark glare. "Stop blaming others for your mistakes. It's getting old."

Tillie's mouth fell open in abject surprise. "How can you blame me for this?"

"I'm familiar with your work." Winnie was calm. "What are you going to do about the elemental? It's obvious that Gemini has a plan. If he says Stormy isn't the target of that plan, it's somebody else."

"How do we figure out who?" I asked.

"Let's think about it." Scout adjusted on the chair, giving Tillie an imperious look. "What was going on in Shadow Hills ten years ago?"

"I don't know," I replied. "I was out of town then. You guys would know more. Well, and Hunter." I sent him an apologetic look.

"That was about two years after you left," he started. "You left for college that August." He glanced at me. "I was in the academy."

"Your father was in charge," I surmised. Why was Greg Ryan constantly at the periphery of our lives these days?

"He was," Hunter confirmed. "I'm trying to think what sort of cases he worked. We were not all that close back then. We had ... a falling out."

"Why?" Winnie asked. She didn't look as if she was being nosy as much as curious. "What were you and your father fighting about?"

"A lot of things." Hunter looked uncomfortable. "He was a bit abusive." He avoided looking Winnie in the eye.

Winnie's expression turned dark. "I didn't realize. I guess I knew a little. Terry mentioned that he tried to step in when you were younger because he always thought you were a good boy and your father was a jerk. I didn't know the rest."

"Probably because Terry knows I don't want my story shouted from the rooftops." Hunter said. "I don't want to dwell on my father. He was a jerk, but I don't see how this could have anything to do with him."

Winnie looked as if she wanted to push the matter further—like get a home address to track down Greg—but she cocked her head. "Ten years ago was before we switched the name of Walkerville to Hemlock Cove. Bay was at college. She stayed south and moved to Detroit after she graduated.

"Thistle and Clove were still here," she continued. "I believe Thistle graduated the same year the Eatons disappeared." She tapped her bottom lip. "That story made the rounds up here, but not for very long. I thought it fizzled because the kids were eventually found and returned to their mother."

"I wonder if a lot of people thought that," Scout mused. Tillie was making a show of trying to crowd her out of the chair—starting a slow roll over one of the arms—but Scout still refused to move.

"Would it matter?" Hunter asked. "Why do you find that important?"

Scout shrugged. "It's interesting that the story died down so quickly. Most areas, especially areas as sparsely populated as the towns up here, would cling to a story like that for years. It would be the biggest thing to happen in decades.

"Heck," she continued, leaning forward so she missed Tillie trying to plant her butt in Scout's face, resulting in Tillie sliding off the arm of the recliner and hitting the wall. "Most towns would've turned the disappearance of the Eatons into a huge cautionary tale for teenagers."

"An urban legend," Gunner added. He had flour on his nose and determination on his face as he worked on decorating the crust for a second pie.

"The Eatons are an urban legend?" My forehead wrinkled as I tried to wrap my mind around it.

"They would be in a different town," Scout replied. "Think about it. Two teenagers. Warring parents. Other parents would've turned it into a 'this is what happens when you don't obey your parents' situation. They would've enhanced the story, pretended Shauna was meeting a date, and so on."

She was right. "Was that because we're dealing with an elemental?"

Scout held out her hands. "I'm not sure how all of that works. Aquarius was less than informative, and none of our people know anything about the zodiac elementals. They're enigmas because they don't come out to play very often."

"Rooster said they used to come out and play a lot more than they do now," Gunner offered. He was using a cookie cutter to shape dough for the top of the pie. He really did look as if he were having the time of his life. "Supposedly they enjoyed being out quite a bit until about a century ago. Ever since then, they've been quiet."

"What happened a century ago?" I asked.

"I know someone we can ask," Evan volunteered. He was edging closer to Scout, sensing that Tillie was going to lose it if his best friend didn't cede the chair to her. If Tillie started throwing around her magic, things would get messy.

"Who?" Hunter stood ramrod straight. Did he think Evan was going to suggest talking to Greg?

"There's one person who might know what happened a century ago to change things up with the elementals," Evan replied. "She's close."

I didn't catch on, but Bay did.

"The vampire apex," she said, jogging my memory.

A vampire apex had moved into the area several months ago. She wasn't always forthcoming, but she had answered our questions on more than one occasion. Esther's fate was tied to the fight Scout would ultimately engage in with the lamia apex.

"Do you think she'll help us?" I asked.

Evan shrugged. "We're already in Hemlock Cove and she's at Hollow Creek. Why not ask her?

"It's not a bad idea," Bay agreed. "In fact—"

She didn't get a chance to finish because Tillie made her move on Scout and jumped on the pixie apex's lap. Tillie gripped each armrest of the chair and balanced herself on top of Scout. "Ha!" She managed to maintain her position despite the pixie witch trying to buck her off. "I win!"

Winnie glared at her aunt. "Is this really something you want to be excited about? You're sitting on another witch in a recliner. Is that really winning?"

"Oh, stuff it." Tillie looked so happy with herself I couldn't help but smile. "I won. You should all bow down to me."

Beneath her, Scout let loose a growl. "She's far wilier than I gave her credit for. I didn't see it coming."

Bay chuckled. "I told you. Even when you think you're going to win, don't bet on it. She'll always come out victorious."

"I thought this one time." Scout shook her head. "I guess I'll have to plan better next time."

Hunter cleared his throat to draw everybody's attention . "Are we going to see the apex after dinner?"

"Do you have a better idea?" Evan asked. "She might know things about the zodiac elementals."

Hunter didn't look thrilled, but he didn't argue. "I really hope she knows something."

25
TWENTY-FIVE

I found Hollow Creek creepy and hung back as Bay and the others splashed through the water.

"What's wrong?" Easton asked as he matched my pace. His eyes were forward for the trek across the water, although he cast the occasional smile toward Evan when the vampire purposely splashed Gunner before taking off like a blur.

"What makes you think anything is wrong?" I asked. I thought I was doing a good job of covering my worry.

"Your face shows every emotion you're feeling."

"No, that's Scout." I vehemently shook my head. "She can't hide anything."

"Scout too," he agreed. "You feel things deeper than most people. I can tell you're feeling something important right now."

"I'm wondering about what I did with the Eatons," I admitted.

"What you did with the Eatons was great."

"Am I supposed to do it? I don't understand my own magic."

"Your development was thrown off right from the beginning."

"Kind of like the Eatons." I was going for a joke, but it was so apt, I had to pull up short and think about it. "Actually, just like the

Eatons." I focused on Easton. "Is it possible their development being off has anything to do with our development being off?"

"I don't see how," he said. Then he seemed to think it over. "It is weird though."

"Parallels." I rubbed my cheek. "Will Esther know anything about this?"

Easton shrugged. "Can't hurt to ask."

Our party was bigger than I thought—Landon and Hunter refused to be left behind—and we made a lot of noise as we traipsed through the foliage behind the creek. I wasn't surprised when Esther's minion—a little troll-looking creature name Bixby—appeared at the head of the trail that led to her cabin.

"No trespassing," the creature barked at Scout, who was in front of the line.

She'd once tortured the little beast by making him listen to *Designing Women* diatribes and the *Dawson's Creek* theme song over and over again. They hated one another.

"Oh, it's my little tadpole." Scout made a big show of trying to hug the minion. He dodged her.

"Don't touch me, foul creature," he barked.

"You don't have to go overboard to pretend you don't love me," Scout teased.

"I wish you'd fall into a pit of cow manure and never climb your way out," Bixby shot back.

"And I want to cover you with butterfly kisses and throw you in a Jello pit at a strip club to see how much money you can make." Scout batted her eyelashes at him. "That's how much I love you."

Bixby looked offended. "Don't ever say anything like that again."

Scout made fish lips. "Give me a kiss, little guy." She recognized she was driving him to the point of no return but didn't care. "Give mommy a big old kiss."

Before Bixby could unload his real feelings on Scout—it always happened—a chill settled over the trail. Up the slope, Esther stood in an ankle-length dress, her long hair pulled back in a severe bun. She didn't look surprised to see us.

"There's quite a group of you tonight," she noted as her gaze bounced between faces. "Eight of you. Too many for my small cabin."

"Send them away," Bixby hissed.

Esther ignored him. "A bonfire might be nice." Her eyes moved to me. "It is fire bringing us all together tonight, isn't it?"

"Actually, it's an air elemental if I'm not mistaken," I replied.

"A demon is a demon," she replied. "Come along. We have much to discuss." She glanced down at Bixby as the minion scampered to catch up with her. "Why must you always fight with the pixie? I don't understand why you can't be the bigger person."

"You've met her," Bixby groused. "She's horrible."

"I find her amusing."

"No, you don't." Bixby shook his head. "You're beautiful and ethereal. She's the gunk you dig from between your toes."

"I really am going to kiss you," Scout warned. "I might use tongue."

"Don't do that," Gunner complained. "I'll have to rip his limbs from his body and whack him in the face with his own arms if you do that."

At the top of the hill, Esther sent Evan, Easton, and Gunner for wood. Then she took Bay and I inside to gather refreshments. By the time everybody had regrouped, the fire was roaring.

Esther glanced around. "This is very nice." She lifted her head, as if scenting the air, then sighed. "You're here because of Gemini." It wasn't a question.

"You're familiar with his work," I replied.

"He's always been a bit of a pain," she acknowledged. "Of course, there are worse elementals."

"Which are worse?" Scout asked. "Just in case we run into them."

Esther's lips twitched. "Always looking for a fight, aren't you?"

Scout shrugged. "It seems the fights always find me."

"Well, if you ever see Virgo, Aries, and Capricorn, I'm sure the fur will fly."

"All men," Scout guessed.

Esther shook her head. "Capricorn takes the visage of a woman. Keep in mind, they can look as they want."

"We met Aquarius," Bay volunteered. "She's fought Gemini a few times."

"Those two get along like oil and water," Esther agreed. "I find Aquarius to be a little..." She waved her hand. "She's very into herself."

"We're all Aquariuses," Scout said, gesturing between Bay, me, and herself. "She found that interesting."

"As do I." Esther cocked her head. "Powerful witches are often born under the sign of Aquarius."

"It's the best sign," Scout said.

Esther snorted. "You always have to be the best at everything."

"Pretty much," Scout agreed.

"There is no sign that dominates others. Certain traits are associated with various signs. Aries is considered the most powerful because he's a risk taker. Taurus is up there, along with Capricorn."

"It's interesting that Aries and Capricorn are also in the meanest group," Landon mused.

Esther nodded. "To be successful in business, you must be ruthless. Aquarians tend to keep to themselves more and are fine not socializing. To be a successful actor or actress, you need to socialize. There is one notable exception."

We waited for her to finish.

"Many successful musicians are Aquarians," she continued. "They tend to march to the beat of their own drum and that makes for breakout artists. Aquarians are also high on the successful athlete list. They often have inherent ability that can't be matched." Her eyes moved to me. "That's why some of the most successful artists in the world are Aquarians."

I didn't like her staring at me so hard. Discomfort rolled through me. "I'm not sure what this has to do with what's happening."

"It might not have anything to do with it other than the fact that Aquarius is big on balancing the social scales," she explained. "The reason Aquarius is so often fighting with Gemini is because Gemini doesn't care who he stomps on."

Bay cleared her throat to draw Esther's attention. It was as if she realized I was uncomfortable being the center of the apex's attention. "We've done some research and found Gemini has been at the root of what could be termed religious wars. Even Prohibition, in a way, was a religious war."

"Gemini thrives on the theater of it all when people fight over religion," Esther explained. "People believe fiercely, so when their beliefs are challenged, they fight tooth and nail to prove they're right. That's human nature."

"Is Gemini a true believer?" Evan asked.

"He'll tell you he is."

Evan's eyebrows moved toward one another. "That's not what I asked."

Esther regarded him for an extended beat, then sighed. "I met Gemini the first time about three-hundred years ago during the first Great Awakening. It was a response to Enlightenment, a European movement that focused on science and reason over religion. Why do you think Gemini wanted to halt that?"

"Because it's easier to get people riled over religion than science," Evan guessed.

Esther nodded. "People argue scientific facts all the time now, as if they're fluid. Back then, that didn't happen. Gemini wanted to fire up all the believers to make sure that science didn't get a foothold."

"To what end?" I asked.

Esther held out her hands. "It's always hard to tell. Gemini's dual nature makes him an enigma. One day he can be the best friend you've ever had. He loves drinking and carousing and having a good time. The next he can be a sullen monster screaming at you for looking at him wrong."

"He almost sounds schizophrenic," Landon mused. "Is he the elemental with a personality disorder?"

The question made Esther throw back her head and laugh. "You're funny," she said when she'd recovered. "That could be true of any of the zodiac elementals."

"What are the zodiac elementals?" I asked. "Are they demons?"

Esther lifted one shoulder. "That is not an easy question to answer. The word demon is thrown around far too often. The zodiac elementals came into being long before me. Some say they took on the personalities of the zodiac, but I don't know anyone who could prove that. Other than the elementals themselves, and they're not saying."

I nodded. "Do you consider them demons?"

"I consider them their own thing. They used to be much more powerful. My theory is that they could control the masses easier when people believed the stars governed their lives."

That made a strange sort of sense. "What is Gemini's goal this time? This is an odd place to start a religious uprising."

"It is," Esther agreed. "Also, it isn't. This area has become a hub for some of the most powerful beings in the world. You have a necromancer who has almost limitless power ... or will one day." She pointed at Bay. "Raising the dead is a very powerful ability."

Bay blanched. "He's here for me."

Esther shook her head. "Not specifically for you. He's here for all of you."

My heart sank. "I don't understand."

"Bay is a necromancer. Scout is the pixie apex. I'm here ... not to toot my own horn." She smiled at me. "Then we have a hellcat, but they were supposed to be extinct. When you add in the mage, who isn't far away, and the nexus in Hawthorne Hollow..."

"That's a lot of magic," Hunter murmured.

"A great deal of magic," Esther confirmed. "We have gnome

shifters, a day-walking vampire with a soul, the lamia apex bent on destroying everything."

"She's on another plane now," Scout interjected.

"She'll be back. You can't believe it will be that easy."

Scout shook her head. "If the prophecy is right, we'll be bringing the new loa in for that fight as well."

Esther grinned. "I'm very eager to see how that works out. The loas have been working on organizing their future for a very long time. They're so invested that Baron and Brigitte are spending huge amounts of time with your friend."

"I don't think that Poet likes it that much." Scout made a face. "You're saying that Gemini is here because he knew we would all be here. How does that work with their arrival? It's been suggested that their arrival was flubbed."

"Gemini's determination to come as twins—something that weakens him even as he believes it strengthens him—has made for more than one difficult entry in his past," she said. "Whenever that happens, the destruction is ten times worse."

"Why would he have been interested in coming here ten years ago?" Easton asked.

"It's possible he wasn't aiming for ten years ago. It's possible he was aiming for now, when all of you were finally grouped together. Ten years for an elemental is nothing."

"They were born," I argued. "They would've had to age through the system. Maybe they were supposed to come sooner."

"That too is a possibility," Esther acknowledged. "Their original plan may not matter. They've got something in mind, and that's what should concern you."

"They said they weren't here for me yet," I volunteered. "When we fought them at the river today, they stressed that I wasn't their target."

"They could've said that because you easily dissipated their fire magic," Easton argued. "You may have frightened them."

"That seems likely," Esther agreed. "I have a theory about their overall plan."

I sat straighter.

"We're always interested in theories," Scout said.

"The spring equinox is tomorrow," Esther explained. "Gemini's power will peak with the equinox. They're hobbled because their entry was flubbed. They need a power boost."

My heart sank. "You think they're coming for our powers."

"That would be my guess." Esther's eyes moved to Scout. "They'll fear you. Stormy's power is flashier. They like fire magic and they understand how to use it."

"They're going to try to steal Stormy's magic tomorrow?" Hunter demanded. "We can't let that happen."

"They'll need gnome magic to help them," Esther replied. "They can't do it on their own, even with the equinox boosting them."

"Me," Easton realized. "They're going to kill me and steal my power to get to Stormy."

"You're not the only gnome in the area," Esther replied. "It wasn't your sign broadcast in the sky last night."

A sinking feeling threatened to take me over. "Weston."

Esther nodded. "He's a much easier mark."

I got to my feet. "They were never here to work with Weston. They're here to kill him."

"And then you," Esther agreed.

Hunter raised his hand. "You said they wanted to steal Stormy's powers."

"She won't survive the process." Esther was matter of fact. "Neither will Weston. I doubt you're all worried about saving him, but if they get his powers, Stormy will be in grave danger. She's not yet ready to fight that sort of magic."

"Then we have to save Weston." Evan was grim. "I didn't have that on my bingo card for tonight."

"Do we even know where he is?" Landon asked. "I thought he was in hiding."

"He's at Monica's house," I replied. "I talked to him a few hours ago."

"Hunter's ex-girlfriend?" Landon glanced at my fiancé. "That's some bad luck."

"It's going to turn into worse luck if we have to storm in there and magically protect Weston," Hunter muttered. "Monica is not going to be happy."

"It'll be worse if he dies and she has no idea why," I argued.

"Well, let's go get him," Scout said. "If tomorrow is the equinox, they're going to try to kill Weston tonight. Once they have his magic, they'll go after Stormy."

"We still don't know their ultimate goal," I said.

Scout shook her head. "It doesn't matter. If we can stop them from absorbing Weston's powers, we'll knock them out of the game. They'll have to go back where they're from and regroup."

"Can't we just kill them?" Landon almost looked disappointed.

"They're zodiac elementals," Scout replied. "We can only stop them for now."

"So we need to go to Monica's house." I wasn't looking forward to that. "I guess we might as well get it over with."

"Take heed," Esther warned as we started for the hill. "Gemini is sneaky. Even if he's not firing on all cylinders, he's still dangerous." She leaned forward. "And one side of his personality is willing to lose everything to win."

26

TWENTY-SIX

W e headed to Shadow Hills, my anxiety through the roof. Hunter and I rode together. Gunner and Scout caught a ride with Bay and Landon.

Hunter kept his attention on the road as he drummed his fingers against the steering wheel.

"You can talk about it if you want," I offered. We were still fifteen minutes from our destination, and I couldn't stand the silence. "It's okay if you're worried about Monica."

He sighed. "I don't want you thinking there are residual feelings."

"I know you cared about her."

"It's really not about that. I knew it wasn't a forever relationship —none of them were—but she's already been hurt because of me."

"Because of me," I corrected.

He sent me a steely look. "Not everything is about you, Stormy." He patted my thigh to let me know it wasn't an insult. "Everything that happened to Monica was because of me."

"It doesn't really feel that way," I hedged. "I mean, if I hadn't come back—"

"We still wouldn't have lasted," he insisted. "My relationship with Monica ended early, but I was already drifting before you returned. If anything, I stretched out the relationship because you were returning."

"You wanted me to see you happy," I surmised.

He opened his mouth, then shut it. "I guess that's fair," he said. "Believe it or not, getting back together with you wasn't on the top of my to-do list when you showed up. For a long time, I was bitter about losing you."

"When news broke I was coming back, I bet everyone in town was on you. They wouldn't have looked at it as giving you a hard time, but that's how you viewed it. They were torturing you by suggesting you were going to run back to me."

"I did run back to you."

"I gave you a little push."

He emphatically shook his head. "The second I saw you, all of those feelings I'd been trying to ignore for years came rushing back. Turns out, they hadn't been lost or even changed. They'd just been hidden."

"And Monica paid the price for it."

"I'm not sorry we're together. We belong together. I'll never believe otherwise. But I wish I'd done things differently with her. In an ideal world, I never would've gotten involved with her in the first place. Then I stupidly doubled down when I heard you were coming back. Deep down, I knew that I wasn't doing right by her, but I needed a shield so I didn't drop to my knees and beg you to come back."

"You would not have begged."

"I don't know. I felt like my heart was going to beat right out of my chest the first time we talked. Of course, there was a dead body to deal with and that gave me something to focus on."

"You played your cards close," I offered. "I had no idea you still had feelings for me that first conversation. In fact, I almost wished you'd said something nasty to me at the time. If you hated me, it would have meant there were still feelings. You were more ... indifferent."

"That was all an act. It took everything I had not to pull you close and start kissing you right there."

Uncomfortable, we fell into silence for a few seconds.

"You probably shouldn't have assured Monica that my return wouldn't change things," I said finally.

"I said it over and over. I remember the first time she brought it up. It was about two days after I'd heard you were coming home. I'd been a little, I guess standoffish. I was trying to figure out how I felt.

"I knew then that I was excited for you to come home," he continued. "I hid it behind a mask of indifference, but I wanted to see you again. I wanted to see if that zing was still there."

"But you didn't tell Monica."

"That would've been an uncomfortable conversation. In truth, I didn't talk to her much about you. Occasionally, a story would bubble up when we went to a festival or something, and before I even realized what I was going to say I would be like, 'Stormy and I used to come here every year, and we had a ball.'"

I grimaced. "I bet that didn't go over well."

"She was good about not overreacting. She never got accusatory, or asked if I still had feelings for you. I knew she'd heard stories—everyone in Shadow Hills runs their mouth—but I figured it was best I kept mentions of you to a minimum. That was easier for her—and me."

"When news broke that I was coming back, it was probably like an explosion," I guessed.

"At first, only a few people knew," he said. "I think your grandfather told me the way he did so I could have some time to absorb it. Then word began to spread. I'm not sure who told Monica, but it was somebody in the coffee shop.

"I could tell by the way she was looking at me that she had something on her mind that night," he continued. "She cooked dinner. I was doing something on my computer for work. Normally, she played music while she was working in the kitchen. She didn't that night. When I sat down at the table, I thought she was going to break up with me." His smile was rueful. "I would've been okay with that. Instead, she said she'd heard you were coming back."

"She was testing you," I realized. "She wanted to see if you'd heard."

"And she was disappointed when I said I knew you were coming back. She seemed to be searching for something to say. Finally, she asked if I was upset."

He lifted one shoulder in a shrug. "I said that I hadn't given it much thought, which was an out-and-out lie. Once I heard, that was all I thought about, to the point it was difficult to even do my job.

"She took it at face value that night, but then people in town kept going at her," he continued. "They told her they were sorry about the breakup, even though it hadn't happened yet. They explained that you and I were inseparable, and I'd been broken-hearted when you left. All the while, I kept saying it wasn't a big deal."

"I don't want to be obnoxious, but you kind of gaslighted her," I said.

"I didn't mean to. It wasn't intentional. I really did convince myself that I was going to keep my distance from you ... right up until I saw you again." A soft smile played over his lips. "You were tired and freaked out from finding a body and utterly beautiful at the same time."

"That's kind of sweet," I teased.

"It was like a punch in the stomach."

"For me too. I thought you were going to be mean. When you weren't, when you were removed from the situation, that hurt worse. I think I wanted somebody to be mean to me because I was angry with myself. You made a good option. Then you weren't mean to me."

"No matter how angry I was, or hurt, I could never be mean to you." He was solemn. "You were my everything when we were kids.

When I was going through that stuff with my father, you were the only thing I had to cling to."

His honesty filled me with guilt. "And then I left."

"Don't." He was firm when shaking his head. "We wouldn't have had a shot if you didn't leave. It had to happen. It hurt, but we both went through what we needed to go through to get to where we are now. I wouldn't change where we are now for anything."

"But you would change how things ended with Monica," I said.

"I should've broken up with her right away when I heard you were coming back," he acknowledged. "Dragging things out the way I did was unbelievably cruel, and I do wonder if the way I treated her will haunt me for the rest of my life. It feels as if I shouldn't be allowed to be happy because I broke her."

"And now our problems are her problems ... again," I said. "She's fallen for a gnome shifter targeted by elementals, and that's on us."

"What was the alternative, Stormy?" He was matter of fact. "If we'd told her the truth, she either wouldn't have believed us or would have accused us of targeting her. We were in a no-win situation."

I didn't disagree. Still, this felt like it was our fault. "What do we tell her?"

"We should ask for Weston."

"She's going to be upset."

"Do you see a way around that?"

Unfortunately, I didn't.

BAY, LANDON, GUNNER, AND SCOUT STAYED in Landon's vehicle when we parked in Monica's driveway. Her Jeep was there and lights were on inside the house. There was no one else in sight, so the others stayed and allowed us to tackle Monica.

She was confused when she opened the door.

"Oh, no." Her hand flew to her mouth. "Is it West? I knew he'd been gone on his run too long."

I took a moment to absorb her reaction. "He's not here?" I blurted.

She shook her head. Her hand fell. "Isn't that why you're here?"

"We need to talk to him," Hunter replied.

"He's not hurt?"

"We're not here to give you information on West," I replied. "We need to talk to him."

"West went out for a run," Monica replied. "Three hours ago. He should've been back. It usually doesn't take him more than an hour to get his workout in." She paused. "He's in very good shape."

The comment was directed at Hunter. Was she trying to make him jealous? When I thought about it from her perspective, I didn't blame her. She wanted to hurt Hunter because he'd hurt her.

"Monica, I get that we're the last people you want to see on your front porch," I started.

"You get it?" Monica arched an eyebrow. "What is it you get, Stormy? Do you get that I don't want anything to do with the two of you yet you're constantly in my life? What were you doing here earlier? Why did you come here to see West out of the blue? It wasn't because you heard he was an author. You don't write any longer."

The writing dig somehow hurt more coming from her. As for the rest, she had a right to know, but we were in no position to explain. Before I could decide how I wanted to respond, Hunter did it for me.

"Monica, we need to find West because we believe he's in danger." Hunter's tone was even, his cop face in place. "We're not here to cause problems. We're not here to upset you. We need to talk to him."

Anyone else would've taken Hunter at his word. Monica had too much history with him—and me for that matter. She folded her arms across her chest. "I'm not helping you."

"You have to, Monica," I insisted. "It's important. We need to find West."

"How do you even know him?"

I chewed my bottom lip. I didn't want to lie—that would only make things worse over the long haul—but the truth right now would ruin her.

"If West wants to explain to you how he knows us, we'll leave him to do that," Hunter said, catching me off guard. "I guarantee he hasn't told you the entire truth, but we're not here to implode your relationship.

"We're here to talk to West about a serious matter," he continued. "We can't tell you why we want to talk to him. It's too convoluted, and we don't have time. You need to have faith in me that I wouldn't come here unless it was absolutely necessary."

Monica eyed him with unveiled annoyance. "I don't have faith in you. Why would I? Everything you ever told me was a lie."

Weariness wove its way through Hunter's voice. "I get why you think that. I don't blame you for hating me. All I can say is that I never meant to hurt you."

Monica's eye roll wasn't lost on Hunter.

"I'm serious," he insisted. "I wasn't lying to you when I told you the things I told you. I just ... didn't see the truth myself."

"Will you listen to yourself?" Monica exploded. "You are unbelievable! You act as if I'm sitting around pining for you almost a year later. Well, guess what, Hunter? I've moved on. You're the one knocking on my front door looking for my new boyfriend." She sent me a pointed look. "Doesn't that bother you?"

Given the limited information at her fingertips, it didn't take a genius to understand why she'd jumped to that conclusion. I kept my voice low when I spoke again.

"Monica, we can't explain what we're doing here," I said. "It's a very long story, and quite frankly, it's West's job to tell you. Suffice to say, though, we would not be here if it wasn't important."

She cocked her head. Perhaps she sensed I was telling the truth. She exhaled heavily. "Does this have something to do with the other stuff you do?" Her voice was barely a whisper. "Is West involved in all of that too?"

"Not the same way that Cliff was involved," I assured her. "I need to talk to him. We believe he might be in trouble. I can't tell you more than that."

Monica blinked, then turned to Hunter. His expression was carved from granite, so she turned back to me. "I told you I don't know where he is. He went out running. He's been gone too long. Maybe whatever you're worried about has already happened."

"Where does he run?" Hunter asked.

"I don't know," Monica said. "He doesn't say, and why would I ask? It's not important."

"We need to find him." Hunter planted his hands on his hips and turned away, scanning the street.

"Are there running trails around here?" I asked. "Where did you run when you stayed with Monica?"

He considered it for several seconds. "The park," he said finally. "There's a running trail around the pond. Two laps is a mile."

"West did mention the ducks at the park," Monica offered.

I shot her a reassuring smile. "We'll find him. Everything is going to be okay." I couldn't make that promise—for all I knew, Weston might already be dead—but I had to put her at ease. "Stay here, and I'm sure he'll be back before you know it."

"And if he's not?" Monica challenged.

I didn't have an answer, so I lied. "Have faith."

"Oh, right." She threw her hands into the air. "I'll just have faith in you guys."

"Do you have a choice?" Hunter asked.

Monica frowned. "I guess I don't."

27
TWENTY-SEVEN

We congregated on the south end of the park. Scout wanted to barrel in, fingers blazing, and take out the elementals. Hunter and Landon insisted on a more moderate approach.

"We need to know what we're dealing with," Landon said. "We don't want anybody getting hurt."

"Weston might already be hurt," she argued.

"He might not even be with them."

Scout's eyes narrowed. "You remind me of this guy who was in charge at the third group home I lived in. He smelled like bacon twenty-four-seven. Just for the record, that's not a compliment."

Landon didn't back down. "You're used to getting your way. I understand that you're powerful and you like to fight, but you're not the only one here."

"Besides," Bay added, "Aquarius said Stormy was her proxy. She knows something that we don't know."

All eyes turned to me, and I shrank back. "I don't know what she knows."

"We need to figure it out." Landon glanced at Evan. "Can you get in there and look around without them knowing?"

Evan shrugged. "Probably."

Evan sent Scout a sly smile. "Guess who gets to go in first."

"You suck," Scout muttered.

Evan chuckled, then jumped into the nearest tree. He liked to swing between branches. Almost no one expected a vampire to drop in from above.

Once he was gone from sight, I looked to see what Hunter was doing on his phone. He'd pulled up a map of the park. "It's pretty big," he said. "There's a pond in the center. There's a lot of open ground to cover."

"There are only two of them and one of them is nutty," Scout countered.

She tapped her fingers on the hood of Landon's Explorer. "You realize that they may have already spotted us? They could be killing Weston even as we speak."

Easton balked. "Why must you always be such a ray of sunshine?"

She shrugged. "I'm just saying that sitting here and doing nothing is a bad idea. I—"

Evan dropped down next to us.

"There are two people tied to trees about a quarter of a mile in," he said. "They look pretty beat up."

"Shauna and Eli?" I asked.

He shook his head. "A man and a woman. They look to be in their late forties. The woman reeks of booze."

"Sandy and Craig?" I wondered aloud.

"I don't know what they look like."

Hunter tapped his phone screen and pulled up a photo of Sandy.

Evan was grim when he nodded. "That's the woman."

Hunter then showed him a photo of Craig.

Evan nodded again.

"They brought their parents here?" Bay's forehead creased. "Why?"

"Maybe they're angry because they have crappy parents," Hunter suggested.

"They're not really their parents," I argued. "It sounds as if Eli and Shauna hijacked Sandy so she could give birth to them."

"I don't know," Evan admitted. "There must be a reason they chose Craig and Sandy."

"What about Weston?" Easton asked. "Did you see him?"

"No, but he's been here. I scented him."

"Do we go after the parents, or leave them?" I asked. Even asking the question made me feel guilty, and I came up with my own answer before the others could respond. "We have to go to them."

Bay nodded. "We don't have a choice," she said. "They might be crappy parents, but we can't leave them to die."

"What if it's a trap?" Landon asked.

"Then Scout will get her way, and it will be war." Bay offered up a shrug. "Do you have a better idea?"

Landon nodded without hesitation. "You can send ghosts in to release them and we'll see if it triggers a trap."

Bay looked caught off guard. "I guess I could do that." She looked at Scout to garner her opinion.

"If we're going to do this the safe way, that seems the best idea," the pixie apex said. "I prefer my rescues to be hands-on experiences, but let's be as safe as possible, by all means." Her sarcasm was impossible to ignore

Bay raised her hands. "*Come*," she intoned in the dead voice she used to call ghosts.

Three of them, including Mrs. Parker, appeared.

I smiled at her. "You're still here."

"I can't leave," she replied simply. "I'm stuck here ... apparently forever."

"No, you're not," Bay said. "I'll help you cross over once we're done with this."

Mrs. Parker managed a smile. "You can do that?"

"You would be surprised what I can do. For now, I need you three to do something for me." Bay laid out her simple plan. "You can't be hurt," Bay told them as she finished. "Get the parents off the trees and herd them in this direction."

Mrs. Parker bobbed her head. "Evil won't win tonight." With that, the ghosts took off in a blur.

"I'll head in to offer help if necessary," Evan said. "You guys wait here. We need to know what's going on. Craig and Sandy are the only ones who can help us before we make any decisions about Gemini and Weston." He shot an apologetic look toward Easton. "It won't be long now." He disappeared just as fast as the ghosts.

Because I was antsy, and needed to do something proactive, I sidled over to Easton. "I know you're worried," I started.

"I shouldn't be." Easton looked bitter. "Technically, he's my enemy. He's my cousin—and a member of the brotherhood, so also my brother—but we weren't always enemies. There was a time..."

Easton's relationship with Weston was difficult to grasp. There were times I'd wanted to ask him about it, but he was secretive, and he didn't often want to talk about his feelings. His entry into this world had been messed up, much like that of Eli and Shauna.

"We'll find him," I said. "I promise, we won't abandon him."

"Have you ever considered that we should abandon him?"

I shook my head. "I mean, I don't like him, but he's important to you." When he didn't respond, I took it a step further. "And you're important to me."

"I thought I was a pain in your ass."

"You are," I replied. "That's the way it is with family. I won't lie and say you handled everything correctly when you entered my life —and there are still times when I mourn the cat—but you're stuck with me."

He rested his forehead against mine. "Everything is messed up. Nothing happened as it was supposed to."

I patted his arm, then turned to Bay. "Easton's entry was flubbed. Gemini has tried to enter twice. Is that a coincidence?"

Bay considered it for several seconds. "It could be," she said. "But when you're a witch you learn early not to believe in coincidences."

I exhaled heavily. "Something isn't right." I was still thinking about it when the sound of footsteps became apparent.

Everyone who had been grouped around the vehicles waiting went ramrod straight as Sandy and Craig appeared, Evan was between them. He had an arm around Sandy's waist because she didn't look steady on her feet. He wasn't gentle with her when he led her closer to us and unceremoniously dumped her on the ground.

"I think Gemini is still in there," he said. "I can smell Weston. I know he hasn't left the park. There's an eerie sense of dread hanging over the space. We're definitely not alone."

"How about them?" I gestured toward a dazed Craig, who lowered himself to the ground next to Sandy.

"They're beaten up some," Evan replied. "They might be dehydrated."

"I have bottles of water." Landon headed for the back of his Explorer, returning with two bottles of water. He handed one to me, then hunkered down in front of Sandy and cracked the other. "Drink."

I took the other bottle of water to Craig and did the same. It took several seconds for his gaze to sharpen on me.

"I know you," he said dully.

"I have some questions for you."

"I don't know ... I don't understand..." Fear flooded his eyes. "They're even worse than I thought."

"We need to know what happened. How did you end up here?"

Craig spoke in a whisper. "They came looking for us." He seemed terrified, but something was off.

Scout squatted down next to me. "Listen, little man, I'm going to tell you something." Her hand caught fire and pink flames illuminated Craig's face. "We've dealt with enough nonsense." Her tone was icy. "I don't know what's going on with you. I honestly don't care. You're going to tell us, because we're all that stands between you and death.

"You might have been strung up there as a trap for us, but you weren't getting out of that situation alive," she continued. "We saved you, and you owe us. Now tell me what's going on."

Craig swallowed hard, then glanced at Sandy. When he spoke again, he was still frightened. "We're muses," he said, rubbing his forehead. "Gemini sent himself to us as a joke. It was supposed to be funny. The entry of the twins was botched, and they grew to be monsters. He wants to call them back—that was the original plan—but they refuse to go. They escaped, and until they reappeared on that road we had no idea they were still out there."

Sandy made a hiccupping sound as she sobbed.

"You're muses?" I asked.

Craig cocked his head, annoyance obvious. "You're a witch. Why are muses so hard to swallow?"

I looked to Bay for help. Scout swooped in. "You're not one of the original muses." She gave Craig some serious side-eye. "They're powerful. You're not powerful, which means you're pretty far down the line."

"Does that matter?" Craig challenged. "We were assigned here. You get freaky deaky with your witch stuff and need somebody to keep you in check. Gemini sent the twins to us specifically because he wanted to have part of himself in position here when you all arrived. There was just one problem."

"They arrived early ... and without one another," Sandy said dully. Her eyes were red-rimmed when they landed on me. "Eli was first, and there was clearly something wrong with him. We didn't know what to do, so we took care of him and waited for word from Gemini. Then Shauna appeared—I wasn't even pregnant at the time and then suddenly I was overnight—and we had two babies.

"Two odd babies," Craig agreed.

"They were monsters," Sandy said. "There was something wrong with them from the start. Eli liked torturing things. Bugs, animals, the occasional human. He didn't care. Shauna liked showing strangers terrible images in their heads. They were abominations."

"We spent hundreds of years together," Craig said, gesturing between Sandy and himself. "They destroyed our marriage for fun. Gemini kept trying to get them to cross back over so they would be destroyed and he could start again, but they refused."

"I don't understand," I interjected. "Aren't they Gemini?"

"They're representations of his power," Craig replied. "Gemini rarely comes here. He creates a set of twins to do his bidding."

"And this set is defective," I surmised.

"Very." Craig was grim. "Gemini came to me with a plan to force them over. I took them to the spot where they were supposed to go. Something happened that day, though. They didn't end up where they were supposed to. Sandy and I had to scatter because we knew they might return."

"And they would be angry when they did," Sandy whispered.

"So you stayed split up?" I asked. "Why not run away together?"

"They ruined us before we came to the decision to send them away," Craig replied. "The love we shared is gone."

"Love doesn't just disappear," Hunter argued.

"You're too young to know anything about love," Craig said. "You act as if we made this decision without serious thought. We didn't start aging until we separated. It's part of our life cycle. As long as we're together, inspiring others, we thrive. When that stops..."

"It doesn't matter," Sandy said. "We cycle again. Those twins need to be destroyed so they can cycle again."

"If they didn't go to the intended plane the first time, where did they go?" Scout asked. "I can open plane doors. If we need to shove them through, we can."

"The second you came to see me, I went to check the door," Craig said. "It's gone. They destroyed it. I think they might have been trapped on the threshold and it caused another time blip. That door is destroyed."

"Then why did they bring you here?" Landon asked.

"They needed to set a trap," Craig replied. "You're the one they want." His gaze landed on me. "They also wanted to dole out payback. They're even worse than I remember. Eli isn't there at all, and Shauna, well, she's even more evil."

"Gemini can't control them," Sandy said. "They have to be destroyed."

"And then what?" I asked.

"Their magic returns to Gemini and he starts the whole cycle over," Craig replied. "There's nothing you can do about that. The magic belongs to him. You have to get rid of them. Nothing has gone their way, and now they're prepared to punish anything and everyone because of it. Just like anything else, they don't want to die."

I pressed the heel of my hand to my forehead. "They're going to kill Weston, take his magic, and then come after me."

Craig swallowed hard. "That's the plan. They need fire magic to bolster them. Shauna thinks it's the only thing that will balance Eli, and without his help she's a sitting duck."

"They're in that park?" I pressed.

He nodded. "They expected you to come. They thought they would have more time. Like everything else, their timing was off."

I sighed and briefly shut my eyes. "Then we shouldn't keep them waiting." I lifted my gaze until it locked with Scout's. "It looks like you're finally going to get your wish."

She pumped her fist.

"Let's do it," I said, resigned. "We can't drag it out any longer. There's no going back."

28
TWENTY-EIGHT

W e left Craig and Sandy behind. Landon could've taken them into custody, but it wouldn't benefit anyone. They were muses who had lost their way, and they were on the decline.

"They've been punished enough," he said as we started across the park, our group spreading out just enough that one magical blow couldn't end us if the Eatons decided to unload. "They were once in love and happy. They lost that. Apparently, there's no getting it back." He shook his head, his eyes briefly going to Bay. "I don't want to punish them any further."

"They're punishing themselves," Hunter agreed. He was determined to keep close to me. "They'll never get over what's been done to them. Let them go."

Was he worried the same thing would happen to us? I opened my mouth to ask that very question, but he stopped me with a shake of his head.

"We're going to be happy forever," he said.

My lips curved, surprising me. "How did you know what I was thinking?"

"I know you."

I cocked my head. "I guess you do." I reached out and squeezed his hand. He didn't let go, holding tight.

"How is this going to go down?" he asked. "Are they going to start throwing magic at us the second they see us?"

I imagined they'd throw fire around the park in an attempt to incinerate us and I would save the day. Things were never that easy, though.

"I should do the talking," Scout said.

Bay grimaced as Evan and Gunner snickered. "It's not funny," Bay chided.

"Why would it be funny?" Scout challenged.

"Because the notion of you facing off with an unhinged elemental—and that's exactly what Eli is—makes all of us want to crawl into a hole and hide," Evan replied. He never held back with his best friend. "You tend to let your mouth get away from you."

Scout didn't deny it. "That's why I'm the perfect one to handle this situation."

"We should let Stormy handle it," Bay countered.

I was so caught off guard, I almost tripped and planted face first on the pavement. I shot her a bewildered look. "Why me?"

"This is technically your fight." Bay sounded utterly reasonable. "Aquarius made you her proxy for a reason. It's the fire magic. Weston is tied to you. You can control their fire. That makes you the central figure here."

"She can still be the central figure if I'm the mouthpiece," Scout argued.

Bay shot her a quelling look. "You just want to mess with them."

"You say that like it's a bad thing."

Bay shook her head. "This is Stormy's show."

Hunter's reassuring squeeze of my hand calmed me. "No pressure, though, right?" I tried to be chipper.

She grinned over her shoulder. "I know this is all new for you, but you'll do great."

"I think you're the only person who believes that," I countered.

"That's not true." Hunter shook his head. "I think you're going to do great."

"So do I," Evan added.

"I always think you'll do great," Easton reassured me.

I had to fight the urge to roll my eyes. They were trying to bolster me—and I appreciated it—but I remained skeptical. "What about you?" I asked Scout.

Her smirk was devilish. "You've got this," she said without hesitation. "You won't be as flashy as me—"

"That's not a bad thing," Bay chided.

Scout ignored her. "You'll be fine. If you need help—or somebody to be obnoxious—you have us. Remember that you've already handled them. If you'd been better prepared you would have been able to take them at the river. You weren't expecting to so easily handle their fire, and that resulted in them slipping away. It won't happen a second time."

That was true. I'd expected a battle. I'd corralled them quickly when faced with their fire. "I guess I'm just nervous," I admitted. "They're elementals. They've been around for thousands of years."

"But one of them is messed up, and their power is split," Scout said. "They're not a full elemental. Make sure that you no longer look at them as if they're children."

That was a good point.

"They were never children," she continued. "They were always monsters."

"It does make me wonder," Bay said. "Were they looking for Stormy when she found them on the road that day? Were they drawn to her?"

"I've been thinking about that," Scout said. "I think they were confused from their trip. They were trying to correct a wrong, but it didn't work out. It was just a coincidence."

"I thought you didn't believe in coincidences," I challenged.

She lifted one shoulder. "I don't think it's a coincidence that they came back here. It's not a coincidence that they were trying to time their arrival when magic was strong in this area. It is a coincidence that they crossed paths with Stormy when they did."

"They were lucky," Evan interjected. "Imagine if they had crossed paths with Scout first. They might not have even made it to the hospital."

"I can't imagine myself killing two kids, even if I were suspicious of their origins," Scout argued. "But point taken."

"I guess it doesn't matter," I said, letting out a sigh. "We're here, and we have to deal with it."

Scout didn't get a chance to answer because Shauna appeared on the sidewalk in front of us, stepping out from behind a tree. "Yes, we all have to deal with our current predicament," she drawled. "You're early."

So, she wasn't expecting us just yet. Did she know we'd found the muses? "Something tells me we're right on time," I countered. Immediately, my gaze went to the trees looking for Weston. If he was here, I didn't see him. "We're looking for someone."

Shauna rolled her eyes. "You're looking for the gnome. Do you think I'm stupid?"

Scout's hand shot in the air like an eager student wanting to be called on. I shot her a "now is not the time" look, but she rolled up to her toes and kept waving her hand.

"What is she doing?" Shauna demanded.

"If I don't call on her so she can run her mouth she's going to lose her cool," I replied.

"This is her being cool?" Shauna demanded.

I motioned toward Scout because I really did think she was going to blow a gasket.

"Whew." Scout's face was red from holding her breath, and she pressed her hand into her side, as if nursing a cramp. "What was the question again?" she asked.

I made a face, then returned my focus to Shauna. "What do you expect to happen here?"

"I expect you to turn around," she replied. "I expect all of you to march out of this park."

"Or what?" Scout challenged.

"Or we'll kill the gnome."

I remained rooted to my spot. "If we leave, you'll kill him so you can use his magic against me."

"I take it you ran into Craig and Sandy." Shauna threw up her hands. "I told Eli to use them to set a trap."

"I don't think you want to put your world domination plotting in Eli's hands," Scout offered. "Where is he, by the way? I kind of want to see him."

"Why?" Shauna folded her arms across her chest. "He's not a zoo animal."

"He kind of is," Scout countered. "He's like the monkey that throws poop at the glass and then rubs his face all over it to intimidate the zoo goers."

Shauna's slow blink had me gripping my hands into fists at my sides. Was she about to blow? "He's not that bad," she said finally. Her tone told me she was offended on her brother's behalf. The two beings who had been created out of nothing would cease to be after tonight.

"We have to deal with this," I said, jerking myself out of my reverie. "We can't let you kill Weston."

"Then go." Shauna showed me her teeth when she smiled. "If you want to save him, leave."

"You'll kill him," I shot back.

"Maybe we won't." She shrugged. "Maybe we'll let him live."

"Your whole plan is to kill him, then use his magic to go after me tomorrow during the solstice." I was becoming frustrated. They weren't real children and yet dealing with them was as annoying as dealing with teenagers.

"Who told you that?" Shauna demanded.

"Let's just say that we've talked to people much smarter than us, and we understand what's happening," I said.

She ran her tongue over her lips. "I feel there's no way for me to win," she said finally.

"There's really not," I acknowledged. "We outnumber you. The only person you have backing you up is a deranged elemental." I held out my hands. "Perhaps you should leave willingly."

"Where do you suggest I go?" Shauna challenged.

"Away." I shrugged. "You can take Eli and..." I trailed off. I didn't know what to tell her. We couldn't just let them go. They would become a threat that someone else would have to deal with.

"I can see you're figuring it out too," Shauna surmised. "You can't let me go, and I won't sit back and let you kill me. It's going to be a battle."

"Yes, well..." Before I could finish it out—I didn't know what I was going to say—what could only be likened to a Molotov cocktail, only of the magical variety, smashed against the walkway in front of me. Orange fire erupted and built like an inferno, racing to surround us like the same traps I'd learned to make in Hemlock Cove.

I caught the fire and managed to keep the circle from closing. When my breathing became even, I pushed back.

From the darkness, a loony laugh erupted. I saw Eli through the flames. His eyes were wild with excitement, and there was soot on his cheeks.

"I've got him," Scout announced as she burst through the opening of the fire circle and raced toward Eli.

He saw her coming, let loose another giggle, and then bolted toward the trees. Gunner didn't bother announcing his departure. Scout might've been the powerful one, but he wasn't going to leave her to fight an elemental without backup, even if that elemental wasn't all there.

Evan looked momentarily torn, his gaze flicking to watch Gunner and Scout disappear before returning to me.

"You can go," I promised him.

"You've got this," he assured me, looking relieved. "You have

Easton and Bay. They're the reasonable ones." He left the circle without a backward glance.

That left our teams evenly split.

"This is not how I wanted this to go," Shauna said. I'd momentarily lost sight of her when dealing with the fire, but she was back, and she was no longer alone. Weston was with her. He was bound with a glowing rope, and Shauna had a knife pressed to his throat.

"This ends now," Shauna announced.

Hunter and Landon were behind Easton, Bay, and I. There was nothing they could do to fix this, so they wisely remained quiet.

I looked at Shauna and Eli as children. They had never been children, though. Gemini used magic to create them. They didn't have souls. They weren't real. Not in any sense of the word. When they were snuffed out, the world wouldn't even remember them.

On a sigh, I closed my eyes. When I opened them again, the flames Shauna and Eli had conjured were gone.

Her eyes went wide when she realized what I'd done. "I'll kill him," she repeated, dragging Weston in front of her.

Evan dropped Eli's body from the tree above. The dead boy's body bounced when it landed.

Shauna blanched when she saw her counterpart was dead. "How...?" was all she managed to get out.

"It doesn't matter," I replied. "This visit was screwed up from the beginning. I'd like to know in what period you intended to arrive, but I'm not sure it matters now."

Shauna's eyes were dark slits of hate. "You think we came for you," she hissed. Her eyes were on Eli, and it was obvious she realized she'd lost. The only question now was how much damage she would do on her way out.

"Me personally?" I challenged. "Doubtful. When you found out there was a hellcat present, you thought you could use my magic to fix what went wrong with Eli. You had access to fire magic, and it just made sense to you."

She continued to stare.

"The things going on around me garnered your attention," I said. "You're interested in the nexus, and the apexes ... and everything else that happens around here. But I don't think you were aiming for this time."

"No, not this time," Shauna agreed. "We were supposed to be here before you banded together. You're too strong now. It's too late."

Bay stirred. "And who sent you to get to us before we became strong together?" she asked.

Shauna jerked up her chin, realization washing over her. She'd said too much. "It doesn't matter." She sounded tired now. "It's too late."

"It is too late," I readily agreed. "Just out of curiosity, though, do Sandy and Craig know why you were sent here?"

A smirk tugged on the corners of Shauna's lips. "Why not ask them?"

"I will." *If I can find them again,* I added silently. "It's best that you give us Weston now. You're done. You can't come back from this. There's no sense in dragging it out."

"That's easy for you to say." Shauna's vitriol was palpable. "You're not about to die."

"You could've fled when you returned and realized nothing was fixed. You could've gone into hiding and lived out the rest of your life. Instead you decided to come after us."

"We had a mission," Shauna said. "We had to try." She was weary.

I took an involuntary step forward, pity for her momentarily overwhelming me. "Shauna—"

"Don't." A ring of fire erupted around Shauna. Her eyes were glassy as she raised her chin. "There's nothing you can say to make this better."

"You have to give us Weston," I insisted.

"You would be better off if I killed him," she said. "You can't see it yet, but I can."

"Maybe so, but he's coming with us."

Shauna grinned. "How are you going to get him?"

I choked out her fire with a small hand gesture, then watched with detachment as Evan darted close enough to knock Shauna's hand away and grab Weston. He heaved the gnome over his shoulder and then flitted away again, leaving Shauna exposed.

"Great," Shauna muttered.

I built the cage this time. It was the same one I'd created when training with Bay and Tillie days before. Shauna's eyes went wide when she saw it. Then, when she touched her finger against it and realized her skin had died—the same way Tillie's had—all the fight went out of her.

"We would offer you a deal, but there's nothing you can give us," Scout said as she appeared behind Shauna. Apparently, the fight with Eli hadn't taken much out of her because she looked flawlessly put together. "You don't know what you were fighting for anymore, do you?"

Shauna held my gaze. "Just do it," she ordered. "I'm tired of this world. Nothing worked out as it should."

I hesitated—could I really do this?—then steeled myself. I had to protect the people I loved.

"I hope the next rebirth goes better," I said.

Shauna snorted. "It won't matter to me. You don't get two shots at it."

I collapsed the trap on her. She screamed when the fire hit her. My only solace is that it was fast.

Her scream was still an echo on the wind as we all stared at where she'd stood. Then our world erupted into an even bigger problem.

"What the hell was that?"

29
TWENTY-NINE

Monica, her eyes wild, stormed forward.

"What in the hell was that?" she demanded.

I went slack-jawed at the sight of her.

"Did you follow us?" Hunter demanded. He managed to act as the affronted party despite what had just happened.

Monica shot him an incredulous look. "Are you kidding me?" She rushed to Weston, her face pale and her fingers gentle as she brushed his hair from his face. She gave Easton a dirty look when he hunkered down to check on Weston, removing the ropes that were no longer magical. "I've got it."

Easton gave her a long look, then glanced at me. He was trying to communicate his disgruntlement, but there wasn't much I could offer.

Scout took control. "You have to let us check him." She knelt down next to Weston and pressed her hand to his forehead.

Weston's dazed eyes lifted to lock on her. "Pixie," he said.

"Actually, I identify as a witch," Scout replied. "You seem okay, despite being eternally stupid. Did they zap you magically?"

Weston nodded. "They were going to kill me."

"You don't have to worry about that any longer." Scout flicked his cheek for some reason I couldn't fathom. "We still might kill you if you're not careful."

To my surprise, Monica slapped Scout's hand away. "Don't touch him," she hissed. "I'll call the police."

Scout looked caught between amusement and annoyance. Thankfully, amusement won out. "Okay, then." She got to her feet. "He should be fine after resting."

I nodded because I didn't know what else to do. Monica showing up threw a wrench into everything. I flicked my eyes to Bay to see what she was thinking and she appeared just as flummoxed.

"What was all of that?" Monica asked. She kept stroking Weston's hair. "What are you people?" Her eyes were accusatory when they landed on Hunter. "Is this why you left me for her? Are you all ... monsters?"

"Monsters is insulting," Gunner offered. "In case you didn't notice, we saved your boyfriend. The monsters had him trussed up like a Thanksgiving turkey."

Monica didn't look convinced. "Why should I believe you?"

"Because your boyfriend is beat to hell and we rescued him," Gunner replied. "Deep down, you know we saved him. Let's shelve the histrionics."

Scout looked around the park. "Shauna is gone. We still have his body to deal with." She gestured toward Eli.

"What did you do to him?" Landon asked. He kept casting the occasional look to Monica, as if debating what to do.

"He kept trying to set fires while we were chasing him," Evan replied. "I got behind him and stopped him from setting more fires."

Landon didn't ask for specifics. Evan had killed him—something Scout would whine about for weeks—but he couldn't volunteer the specifics in front of Monica. "I'll call my office and have them pick up the body."

"Your office?" Monica demanded. "Where do you work?"

Landon pulled out his badge.

"FBI?" she sputtered. "Are you kidding me?"

"No."

Monica wet her lips. She looked as if she was about to pass out. "I don't understand any of this."

"We can try to explain," I offered.

Scout made a slashing motion across her throat to silence me.

"We can't leave her to fill in the blanks herself," I argued. "She's already painted us as monsters."

"You killed that girl," Monica hissed.

"She wasn't a girl," I replied. "She wasn't..." How could I explain this to her? What would she think if I told her Shauna and Eli were an elemental demon called Gemini and they were trying to kill Weston to get his magic so they could kill me?

Weston cleared his throat. "I'll talk to her," he said as he struggled to a sitting position. He'd gotten some of the color back in his cheeks.

"What, exactly, are you going to tell her?" I demanded.

"I'll talk to her," he said pointedly. "Don't make things worse."

Could they get worse? I pictured Monica spreading stories around town. She would tell Phoebe, of course, and when Phoebe was done with the tale, everyone in town would look at us differently.

"Just let me handle it," Weston insisted. He sent Easton a grateful look when the other gnome helped him up from the ground. "She'll understand when I'm finished."

"We shouldn't let them leave together," Scout supplied. "It's too dangerous."

Monica huddled close to Weston, sliding her arm around his waist. "Are you going to kill us too?"

I took pity on her. She was terrified. If I were in her position a year ago, I would've been horrified to the point of crapping my pants. "Nobody is going to be killed," I replied.

Monica sent an incredulous look to Eli's body. "How can you say that with a straight face?"

"Because I understand what happened here," I replied. "You don't."

Monica stared me down for several seconds, then tugged on Weston. "We're leaving. Don't you dare try to stop us." There was a warning in her gaze. "I'll call the police."

"I am the police," Hunter reminded her.

Monica was haughty. "There are other types of police. I don't trust you. You were in on it."

"I'm with the FBI," Landon reminded her.

"I don't know you." Monica was pale.

"Let them go," I instructed.

Scout shot me an "are you kidding?" look. "We can't let her go. She'll spread our business all over the place."

"She won't," I replied. I trusted Weston to get this situation under control. It might be a mistake—at the very least, naive—but I didn't see that I had another choice. "It'll be okay." When I glanced at Bay, I found her nodding in agreement. "You can go," I said to Monica.

"Thank you so much for your permission." Monica practically dragged Weston away from us. "You all need to stay away. I'm not kidding, stay away."

Everybody remained silent as they walked back across the park. Monica had likely parked in the same spot we had, so she had a bit of a hike before her. Carrying Weston would make it even longer.

"Is it really a good idea to just let her go?" Scout asked when they were out of earshot.

"You have a better idea?" I challenged.

Scout bobbed her head. "We could've modified her memory."

"I hate doing that," Bay moaned.

Scout refused to back down. "She's a danger to all of us. We'd be safer if she didn't know."

"She already knew about the magic, at least in a limited capacity," I argued. "She didn't say anything after the first time."

"That was before you burned a teenager to death in front of her."

"She wasn't a teenager." Frustration reared up and grabbed me by the throat. "Stop calling her a teenager."

Scout held up her hands in supplication. "I'm not accusing you. I know exactly what she was. I'm just saying, from her perspective, that was a teenager."

"Weston will handle it," Easton volunteered. He looked shaken but determined. "He'll tell her just enough to keep her quiet."

"You sound pretty sure of that," Bay noted.

"He's good at what he does, and we've been protecting ourselves for a long time," Easton replied. "He said he could handle it. I believe him."

I nodded. "So do I. We have to give him a chance. If it doesn't work, we'll modify her memory."

"It will be too late," Scout argued. "She'll have told anyone who will listen."

Landon challenged, "Do you really think everyone in town will believe that three witches, one gnome shifter, one vampire, one FBI agent, and one police officer walked into a park and killed two teenage monsters?"

"It might make for a joke if you put us in a bar," Gunner volunteered. He shrank when everybody glared at him.

Scout shook her head before planting her hands on her hips and focusing on Landon. "You're not worried? You're the biggest worrier in this group."

"We have no choice but to see how this plays out." Landon was matter of fact. "We have to trust that Weston can do what he says."

Scout didn't look convinced. "I still think this is a bad idea." She glanced at Evan, and they seemingly had a silent conversation. Ultimately, she sighed. "You guys are going to be in greater danger. She has no idea who we are."

"It'll be okay," I insisted. I needed to believe that. "We just have to play it out. The important thing is that Eli and Shauna are no longer a danger."

"But we don't know why they were here in the first place," Scout shot back, "but this is your show." She blew out a sigh and shook off her irritation. "Anybody want to order pizza?" she asked. "I could use a snack."

Gunner's hand shot in the air. "You're speaking my love language, baby."

I didn't think I was hungry until my stomach growled. "I could eat," I said, surprising myself.

Hunter slung his arm around my shoulders. "Me too." His lips brushed my temple.

When we were alone, in the safety of our bed, we would unpack everything that happened. We were nowhere near out of this, but the big threat had been thwarted.

"I'll get a team here," Landon said. "Give me thirty minutes, then we'll get that pizza." He shot Bay an encouraging smile. "All in all, things didn't go too badly tonight."

Bay smirked. "I love how your scale slides."

"Sweetie, you no longer smell like rancid pickles. That's a win."

We had won the battle. We still had a war before us.

Printed in Dunstable, United Kingdom

68529769R00150